Catching Serenity

EDEN BUTLER

Copyright © 2016 Eden Butler

All rights reserved.

ISBN: 1530829658

ISBN-13: 978-1530829651

All rights reserved as permitted under the U.S. Copyright Act of 1976. No part of this publication may be reproduced, distributed, transmitted in any form or by any means, or stored in a database or retrieval system, without the prior permission of the Author. For information regarding subsidiary rights, please contact the Author Publisher.

Edited by Sharon B. Browning

Copy Edited by Judy Lovely

Cover Design by Steven Novack and Tee Tate

Illustrations by RN Laing

This book is a work of fiction. Names, characters, places, and incidents are the product of the author's imagination or are used fictitiously. Any resemblance to actual events, locales, or persons, living or dead, is coincidental. The author acknowledges the copyrighted or trademarked status and trademark owners of the following word-marks and references mentioned in this work of fiction.

PRAISE FOR EDEN BUTLER'S WORK

the Serenity Series

"I loved this book! The hero is a tatted up Irish rugby player who has traveled to the states to play for college. Like the heroine he has a tragic past and when Autumn and Declan meet sparks fly! Nice to read a book that is anything but predictable." —*Kele Moon, author of the Battered Hearts series*

"This book explores emotional heartache, but on different levels. It's not just about romantic love, but about the love of family (and "family" takes on a whole new meaning. It encompasses friends, too). From disconnect to possible re-connect. From old scars that refuse to heal, to potential emotional mending. You'll feel it, deep." —*Maryse Black, Maryse's Book Blog*

"Eden Butler has captivated my heart. From the town she created with its love of rugby to its foundation of friendship and family, I find I wish I could hop on a bus and stay there a while. The characters as flawed yet beautiful, broken yet unbelievably strong. Layers of intense feelings are still trapped in my heart." —*Nichole Hart, Sizzling Pages Romance Reviews*

Catching Serenity

the thin Love Series

"There is a bold mission when [Butler] puts pen to paper to grab our attention, open our hearts, and engage our imagination. Butler didn't hold back with crafting these characters from different cultures, tossing in some major adversity, and challenging them to dig deep for inner strength. At the end of the day, Thin Love is hearty blend for the soul." —*Michelle Monkou, USA Today*

"Read [*Thin Love*] in one sitting! Without a doubt, my favorite dynamic of bad boy meets feisty good girl. Superb writing!" —*Penelope Douglas New York Times bestselling author of Bully and Until You*

"I felt so connected to these characters and this story that it almost felt too personal to share it with anyone. But rest assured, I will be shouting the praises of *Thin Love* and Mrs. Butler from the rooftops so that I can make sure others experience what I have." —*Lori Westhaver, Red's Book Blog*

"*Thin Love* is more than just a book. It's more than a story. It's a journey—an experience that grabs you by the gut and won't let go until it's ready to release you. And damn, what a release it is. Eden Butler nailed it." —*Lila Felix, bestselling author of Love and Skate*

"We LOVED this book [*Thick Love*] and would recommend it in a heartbeat!" —*Totally Booked Blog*

Crimson Cove

"Eden is continually proving herself in the ranks of every genre of romance, no matter the plot, type or setting, she will pull you in. Prepare yourself." — *Trish Leger, best-selling author of the Amber Druids series*

"When the twists and turns started coming, [in Crimson Cove] I had to hold on tight. Mrs. Butler did not hold back in that department. Great job." — *Jennifer Sons, Through the Booking Glass Blog*

"A wonderful standalone that will entrance you and captivate you from start to finish. I cannot stress how much I enjoyed reading this. #oneclicknow" — *Kawehi, Kawehi's Book Blog*

ALSO BY EDEN BUTLER

Chasing Serenity, (The Serenity Series Book 1)

Behind the Pitch, (A Serenity Series Novella)

Finding Serenity, (The Serenity Series Book 2)

Claiming Serenity (The Serenity Series Book 3)

Thin Love, (Thin Love Book 1)

My Beloved, (A Thin Love Novella)

Thick Love, (Thin Love Book 2)

Swimming in Shadows, (A Shadows Series Novella)

Shadows and Lies, (The Shadows Series Book #1)

Crimson Cove

DEDICATION

For Grace L. who fought a warrior's battle.

Your life and legacy is felt everywhere, every day.

Rest well, sweet girl.

PLAYLIST

You Ain't Alone by Alabama Shakes

I Let You Go by The Lone Bellow

Hold Back the River by James Bay

In My Veins by Andrew Belle

Heartbreaker by Noah Gundersen

My Love by Sia

9 Crimes by Damien Rice

Baby by Warpaint

Let it Go by James Bay

To Be Alone by Hozier

Cigarettes by Noah Gundersen

Make It Rain by Ed Sheeran

"To hurt is as human as to breathe."

—J.K. Rowling, *The Tales of Beedle the Bard*

Love is a motherfucker

Love. It breaks your heart.

It fills the fractured pieces, the ripped and shredded shards
because,

in the end, there is no pleasure without pain.

There is no light without dark.

This is the story of that darkness and the love that fought like hell to breathe.

You have been warned.

INTERLUDE
the Day before

Quinn O'Malley is the pall I keep in front of my eyes. He is the perfect mask that dulls the ache of certainty.

And I am his.

We are together in this—using each other as balms, the quick numbing relief needed when the day ends too quickly, when the doctors' voices become too quiet, too soft.

Quinn is my buffer from the ugly truth that runs toward us and Christ, what a beautiful distraction he is.

My body buzzes, hums with the temporary joy orgasms give. It won't last, that's not how numbness works. But in the quiet, the small seconds that lengthen around the room, I pretend that it will last. I pretend that I am flying, soaring, not part of the weight that keeps me to the earth or the heartache I feel inching closer to me every day.

Eventually, that buzz dims and the call of that man sitting near the window, naked, focused, is too much to ignore. He is beautiful, after all. I mentioned that.

He doesn't hear me. The music—Damien Rice pumping from the small iPhone dock next to his fine leather wallet and vintage Ramones tee—interferes and there is no bed, no springs that creak and whine when I leave the huddle of our clothes. This forgotten warehouse is a paltry place for an indiscretion or, maybe the perfect one.

The light is dim, shadowed behind the low sliver of moonlight that peaks between the makeshift curtain of one of Quinn's shirts and thin, coffee-stained newspaper. His silhouette is perfect, lithe. He never works out, is too casual, too cool for something as mundane as exertion other than the kind we make together.

If I were the woman I'd been before, I'd slip behind him, push at the charcoal pencil in his hand, insist that he forget whatever character he's bringing to life on that white page, dust away the black lines that darken his knuckles. That Sayo McIntyre would slide her long arms and longer legs around Quinn's slim waist, she'd let the warmth of her skin, the graze of her nails slip against his cool body, against the pale flesh.

She'd take him because the mood had struck.

But I haven't been that girl for a long time. I haven't taken anything that wasn't offered up to me.

Not since Rhea stopped smiling.

Not since my little cousin began to live at the hospital.

Not since nothing I did, nothing I gave, helped in the least.

"You can stop staring, love."

Months it's been and still the gruff lull of his voice, that deep resonance of Ireland thick in his accent twists my belly until I can almost forget I am logical, that I have self-control.

"O'course," Quinn says, not looking at me so much as

glancing in my direction, "were you to keep staring, maybe step a bit closer, I could paint you again."

There is a thin coat of red paint, acrylic and flaking, splotched up my arms with thin lines of black layered in the bend of my elbow and across my stomach. It's the brightest color my skin has seen in months. Long gone are my vibrant colors—no more Hello Kitty pink shirts, no more purple headbands that clash with my dyed pink hair. Quinn had painted me an hour ago and though I know I should have; I hadn't stopped him. Hell, I hadn't even wanted to stop him.

When I remain silent, those wide blue eyes glance my way again, this time smoothing over my body like it was their right, like Quinn knew exactly what his attentions did to me.

"Red looks good on you."

The Sayo from before would yell at me for how easily one look, the slightest beckon of his eyebrows bending up has me coming to him, has me forgetting the fight I've always put up when Quinn wants me. But here the fight in me is a lesser thing, like something that sticks in my head—an appointment not important enough to keep.

I fit atop him with one slip of his arm on my waist, with his charcoal smudged fingers leaving impressions of black, lines the size and shape of his touch up my back and along my ribs. Quinn's lips smooth clear the remnant of red paint, his mouth clears a thick patch between my breasts and that low, hypnotic hum his throat makes is a quiet comfort I tell myself I do not like.

"You're smooth, love." That comes in a whisper across one nipple. "But you burn."

Quinn's voice is mildly awed, cool still, but somehow fascinated that I let him touch me. Like just now with his fingertips flirting down my neck, across my collarbone, he still glances at my face, as though he wants to be certain he doesn't disgust me. And when I stretch my neck, let my face rest against his palm, the tension in his touch eases. "You're like something I know I shouldn't want. A habit I can't bleeding stay clear of."

Quinn squints, gaze focused, doling out a look that tells me he doubts my easy acceptance of his touch. As though it is some trick he expects me to reveal. Really, that blank unfocusing of my eyes is just my subconscious hunting for the mythical, fictional thing that will whisk me from reality. I want a broomstick to fly from this warehouse. I want the Milano and Star Lord to carry my little cousin and me from hospitals and criminally beautiful Irishmen who ask for things that they should not be given. I want The Doctor and that brilliant blue box that offers a reprieve from expectation and responsibility.

But there is no TARDIS that can take me away. I've looked. The skies are empty.

"I could paint you all day." Quinn's touch is like a hit from a needle I know might end me, but I don't refuse. I'm not sure I could even if I wanted to. He's had my head spinning from that first day, all those months ago. He'd stood across the patio and time stopped just with the look he gave me; one that kept the breath thick and still in my lungs. One that promised that my life would not be mine if I let that man touch me.

That beautiful dark haired man who'd been brought from Ireland by his brother, my best friend's boyfriend, had made my time and thoughts secondary, superfluous with one penetrating look.

I'd promised myself he'd never get more.

God, how I've gotten good at lying to myself.

For now, I can forget. I let this beautiful, fit body take me away where the good Doctor and his blue box cannot. Quinn doesn't expect much from me. He gave up trying to elicit my loss of control weeks ago. But that doesn't mean he will give me a half-hearted effort.

"Look at you, beautiful. So small, so fragile." Quinn pulls on my hair because I let him. "I could touch you, never stop touching you, but not how I want. Not as I'd like." He kisses up my ribs, my chest because I never tell him to stop. "I don't want to break you, love."

But I am already broken. I am doll parts. Fractures that cannot be repaired.

"Nothing left to break."

It's only when the kiss he leaves on my collarbone dries that I notice Quinn has stopped touching me at all.

"Sayo. Love."

There is too much tenderness, too much sweetness in his tone. It's different enough that I look down at him wondering what he hides beneath those squinted eyelids. We've discussed this. We've kept to the unspoken rules that have made release and wordless comfort possible. I've managed it by not speaking much. He's done his part by talking to himself or, when he's in a particularly complementary mood, my body.

"Don't, O'Malley."

But that demand goes unchecked. Instead Quinn's attention strengthens and some of that unaffected, cool manner he wants the world to see, slips away. It's in the small stroke of his fingertips on my cheekbone and the feather light brush of his hand down my shoulder. "How broken are you?"

I wait. A handful of seconds that make him squirm. He shifts himself in the wooden chair that totters when he moves. But he does not release me, does not keep the soft inflection from his voice when he clears his throat.

"Enough that there is nothing left for anyone else." I want him to know, to understand what I won't, what I can't, give him. "Take what you want, remember? Take what's left."

There had been many small ground rules, mostly implied, but that one we'd both spoken aloud. When the need arose, and it always did, we took from each other what was necessary. There was no soothing sweetness in our words. There was only sensation and touch and then the retreat to our lives away from each other. Away from the news we both know is coming.

"Aye, I remember." His expression is guarded again. Severe, but that touch remains soft, too gentle for my liking and when I glance at his hand resting on my arm, Quinn exhales, squeezes my bicep because he knows I prefer it.

And then he leans forward, mouth soft and wet, slightly open to take mine. I let him. Tonight I want to be used. I want to feel valuable.

There is nothing I can do to save my cousin.

There is nothing anyone can do.

It is only when Quinn brings me back to that huddle of discarded clothes on the floor, when he covers my body and those long fingers smudged with charcoal—an artist's fingers—are beneath my waist, holding me still, arching my hips, pulling me closer to his mouth, that I start to feel not so broken. It is always this way; the climb toward sensation. It's the ache for emotion that does not consume me. That urge for something that doesn't fucking hurt.

"I could taste you, always." And he does, mouth, lips devouring my body until my eyes close shut from the sensation. His breath is so hot, a whisper against my hipbone. I don't have to look down at him to know that my pale skin, my smooth thighs are covered in Quinn's kisses, in the charcoal from his hands. "Sometimes I think I could never stop tasting you, don't I?"

I don't answer. I never do and he doesn't expect it. That's not why we are here. I keep silent while he fills the room with hungry words, promises that mean nothing at all. But as Quinn's touches increase, as his mouth opens wider, that thick, warm tongue teasing me, making a meal of my body, the sensation and sound of us has me floating, flying from reality, I do something I've never done before.

My fingers are in his hair, gripping, directing, guiding him in deeper, closer, and the low, long moan I make is in contrast with the gentle push of my touch against his scalp, then across his forehead, which stops him as he looks up at me, questioning. It's a look I've only seen from him once. The day we met, when I was quiet, when I'd retreated from the hospital at Rhea's insistence. Quinn across that patio looking at me as though he'd never seen my like. As though I was something remarkable.

And he wanted me for himself.

That's the gaze I get from him now. Just touching him, fingers gentle, nails running in a tender swipe across his forehead, his scalp, has him pausing, giving me that amazed, astonished look as though he cannot breathe, cannot move until I explain myself.

"Sayo…"

But he won't finish. He won't ask me what this small, insignificant gesture means. I won't let him. "Make me forget for just a little while longer."

And he does with his mouth again, with his fingers, with the thick, long strength of his dick and Quinn has me flying, floating without the need of things that aren't here and now. No broomsticks, no magic, no impossible gadgets that keep me from reality.

It is good. I manage to forget that I am not scared. So does he.

It lasts exactly forty-six minutes.

And then, my cell phone rings.

ONE
Ten Months Earlier

"Well, I don't think they should call her the *Goddess* of Thunder."

Rhea sits up in her bed, fussing with the mask covering her nose and mouth to get a better look at the article on the laptop screen and the image accompanying it.

"You don't?" My little cousin glances at me like I am simple. It's her customary 'you're a dumb adult' look obscured only by that paper mask. But I know this kid. I know her expressions better than my own. There is only a pause and then she returns her attention to the article, moving her head to the right as though that would help her form a final opinion. "Why not?" I ask her, pushing the screen back with my thumb as I nestle closer to her.

"It's just stupid. They call Thor, Thor. *Just* Thor. Not 'Thor, God of Thunder.'"

"They do so."

When she gets flustered, mildly worked up, her eyebrows move and the smallest hint of her skin brightening makes her cheeks pink. She does this now, and I'm not sure if it's from her irritation at my teasing or the mild infection that has her skin clammy.

"They don't," she says, wiggling up the mattress to turn her body toward me. "I mean like in regular chats. You think Jane says 'Oh, Thor, God of Thunder, grab me a lemonade while you're in the kitchen.' She just says, 'Hey, hot stuff' or 'Yo.'"

"Hey hot stuff?" She nods, eyebrows pinched together above that pale green mask. "So… no one says 'hot stuff' anymore. Where'd you hear that?"

A small shrug as though she's already moved on, and she slips back down against the pillows. "Dad was watching 'The Dukes of Hazard' again last night while Mama was out at the store."

She's already forgotten her point, scanning the article again. To look at her, anyone would think she was a normal, albeit thin eight-year-old. She is far smarter than she should be, but Rhea has spent most of her brief life reading books and comics while stuck in the isolation of her bedroom or, on the occasions that her platelets were too low or some weird infection took hold of her, at the pediatric ward at Cavanagh Regional Hospital. Marvel.com might be a little above her reading level, but no one can lecture the kid on being a kid. Not when she's always been expected to tackle the cards dealt her like a war weary solider.

"Well, don't say 'hot stuff.'" She offers me only the slightest eye roll and giggle when I give her elbow a soft nudge. "It's not the 70's."

"What should I say?"

"Nothing. You should read your comics and watch *Firefly*."

Her fingernails are thin, barely covering the tips of her fingers when she waves her hand, telling me with one small gesture that she doesn't need me lecturing her. "I'm not a baby, you know."

"Of course you're not. But you have plenty of time for 'hot stuff' and 'yo.'" When those eyebrows lower further, I shoot a quick glare at her, already knowing why some of the shine in those dark eyes has dimmed. "Don't give me that. You're doing fine."

"Two more rounds of chemo and I'm done." She moves deeper into her pillow, forgetting the small challenge I level, the one she hasn't been too eager to take lately. "Again."

I don't like this negative attitude. It's understandable, it's expected, but Rhea thinking even remotely that she won't win this battle goes against everything I know of my cousin. It's simply not who she's ever been.

"Hey," I tell her, setting the laptop on the foot of the bed. "What did I tell you about grumpiness?"

Most kids her age would pout, protruding bottom lip and all. But Rhea isn't most kids. She hasn't been afforded that luxury. "That it's useless."

"That's right and why?"

When I continue to stare, waiting for her response, the kid shakes her head. Crossing her arms is as close to a pout as Rhea will get. "Because all it does is send bad juju out into the world." When I nod, that head shake doubles. "Claire said the catechism teacher told her that there was no such thing as juju or making things real just by speaking them out loud."

"Yeah well, Claire's catechism teacher is Mollie Reynolds."

It's nearly impossible to keep the affected tone from my voice. Mollie Reynolds was an idiot and a huge gossip in high school. "I went to school with her. Trust me, she's a big dummy." A small laugh bursts from her that she tries to conceal behind her thin fingers, despite the mask. I go in for the double kill to keep her laughter loud. "She doesn't even have a library card. I checked." That was the highest offense anyone could commit in Rhea's book, and the tidbit worked. My cousin's eyes widened as though she couldn't believe anyone would do without access to the library.

Mollie Reynolds and her post-high school recovery is easily forgotten as Rhea sits up again, pulling a small stack of comics I bought her a few days back—the covers already smudged from multiple readings—onto her lap.

"So, what can I bring you back from Autumn's?"

"Declan." The kid isn't remotely ashamed of herself. Since Declan came into our lives two years ago, Rhea's been very blatant about her mild crush, as most kids are. She sees no reason to fake offense when I or Autumn tease her about her love for the stubborn Irishman.

"Goofball, he'll be jetlagged."

"He owes me a rugby lesson." Rhea tosses two *Firefly* comics at her feet and I grab one, flipping through the colorful pages while she copies my motion with another Dark Horse comic I can't quite make out.

"He'll get around to it, you know that," I tell her, keeping my voice even. It would be pointless to tell her the same thing my aunt and uncle have been saying for months now. Rhea knows everything she wants to do, especially anything athletic, will get pushed aside until after her treatment. "Declan doesn't welch on his promises."

"I can play, you know." She pauses only for a second, glancing in my direction before she grabs another comic and I make a mental note to stop by Marty's to check out the new arrivals.

"I have zero doubt about that."

It's the small moments like this one, chatting with Rhea, not really saying anything that we haven't gone over a hundred times, that are the sharpest and clearest in my mind. But then when the future is as uncertain as hers, it's these moments that are the most comforting.

Plenty of amazing things come in life. There are some moments that are brought into focus first because they are so monumental. But it is the mundane, the modest pleasures from our lives that matter the most because they remind us that even the simplest of lives can be extraordinary. With my little cousin sitting next to me, I realize how beautiful unexceptional moments really are.

That's why I make a point to spend some time with Rhea every day. The few hours I am with her, sitting and chatting about comics or books or television shows, or the very important topic of Declan Fraser—who Rhea is convinced she's going to marry one day—reminds my cousin that her life can be normal. It is not all doctors and appointments and the medicine that wears her down.

This time together, just the two of us, reminds her of what a normal life is and how remarkable she is to live in it.

She has stopped reading the comic and a glance at her face tells me she's wondering something but still taking a moment to figure out how to ask about it. It's her way, being thoughtful, and it's how she usually gets the straightforward answers she's seeking. This is no typical eight-year-old. There is a very old soul peeking behind those big, dark eyes and that tiny frame.

Her small fingers drum across the shiny cover of her comic before she stops to glance at me. "Do you think Autumn will marry Declan one day?"

It's not the first time she's asked this. It won't be the last, and sometimes I think Rhea believes she'll pull a different response from me if she keeps at it. But Autumn is my best friend, and Declan started proposing to her months after they began dating. There's no way an altar isn't in their future. "Sorry, kiddo." Even with the mask, I pick up her frown as the comic in my hands hits my lap. "That's pretty much a guarantee."

"Oh."

She's too young for wrinkles, but I've noticed the faintest lines creasing in the center of her forehead lately. Worry, stress, they are a part of all our lives now. I should be used to seeing the same expression in the mirror on my Aunt Carol's face. Still, no matter how used to that frown I get, I don't have to like it.

"He has a brother, you know." I can see her cheeks pushing up her lower eyelids under the mask. "And, he's younger."

"How much younger?" Rhea's squint is forced, a little over exaggerated.

"Still too old for you."

A quick raspberry in my direction and she picks up her comic again. "You're no fun."

"Oh? So I can take these back to Marty's?" I reach for the pile of comics—some old school *Gen 13*, some issues of *Buffy the Vampire Slayer* that her illness and its various treatments had kept her from reading regularly. She'd devoured them after only a couple of days of returning home from the hospital, and already they looked old and well loved.

"No, don't do that." When I don't move my hand from the top of the stack, Rhea tilts her head, pleading a little with one look as though that will have any impact on me.

It totally does.

"Fine, but don't be insulting."

"I guess you're *kinda* fun."

The tease works and we laugh, but then the laugh turns into a small cough which turns into a hack, and Rhea sits up, tears off her mask to cup her hands over her mouth, curving her back as the coughing increases.

"Careful," I say, rubbing her back while the phlegm and mucus breaks loose in her chest. "I don't like the sound of that. You need a breathing treatment." But when I make to leave, Rhea grabs my wrist, head shaking frantically as the last of a wheeze keeps her silent. "What?"

"Not yet, okay?" She inhales, hand on her small chest. "Wait for a little bit."

"Why?"

"Just wait until you leave for the barbeque." She blinks, rubs away the moisture on her eyelashes before she smiles. "Just a little bit longer." There is a small whoosh of air that rumbles the pillow when she leans back against it, keeping her palm over her heart.

The coughing worries me. It takes Rhea longer to get over illnesses, with the cancer and chemo weakening her immune system. The bronchitis she had months ago has left a lingering cough, one that requires breathing treatments when the hacking gets too bad. I hate seeing her suffer. I hate feeling useless. "Maybe I should stay, skip the barbeque."

"No. It's stupid here." She barely lifts her hand from her chest and waves, dismissing my argument before I've had a chance to make a good point. "Why should you be stuck here too?"

"Rhea…"

She shuts me up with a shake of her head. "I want you to go so you can remind Declan about my lesson."

Three comics and a box of Kleenex fall to the floor when I reach for a fresh mask for her from the side table. "You just want him to bring your UK chocolate."

"It's so sweet." Rhea's voice is still a bit raspy, the words broken when she speaks, but she seems calmer, even helps me slip the white elastic straps of the mask behind her ears. I don't let her see my frown when even that simple action leaves some of her hair between my fingers.

"Yeah, I know." This most recent treatment is making her hair fall out. It hadn't grown out much since the last round of chemo, but in the past year things had gone well. It had been the longest time since she was diagnosed four years ago that she'd gone so long without the cancerous masses returning. Now her hair came to just below her ears and there were thin spots around the crown. She catches me looking over her scalp and frowns.

"I'm going to shave it."

"Then I will too." I don't hesitate, shrugging like the concept is no big deal.

"No. That's dumb. You have all that pretty pink hair." Rhea grabs the ends of my hair, curling a wave around her fingers. "Why would you shave it?"

"So we match."

She releases my hair and rests again against the pillow. "We match enough."

"If I shave my head then we'll be twins."

"You're just saying that because we're the only ones in the family who look the same."

It's true. Between my parents' rainbow coalition of adopted children—Asian (me), black (my twin brothers, Booker and Carver), Cuban (my sister, Adriana) and Guatemalan (my sister, Alessandra), and Rhea's folks' adopted child, Rhea, and their natural daughter Claire, our family is a weird little ethnic anomaly. Eighty percent of Cavanagh's residents are Irish, including my parents and Rhea's. So our diverse family make up has us standing out. Eight years ago when my Aunt Carol brought Rhea home, I instantly gravitated toward her.

"She comes from Shirakawa-go, Sayo. Just like you. You might even be related."

I hadn't cared if we were. I hadn't cared if she was Japanese or Bulgarian or lily white like my aunt and uncle and my parents. I only knew that little Rhea was the most beautiful baby I'd ever seen and a sudden, blinding need to protect her, to guard her from the world fell upon me. I was still a kid myself, no more than seventeen, and had no clue where I was headed in life. I only knew that this baby was a shadow of my younger self. Maybe she was the echo I left behind in Japan.

Then came the news four years ago, when Rhea had already taught herself to read, when the prospect of day school and Pre-K had the girl twirling around my aunt's den dizzy with excitement: Aunt Carol had spotted a deviation in her Rhea's left eye. Then came the MRI, more exams and the discovery of a brain tumor along the optic nerve. Bilateral optic glioma, inoperable. Chemo, low white blood cell counts, and low platelet measurements, have become commonplace in our lives since then. When the platelets are very low, Rhea is sequestered in her room and everything must be sterilized. When they are very bad, with no sign of improving, she lands back in the hospital.

"I don't want you to shave it." Her voice is quieter now and I adjust her pillows, fluffing them before I rest on my shoulder at her side. Again she picks up one of my pink waves and runs her fingers through the end. "I want to color mine when it starts to come back again."

"What color? Pink?" I tug on a fallen strand of my pink hair from the pillow next to Rhea's head. I should have already gone in for another re-dye, but Rhea's latest relapse had kept me from most all activities that didn't include sitting with her or taking her to appointments while my aunt and uncle worked to find funding for the experimental treatments the doctor's wanted Rhea to try if the current treatments failed yet again.

"No, not pink," she says, stifling a yawn. "Pink is for you."

"Okay, so you want to do red? Maybe orange or green?"

"Purple." She dropped my hair, turning on her side to face me. "We'll be twins but not identical."

"I like that." Another cough begins, but isn't as severe as the last one and she lets me hold her hand. I don't like how cold her skin feels or the way she shrugs off the blanket when I pull it over her shoulder. "Let me get Aunt Carol. You need a treatment."

"Fine…" she finally says, but the word drops off in another rapid fire cough that has Rhea kicking the blankets from her legs and pointing to the metal bin on the floor.

"You want her now?" I ask, handing het the bin as she rips off the mask to spit out the mess her coughing has produced.

She gives me a sideways look full of irritation but doesn't argue. "But then you have to go. I don't want you to be late for the barbeque."

She wants to be alone, something Carol told me she's been asking for a lot lately. The comics, the books, the debates on names of fictional characters just aren't enough anymore. I'm scared nothing will be.

"You want that lesson that bad?" I ask, wiping her mouth with a Kleenex.

"I want that chocolate."

☘

A NEW FALL semester in Cavanagh ushers in beginnings and endings—kids embarking on the start of their college experience, parents subjected to the deafening quiet in their homes where there had once been teenage noise and commotion. With September comes the lingering of summer, the only a hint that the tight grip Mother Nature seems to have on the heat will eventually give way to milder temperatures.

The day has me baking and the six block trek to the house of my best friend's father seems longer with the heat thickening the air. Still, I do enjoy the scenery. Our town is small, no more than 10,000 inhabitants. Residential areas meld effortlessly into the university campus, which in turn gives way to the older part of town that hosts retail shops, pubs and small cafes.

Beyond that lies an even older section of town with smart little well-maintained Victorians and Craftsman, all at least seventy or eight years old. This is where Joe, Autumn's father, lives. Beyond the fence line of his backyard, beyond the reach of this older residential street, are mountainous ranges that peek and stretch so tall that they disappear into the sky, dislodged from view by the billowing sweep of clouds.

I never tire of seeing it in any part of town, but here in Joe's neighborhood the view is the clearest. It's here, at Joe's, that Autumn chose to host a small barbeque for us to welcome her boyfriend, Declan, home properly from his two-week trip to Ireland, where he'd been sent to fetch his newly revealed half-brother, Quinn.

Quinn, who was two years younger than Declan, had spent a big chunk of his deceased parents' estate on drink and women. No, that made him sound like just a run of the mill bad boy. Quinn was out of control. The amount of drinking, drug use, and sleeping around was not only threatening his health and well-being, but was also becoming an increasing embarrassment. Autumn had shared with me horror stories from Declan about how his half-brother would go for days shit-faced drunk or drugged out of his mind, waking up in a bed where he didn't even know the name of the girl—or girls—with him. The estate trustees wanted him out of the country and on the straight and narrow, and realizing that he had an older half-brother in the States apparently gave them the "out" they needed to make sure the estate didn't get completely squandered. I myself had no idea why they thought Declan would be the right person for the job. He barely keeps up with the varsity rugby squad he captains and his final semester studies at Cavanagh University.

But, Declan being Declan, went to Ireland to take care of this unearthed family business anyway.

Despite wanting to see my friends, my steps slow as Joe's small house comes into view. Maybe it's Rhea and her having to undergo chemo yet again that has me hesitating to climb the steps to the front porch. Most days I've just wanted to stay with her. It's why I've taken a leave of absence from my job as library director at CU, why I haven't seen much of my friends in the past few months. It's the worry, the real fear that Rhea's condition will worsen while I'm out, and I won't be there when she needs me, that keeps me anxious.

"Rubbish," Uncle Clay would say. "It's not your job to look after her, love."

That didn't stop me from wanting to.

Uncle Clay would often give me a wink and a nod of understanding, and despite his protests that I shouldn't take so much time from my job, I got the feeling that both he and Aunt Carol appreciated the help I gave them. It isn't an easy thing, tending to a sick child, especially one who has spent more than half her life in and out of hospitals. That obligation becomes monotony. That worry becomes dread. There was no way I was going to leave my aunt and uncle to face that on their own, especially since my little cousin looked up to me the way she did. And not when I knew, deep down, that the time I had with her was limited.

So it's Rhea, yet again, who occupies my thoughts, even as the front door swings open and I'm greeted with Joe's sweet half-smile.

"There she is," he says, sweeping me inside before I have a chance to change my mind about attending the barbeque. "Told Autumn, I did, that you'd be along." A tight squeeze on my shoulders and Joe has me through the den, the kitchen and out onto the back porch before he's even paused speaking. "Knew you'd come to welcome home our Deco, didn't I, love?"

Joe turns, holding up one finger and is down the steps, making for the small table holding cups and bottles of wine, soda and beer next to the porch and I'm left on my own, taking in the neatly outfitted back porch and patio.

A large pergola connects the porch to the back of the house, made of recycled timber that Autumn told me Joe rescued from a demolished barn just outside of Sevierville. My best friend and I helped Joe last spring, decorating the space with dozens of large pots brimming with blooms of fragrant flowers and hedges that line the perimeter of the fence and along the steps that lead to the covered patio. He had complained only mildly about the fairy lights we weaved through the breaks in the pergola and the chunkier solar lights we fastened in the branches and limbs of the large oak that hung nearly over the entire yard and swept against the ground and planked flooring that made up the back porch. He didn't mind so much, Autumn told me, about the palette table and kitchenette Declan helped us build along the side of the house or the repurposed wicker chairs and table Autumn found at a garage sale for fifty bucks.

It has a homey, comfortable vibe, and with the mouthwatering scent of barbeque wafting in the air and the sudden lick of a breeze rustling my hair off my shoulders, I begin to relax, to feel less guilty about being here and not with Rhea. Suddenly, I feel something else on that wind. It isn't the heat of summer that has sweat collecting against my lower back. It isn't even the humidity that clouds in the air, or that replaces that small reprieve of cool air with something akin to a waft of heat from a fire. It is something deeper, more significant, that I feel the second I step off the back porch and onto the patio.

I'm so distracted by the sensation that I don't bother to acknowledge Donovan, Declan's best friend standing at the back of the yard, or pay much attention to the slumping shape of a man I pick up out of the corner of my eye next to him.

Yet something prickles up my neck, like the quick breath of a stranger passing you in the congested crowd of a subway car. I can't quite put my finger on it, can't tell if it is the day, or the excitement that we are all finally back together for the first time since Declan had left for Ireland. Whatever it was leaves me feeling on display, as though something thick, something weighted has taken the air around us and turned it still and faint.

"Here you are, love." Joe offers me a drink, momentarily distracting me from that odd feeling that someone watches. No, not just watches. I am being gawked at, am the center of someone's focused attention. "Now then. How are you?" the older man continues, holding my arm at the elbow. Joe is mildly flirty, but Autumn swears he's harmless. And bored. Very, very bored as of late. "How is your bitty cousin?"

A small squeeze of my fingers against Joe's thick forearm and the man takes a small step back, though he still keeps hold of my hand. "The same, I'm sad to say, but not getting worse, I don't think."

Joe makes the sign of the cross and his grip on my fingers tightens. "Don't you fret, love. The Good Lord has a plan for everyone, even the smallest among us."

I don't argue. There is no need. I'd stopped debating my elders, or their priests a long time ago. Their assertions never wavered, and I've discovered that long held beliefs, those taken on out of tradition and obligation, not research or logic, were the toughest to penetrate. I have no idea why Rhea is sick but I suspect God isn't the one that made her that way. Still, whatever His plan, I couldn't say I agreed with Him.

Joe sips on his beer, shaking his head as he awkwardly tries to defuse the slip in mood, and his toothy grin returns. "Tell me if you've heard this one then... erm... how do you make an egg-roll?"

It's his way, telling jokes that are more corny than funny. It's the only way he knows to offer comfort—with that sweet laugh and silly sense of humor.

"You push it, Joe."

"You do, don't you, love?"

And Joe laughs at himself, nudging me once again as though nothing in life had been funnier than his stupid joke. Joe Brady is one of my favorite people on the planet. He is kind, gentle and always smells of wood smoke and the brandy he isn't supposed to drink. Autumn says the woodsy smell is from the constant landscaping he does, burning limbs and leaves to keep his place and his neighbors' neat when no one else is up to the task. It's hard to remember that Joe hadn't always been good or kind, having left Autumn and her mother for most of her life, but the past two years he's mended fences and has quickly become an important part of our lives. All of our lives.

I take the kiss on the cheek he gives me with as much grace as I can muster. He'd go on telling me corny jokes and trying to convince me of God's plan for Rhea all afternoon if I didn't break away from him.

Just as the wind shifts again, Autumn appears through the back gate followed by Declan with his arms full of cases of beer. "Hey you," she says and I gladly take the hug she gives me. It is long, firm and I smile at her reaction. You'd swear it had been weeks since I'd seen her last, not just this morning when she and I had our customary breakfast with our friends Mollie and Layla.

"How is she?" Autumn asks, brushing her fingers in my pink hair to push away the few strands that had flown across my forehead. My friends worry over Rhea nearly as much as I do. It's hard not to. The girl has an infectious personality and a quick, easy laugh. Two summers ago when Rhea was six, we took her white water rafting in Jefferson County and then stayed at a nice cabin with views of the Smokey Mountains. By lunch the next day Rhea was in love with Declan, and all of my friends were convinced she'd grow up to conquer the world. We'd eagerly agreed to be her minions.

"She still wants your man."

Autumn has a warm laugh, one that isn't forced or faked. I've always loved that about her. "Well, she can't have him." She winks at the man in question as he smiles our way, handing over the cases to Joe to place on the table.

"Which I told her. I even suggested that she set her sights on Quinn since he was younger."

"Oh, honey, I wouldn't wish that even on Heather." With Autumn's curled lip I laugh, shaking my head at the attitude she still has about Heather Matthews, the manipulative bitch who tried to blackmail Autumn into staying away from Declan when he first came to Cavanagh. Last I'd heard Heather had hooked up with Autumn's ex, Tucker, and then later my ex, Sam. Good riddance on both accounts.

"That bad, is he?"

She slips her gaze across the patio, then quickly focuses on me again, seeming unwilling to pay more than a second's attention at Declan's errant half-brother. "Girl, you have no idea." Autumn dips her head, stepping closer as though she is afraid someone will hear her. "He and Declan haven't stopped fighting since I picked them up at the airport. Other than the ride to the store for more beer, we haven't had more than an hour alone this whole time."

"That sucks."

"It really does, friend. Oh but listen to me babbling. You were just with Rhea?" She steps closer, rubbing my back. "How are you doing with all of this?"

I don't want to burden her. Autumn would be mad if I told her that's what I am thinking, but that's just how I navigate my thoughts. Sorting them on my own, fracturing apart what should and shouldn't be done, who to tell about my frustrations and worries, it's all how I manage my life. Autumn has been my best friend since we were kids. I can tell her anything, but Rhea's illness, and focusing on getting her better is far more important to me than harping on how I feel about it all. People get sick all the time. I could easily. There is no reason to burden my best friend with all the things that bring me the greatest amount of fear. So, I deflect.

"She's running out of comics. I've got to pick her up some more."

Autumn knows me too well, manages to keep from frowning, but the glare is there, the worry that I'm not being honest with her. Still, because she knows me, she doesn't dig, doesn't prod into what's really in my head. Now isn't the time.

When Mollie comes through the back gate with her boyfriend Vaughn at her side, Autumn is distracted with greeting them. I take that moment for the reprieve it is, sipping on the beer Joe served me, steeling myself against the questions I know will come.

Mollie greets Joe, mumbles to Autumn about Layla and why she's absent from the party, but I don't pay too close attention to them. My thoughts are scattered, frayed with the continuous urge to get back to Rhea. It's that central focus, that desire that distracts me, that has me forgetting anything until the sensation from earlier returns, the same one that hadn't completely died when Autumn distracted me.

The wind kicks up only slightly, brings a small gust that moves the table cloth on the picnic table and disturbs my bangs again, picking up my hair so that I have to pull the ends together to keep it from flying all around my face, all while feeling the strange sensation of being watched.

I block everything—Joe laughing with Vaughn, Mollie and Autumn's whispered worry about Layla—I am too curious to know where the sensation comes from and how to be rid of it. Shifting my gaze around the patio, I pause only for a second on Joe at the grill and then to Declan and Donovan across the patio, beers in both their hands. And then, just like that, the sensation intensifies and suddenly I find I can't breathe.

There is a small flush moving across my skin, and the fine hairs on my arms and near my scalp stand at attention. As my gaze slips to my left, away from Declan, from Donovan, it lands on the man next to them. And there it stays.

Autumn had described Quinn O'Malley, saying that he was just as beautiful as Declan, just as tall and athletic. But the dark color of their hair, the fierce shine in their eyes is where those similarities end. Where Declan is broad, massive, Quinn is slender, lithe. He has the body of a runner, all long, lean muscle, thick thighs, limbs that dominate, tower, but it is his eyes, the piercing sharp stare that flies straight at me, that has me forgetting who and where I am for a moment. That gaze penetrates, it seduces, it leaves me stunned. There is no real expression on his face. Nothing that tells me he wants me, no smirk or smile, no typical manner that announces what Quinn thinks. There is only that stare and the delicious threat it promises.

In that moment I feel every movement of his gaze, the one that penetrates me, keeps hold of me like I am is a potential conquest. Like I am his to own, a likely possession. That is a feeling I have never wanted, never toyed with needing. Still, I can't help but catch my breath with how beautiful he is.

But Quinn, Autumn has related, is trouble—an entitled trust fund kid with too much money and too much time on his hands. He is the brother Declan never knew he had; the legitimate son of the man Declan's mother had tried to steal for her own. Declan had been raised by his mother and aunt, then by Joe when the situation went bad. But Declan had managed. He'd done what most survivors do: he endured. Quinn, Autumn had said, had never been made to endure a thing but privilege, and he'd squandered a big chunk of his parents' hard earned savings in the process.

Looking at Quinn those revelations echo in my brain. Autumn's voice in my head warns me to stop staring at him. It is Declan's and Joe's heavy brogue that insists I remember what men like Quinn offer—heartache and misery. These are rational observations my brain makes. They are loud, fiercely stern, but that still doesn't pull my attention from that beautiful man. Sire of heartache and misery or not, Quinn O'Malley is a beautiful, *beautiful* man.

One look tells me all I need to know—those fingers are long, uncalloused, meaning he's never done a hard day's work. Those eyes are unlined and no wrinkles crowd around his mouth, meaning he's likely never had a worry aging his face. His mouth is wide, the bottom lip plumper in the center, the cupid's bow pronounced. Quinn's jaw is angular, sharp and his chest and shoulders are finely sculpted, as though some artist had carved him with precision.

Look away, idiot, drums in my head and I finally manage to pull my attention away from O'Malley when Declan and Donovan block him from my view. It doesn't take a Ph.D. to know what they're saying to him and when Quinn spits at the ground and storms into the house, my suspicions are confirmed. They've warned him not to mess with me, probably mentioning how fragile I am, how Rhea's illness makes me worthy of kid gloves—and unwelcome pity.

"Sayo, love," Declan moves to greet me and the frown he hurries to hide as he kisses my cheek tells me he still sees me as delicate.

"How was Ireland?" I mean to distract him, keep that sad little grimace off his face. I even manage a smile, but it feels forced and awkward.

"Ireland was grand. The company, though... ah, well, my brother is..." the Irishman pauses, rubbing his fingers through his hair. "He's a pain in the arse, is Quinn."

"You know," I say, forcing myself to maintain the smile I don't quite mean, "I remember Autumn saying the same thing about you not so long ago."

"Aye, well, I grew on her, didn't I?"

Now I'm the one to frown, but half-jokingly. "Not the visual I want." He shakes his head, laughing at my lame response. "Besides, maybe Quinn will grow on you."

"Oh I'd not hold my breath on that hope, love. I'm likely to suffocate him whilst he sleeps before too long."

"Seems a waste," I say, glancing back at the house, near the gate as Quinn emerges from behind it with an unlit cigarette hanging from his mouth. Instantly my stomach rumbles with a sensation somewhere between excitement and disgust. "Although maybe if you beat him enough he'll start to appreciate how precious life is."

"Sayo…"

I wave at him, disregarding the concern in his tone, offering him a grin. Everyone knows how I feel about smoking, but it's his business what he does with his body. Why should I care? Still, thinking about Rhea hacking and coughing, struggling for a clear breath while Quinn wastes his own, makes me angry, rational or not.

I try to keep from bristling as Declan tries to sooth me. "I'm fine," I tell him, nodding at Autumn when she joins us. "A little maudlin today, is all." I spot Mollie and run to greet her, knowing full well that Declan watches me, likely wondering why I haven't spoken to any of them about Rhea's illness. It's been four years since my cousin was first diagnosed, but only four months since the doctors told our family that the cancer had returned and the tumor had doubled in size.

No one wants to tell the truth. Not when you're a kid and wide-eyed and eager with hope for all the impossible things in life. No one tells you that some kid your age in China sat in a sweat shop, their fingers bleeding, their family starving as they sew together the pink and green swimsuit your mother buys you for your first swimming lesson. No one tells you that in order for you to live in that big white Victorian with the wrap-around porch and twenty foot high ceilings, that some woman in another land had to sign away her rights to you. She had carried you inside of her, but couldn't keep you. Maybe she had loved you, but had signed the paper full of words she might not have been able to read, had signed away the claim she had on you. Just so you could live in that Victorian and wear that swimsuit and eat in abundance. But no one tells you that after all that, you still might have everything taken away from you too.

My parents love me, but even they never told the truth. They never mentioned how tough life forces you to be. They never made me realize what a gamble it is to love blindly, completely. They never told me that loving Rhea as I did would mean I would have to deal with losing her, and that in losing her, I'd lose a part of myself.

Rhea has eyes shaped exactly like mine. She has the same small cow lick at her temple, and skin the exact color of mine. She could have been me at eight, and now I was having to watch her die a slow death. My friends, no matter how much they love me, would never know this. Not really. Yet, they had their own struggles, their own demons to exorcise. I wouldn't bother them with mine.

And so, I don't.

Mollie talks a mile a minute. Laughing when Autumn fusses at Donovan for some other stupid thing he'd done to Layla that had kept her away from the party.

"Wonder if he and Layla will ever figure out that they want each other." Mollie's smile is effortless, sweet, and when her boyfriend Vaughn stands next to her, the affection in her expression only strengthens.

"Didn't take us that long."

"Sugar, I wanted you the second I saw you," Mollie answers, weaving her arm around his thin waist.

"Yeah? So did I."

"Well Layla and Donovan have been doing this dance around each other since they were kids." She takes a sip of her water, head shaking as Donovan withers under Autumn's fussing. "Sometimes I think they'll never get to it."

That was the way of things with my friends: Declan and Autumn carrying on like they needed to touch each other every so often to maintain a normal heart beat. Mollie and Vaughn casting long glances at each other as though they could hardly believe the other was smiling the same smile right back at them. Donovan and Layla being stubborn to realize that all the teasing, all the insults and pranks they leveled at each other, was the longest bout of foreplay to ever happen in the history of Cavanagh. And me, smiling wide, laughing with my friends, loving them for the support they offer, all while hating myself for holding my own burden to my chest because it was mine to carry.

It is dark when I finally leave and Joe has asks twice if I want him to drive me home, just one time more than Autumn and Declan asked. They are sweet. And stubborn and mostly all drunk. So I slip from the house before anyone notices I'm gone, jotting down a reminder in my phone to meet Autumn in two days for a Saturday breakfast she made me swear I'd show up for. She understands that I need space, but that doesn't mean she'll let me keep sequestered for long.

The sweltering heat has eased, but I still knot my hair to keep my neck cool and tangle my pink waves at the back of my head as I move down the front porch steps, breathing easier now that I have left the party and everyone's attention. But then I am accosted by a plume of cigarette smoke that wafts right in my face as I come to the street light on the corner of the sidewalk.

Quinn O'Malley is leaning against the light pole, flicking

ashes on the ground, stretching his arms over his head as he exhales. The light from overhead casts shadows onto the pavement and his silhouette is one of glorious precision and finely honed perfection. Too bad all that beauty is attached to a smoking, entitled asshole.

Though I know it's rude, I pull my collar up, covering my nose and mouth from the stench of the cigarette as I walk behind him, hoping he won't notice me pass.

"This bother you?"

Walk away. Keep quiet and walk away, I tell myself, knowing that it would be sensible to ignore him, that Autumn and Declan have warned everyone what a prick Quinn is.

"Yes," I say unable to help myself, turning around to face him. "It does."

He holds the smoke between his fingers, squinting at me, likely at the small snarl making my top lip quiver before he takes a drag. "And why is that then?"

"Because," I say, "It stinks." Quinn pushes off the street lamp with the cigarette still between his fingers and I try like hell not to notice the thick scent of his cologne cutting through the reek of tobacco. "It's rude to smoke out in the open where someone can pass by you and be subjected to…" I wave my hand in the direction of the cigarette, "that disgusting thing."

"Is it now?"

"Yes." My fingers itch to yank the cigarette from his hand and toss it on the ground. "That stench lingers on your clothes, in your hair, on your breath."

Something about my accusation gives him pause, draws a half smile from Quinn. "Why is that your concern?"

"It's not…"

I try not to watch the slow slide of his tongue against his bottom lip as he takes a step towards me. "In fact, I'd say you're the last one that should be fussed over the state of me or the way I smell." Quinn stands right in front of me and that erotic scent of his cologne drags my thoughts away from the putrid smell of smoke. "My breath, for instance. Unless you're keen to snog me, is really not for you to worry over, is it then?"

A small image flicks through my mind, but I push it aside. "And why in God's name would anyone want to kiss you, least of all me?"

"Not sure, am I? You just strike me as the tightly wound sort. Been a while, has it, love?"

There is the smallest hint of humor in his tone, along with the challenge. It makes me step forward, eager to knock that grin from his face. "That is none of your damn business."

"Nor is me and my fags yours." He lifts the cigarette at me as though I wouldn't know that slang word meant cigarettes before he stamps it out with his foot. "Best you keep to your own business, unless you change your mind about that snog." Quinn is only inches from me now, invading my space, soaking up the air around us and I suspect he is anticipating my upset. Maybe he thinks that being domineering will somehow intimidate me. It does not and I don't flinch, don't move even a finger as he comes closer still with his warm, tobacco drenched breath heating against my face. "Were you to ask, then I'd throw these buggers away without a second thought."

"For a snog?"

A quick jerk of his chin and that humor is gone from Quinn's expression as though he thinks I'm serious. As though he wants me to be. "Snog, fuck, whatever your willing to give up."

He's no different than half the players I've come across at CU. The same attitude, the same smugness and faux vows to give up something they enjoy just for the pleasure of my time or the thrill of my touch. It's all bullshit. The same bullshit that kept me a virgin until I was eighteen and unattached for the most part since then.

I know Quinn O'Malley wouldn't give up anything for me. That doesn't mean I can't lead him on.

I take pleasure in the surprise that registers as I slip my fingers into his pocket, as I pull out his pack of smokes and free a single cigarette. He accepts it when I place the filter in his mouth, though he squints again, moving his gaze from my fingers to my face like he expects me to insult him.

"If a snog from me will keep you off smoking…" I choose not to acknowledge the fuck comment, instead lighting the cigarette and shoving the pack and lighter back into his pocket, "then you best keep at it. My lips will *never*, ever touch yours."

Two slow steps and the scent of him dims. I'm nearly a block away before I glance back. There is a faint plume of smoke lingering about his head, but the cigarette dangles in his hand. He is watching my movements. I feel that on my neck, my face, my body as he watches me and I tell myself as I walk away that I don't care in the least that he does.

TWO

I AM FOUR, nearly five. I don't remember time, how it stretches and moves, how moments are missed, how memories are distorted by the disarrangement of minutes, hours. But I remember hearing the voices. Strange words I don't recognize, people that look nothing like me or anyone I have ever known, and the woman with the green eyes.

The woman that held me on her lap when we left the orphanage and the crying nurses who handed me over. The woman with the green eyes and the curly ginger hair gave me a paper swan, its wings pointed and sharp, and I held it in the car, through the airport and on the plane as we flew and flew over oceans, as the movies played on the screens in front of us, as the green-eyed woman sang to me so I would sleep. And I did. For days, for minutes, I don't remember.

One minute I am in the village with the smell of fish hanging in the air and the clip of small boats knocking against the pier, the easy hum of music sounding beyond the orphanage walls, and the next I am with Mama and Papa, with all the people that look like them instead of me, and who call me "beautiful" and "precious."

They call me by my name, Sayo, they tell me they are my family now, but I don't know what that means.

A year later two boys who looked exactly the same came to our home. Mama said they were my brothers, but their skin was brown and their hair was softer than mine, curly, thicker. How could they be my brothers? One of them, Mama called him Booker, cried the whole night. He cried the whole next day, too, and the other one, Carver, joined him, both of them keeping me from Barney and the fluffy waffles Mama made with lots of butter and thick maple syrup. But then they stopped crying when I gave them my waffles and held their hands while Barney sang on the television. Then my new brothers fell asleep next to me on the sofa, still holding my hands. They weren't so bad when they slept. They didn't cry at all then.

The next year a girl came to live with us. She looked even stranger than Booker and Carver and Mama called her Adriana and she sat in Papa's lap because, I guessed, his eyes and hair were dark like hers, not light like Mama's.

Months later another girl, my sister Alessandra, with lighter skin than Adriana's and eyes that were small like mine. Then there were so many people in our house that Mama and Papa packed big boxes and hid away all my dollies and every one of Booker's trucks even when he cried and cried for them. And then our new home got crowded with all the children, but every night before I said my prayers, after Mama would tuck me in and read me a story and tell me I was her sweet girl, Booker and Carver would come into my bed and hold my hand and then Adriana followed and Alessandra came too until Mama fussed, until she stopped fussing and we stayed with each other when the night came, when the house got quiet.

Until the memories of Shirakawa-go weren't as strong. Until I didn't smell the fish in the air or hear the murmur of music in the echo of the wind, until my only leftover memory was of that paper swan, and my little brothers who held my hands until they fell asleep and the little girls who looked nothing like me, nothing like anyone I knew, curled in ball at the foot of my bed and we slept, my siblings and I, we slept because that was where we felt safest.

Together.

"Sayo? You stopped reading."

"Did I? I'm sorry, sweetie."

I'd arrived this morning to find Rhea upset. Claire, her older sister was acting out. It happened now and again when she felt left out, when Aunt Carol spent too much time focusing on doctor's appointments or how she'd cover the deductible on Rhea's new meds. Uncle Clay hadn't been around much lately, something I knew worried Carol, but still wouldn't complain about. Claire, though, resented Rhea. It was understandable. She was ten and hadn't yet grasped the concept that Rhea needed attention, sometimes all the attention.

"Okay, so," I say, turning the page. "Where were we?"

"The Midnight Duel. Peeves is about to start screaming."

A brief nod and I continue reading from the book, smiling when Rhea rests her head against my shoulder. We'd read *Harry Potter and The Sorcerer's Stone* at least half a dozen times, but my little cousin never got bored with it, could likely repeat what I read verbatim.

"Draco's a snot."

"Duh. He's supposed to be."

She feels warm, like she is courting a fever and I tick off yet another note in my head to mention to Aunt Carol. Turning the page, I let myself travel with Rhea to Hogwarts, losing myself for a moment in the magic and mystery of those darkened, ancient halls and the threat that loomed at Harry's every turn. From my peripheral I notice Rhea's eyes are closed, but she mouths the words as I voice them, each syllable coming out with a reverence only cherished stories are treated to. She loves disappearing into her imagination as much as I do. It takes her away from the things that threaten her own narrow world.

After a moment, once Harry had met Fluffy, Rhea blinks, her eyes going glassy and I know her attention is no longer with me, that she feels distracted, irritated. I doubt it has anything to do with the fight she'd had with Claire. Those come often enough now that they rarely manage to upset her.

Without me uttering a sound Rhea glances up at me, points to the pencil and sketch pad on her bedside table. I know what she wants.

"I was thinking," she says, nodding at the small doodles she'd already made in the book as I thumb through it to find an empty sheet. "Fairies have no colors. Not really."

She does this often—lets her mind run around with random, unconnected thoughts, following her own internal timeline. I'd seen it with my grandfather when I was ten. He'd been diagnosed with lung cancer and after the doctor's visit that had resulted in what was his death sentence, Gramps found it nearly impossible to keep his thoughts organized. He wanted to stroll down memory lane. He wanted to do things he'd never gotten around to. He wanted to read books, watch films that had once meant something to him. Rarely had he stayed focused enough to finish anything.

Rhea, I'd found, did similar things—attention distracted from whatever she was doing, pulled into an idea, an untethered opinion that then consumed her.

"What about Tinkerbell?"

"She wasn't really like the cartoon. I've read *Peter Pan*." Rhea took the pencil from my hand, scribbling without any concentration a form with wings but no flourish, nothing that made the fairy unique at all. It may have been a moth for all the detail she left out. "Even in my books and comics, the only colors the fairies have are on the dresses they wear, maybe in small splotches on their wings. And there are none that look like me."

This was a travesty to her. She had voiced the desire to rectify many times before, on those low days when her mood is somber and her hope is almost nonexistent.

On those days, when her manner is particularly low, like it was now, Rhea stays quiet, still, and demands only one thing. "Paint me," she says and though I can't draw anything resembling a fairy, I can make Rhea smile with my artless, juvenile sketches. That's what I do now, because the chemo is weighing her down, because she has endured so much in such a small lifetime that I would do anything she asks of me.

"Draw me happy."

And I do, obliging, moving my pencil over the paper, arching loops, curling lines until wings have formed, until the flicker of light from her wand spreads over the page and coats the ground at her stick figure feet.

"That's about as good as I can manage, kiddo."

"It's perfect." And Rhea picks up the paper as though the compliment has not been a lie, as though the meager fairy I'd drawn for her is remarkable and not pathetic at all. "It's perfect," she says again and I catch myself trying to touch her, to hold her against my shoulder like I used to do when she was barely four and already sick. But eight, I knew, was far too old to let your big cousin hold you. And so I grab a new piece of paper and hand it and the pencil to Rhea.

"Draw me a hope."

It was the same game we'd had for years. *Draw me a dream that you dream for yourself* I'd ask her and she would, imagining herself onto the page with no hospital beds, no tubes in her nose, no machines a reach away. She would draw herself healthy. She would draw herself strong. No matter how she drew herself, no matter what form those characters took, that Rhea was perfect.

Today she draws herself standing with her toes sunk into the white sand amidst the soft contours of a shoreline. Her skill is greater than mine, her talent raw and untrained but still immense. She draws an ocean laid out in front of that beach, and trees with fat coconuts between the fan branches On that beach she draws two figures, a man and a woman, hands clasped together, smiles wide. The woman has long hair flowing down her back, and in her free hand is a cane that she leans into as though the hunch of her frail back pains her.

"Who is that?" I ask, wondering who she wished she was today.

"It's me. When I'm old. I'm so old that I need a cane."

"And who is that with you? The faceless man?"

"My husband, but he's very old too. We're old together on that beach." She pauses, smiling to herself about something she doesn't share. "We're retired."

The scene makes her happy, and she focuses on adding a bird in the sky and fat, thick clouds. "Your hair is beautiful." I point to the long, wavy hair down the woman's back and the accented tendrils that Rhea lines over and over again.

"It's gray." She sits closer to the paper, concentrating on a second palm tree, making its limbs longer. "That... that's the biggest dream I have," she admits, now coloring in the space of white that makes up the old woman's hair.

"To be on a beach?"

"No," she says forgetting the drawing for a moment to stare at me, that mild grin completely vacant now. "To be gray-headed, Sayo. To… to be an old lady."

I am not prepared for that revelation or how desperate I am to keep the tears from spilling from my eyes. I blink them away, not wanting Rhea to notice. She doesn't want pity. She doesn't want anyone upset because she is sick—she's told me at least a dozen times. So again, I deflect.

"Maybe you *should* try dyeing you hair purple." I tug on my pink hair, waving it a little. "Then we really would match."

For a long time, Rhea watches me, eyes moving, scrutinizing my features, then dropping her gaze back down to the strands between my fingers.

"No," she says, exhaling before she returns to the drawing. "I'd rather have gray hair."

And because she's not watching, I close my eyes because that's what I want too—Rhea very old and very gray. I close my eyes and pray, right then, that God would grant her the time for her skin to wrinkle, to allow time to leave its traces in her forehead, for gravity to drag down breasts that had yet to even develop. I wanted that so desperately for her.

"Do you think it's beautiful?" she asks and I'm not sure if she means the drawing.

"Yes, sweetie, it's the most beautiful dream."

And it is. Dreams are that way when they are heartfelt. When the significance behind them goes deeper than hope, further than a wish. Those are the dreams of the faithful. The ones who haven't completely given up. Rhea dreams beautifully. She hopes fiercely and that night when I went to bed, it was that old lady I tried to see in my head. That gray haired woman and the faceless man who loved her. More than anything, I wanted that dream to come true.

THREE

I WAIT AT Joe's for Autumn as she hustles to the rugby pitch to fetch Declan and Donovan since both their vehicles are out for repairs. That happens when you race your souped-up rides down Cushman's Crossing like bored teenagers and come off the other side of the track with a trip to the auto body shop in your future. The wait, I don't mind. Not on mornings like this when the wind is cool and the sidewalk and pavement is thick with the smell of rain. It reminds me of mornings I'd sit underneath the front awning of the library before I opened it to the public. Those mornings Cavanagh was quiet, the slumber which would give way to hustle and bustle; the easy breath of a vivid, living community that would rise with a burst of energy and not stop until well after the sun set. Most of my days were full of requests from professors or students complaining about their coursework. Before all that started, I'd take a second, brimming hot cup of coffee in hand and sit out on the benches, watching my hometown as it came to life. It calmed me, prepared me for what would come next.

Two squirrels move across Joe's front yard, scampering toward the large pine tree near his driveway. I smile at the way they chase each other as I stretch my legs out over the front wooden swing, my back against the armrest. The storm that passed through is dying and the steady thump of rain against the roof has me shutting my eyes, breathing in the sweet scent of wet grass and honeysuckle from Joe's back yard. Cavanagh is beautiful, that much I know without opening my eyes. Beyond the cityscape, past the tall buildings and the stadium on campus, there are the lush, imposing mountains that seem to stretch and curl around the town. Cavanagh sits in the center with those mountains acting as sentry—black rock that touches a purple and yellow sky, protecting us.

The university library was my sanctuary—a comforting, imposing structure filled with histories, with the knowledge of a thousand lifetimes, and I was its keeper. I miss it. Rhea's illness, my need to be with her, keeps me from my office and the large oak desk that fills my office. It keeps me from the rows of Funko Pop! figurines of every conceivable fandom I cherish lining the shelves and window seals. It keeps me from the looming size of that Grecian building, the long row of galley windows, even the cobblestone entranceway that spreads out at the front entrance, and leads to the brightly blooming mums and wild flowers in the planters along the steps.

Sometimes I think I'll go back. Sometimes I think I need to, but as the Chancellor told me, family is essential. Family is first. Ava would say that. She's just as much family to me as Autumn, Mollie and Layla are. Still, I tried not to take advantage of our relationship when I asked her for a leave of absence. She understood, but I still felt guilty about it.

The creak of the screen door opening pulls me out of my thoughts; Joe comes out to the porch, his hands full of two steaming mugs. "Still pissing rain?" he asks, offering me a mug of coffee.

"It's slacked off a bit. Thanks," I say, tipping my cup for a quick toast.

He leans against the porch column and sits on the railing, gazing at the thick rainclouds that are moving at a snail's pace away from town. "It'll be gone in half an hour." Joe motions with his mug to the sky. "I hope Autumn will be wary of the slick roads."

"She's been driving for ten years, Joe." He shrugs, dismissing me with a smile. I lower my foot, moving the swing when it slows. "You've been back two years and you still don't quite get that your little girl isn't a kid anymore."

Joe doesn't look offended, doesn't glare at me at least and when he shifts his gaze in my direction, I offer him a smile of my own, loving the way one dimple dents in his cheeks. "Ah, I know that well, love. Too well." He takes a breath, rubbing his neck. "Before too long Declan will finally convince her to accept his barmy arse and she'll be married and likely off to Bridgett knows where."

"You could go with them, you know." The thought comes to me from nowhere and as soon as I mention Joe leaving, I frown. I don't want anyone to leave Cavanagh, least of all my best friend, but I'm no fool. None of them will stay here forever.

"Aye, but I'd only be in the way."

"Joe, you've spent most of her life not involved." I pull my feet up and pat the empty spot on the swing for the old man to sit down. He does, reluctantly but keeps silent. "Don't you think she'd want you around when she starts having babies?"

"Babies?" I had no idea his eyes could get that round and the amazed, loud laughter is out of my mouth when that wild fear and worry hardens the muscles around his mouth.

"That's generally what happens when people get married. Especially people like those two."

"What do you... *oh aye.*" Some distasteful image must jump into Joe's mind when I paint that picture and he wrinkles his nose, then rubs the palm of his free hand against his eyelids as though that would take away the image. "Well. What's that got to do with anything?" He watches the trees move in the breeze, ignoring his coffee as it rests on his thigh.

"You're the only parent she has left." I grab his hand to make him look back at me. "And she loves you. Declan loves you, too. You're the only father either of them has ever known. Of course they'd want you around when they start a family."

That soft smile, the ease of tension in his features makes Joe look younger, calmer and I get some small glimmer of pleasure that I'd somehow comforted him. Still, Joe seems distracted by the thought of leaving Cavanagh again.

We both watch the rain slide against the railing and down the steps, and Joe seems a little lost. "I couldn't just... leave..." he glances up at the house.

"It'll be here for you when you get back. I'll keep an eye on it."

"You, love," Joe says, tapping my leg, "should be out seeing the world."

"I'm not going anywhere, Joe. Not any time soon."

Joe's gaze is hard, I feel the weight of it on the side of my face as I stare out beyond the porch, to the neighboring house and the small Yorkie that runs through several puddles on the lawn. But Joe is not one to let anyone he cares for bear a burden on their own. For all his past mistakes, he is a good man and I take the comfort he offers when he slips his hand, still warm from his mug, over mine.

"Thanks," I whisper, squeezing back against his fingers.

The Yorkie vanishes beneath the covered carport attached to the neighbor's house and Joe and I stay silent, keeping to ourselves as the weather and traffic around us turns into a quiet hum, until the warmth of his touch grows cooler the harder the wind blows.

Then Joe's cell phone chirps, breaking our reverie. He excuses himself with a quick, "Give me just a moment..." and then I am alone again with the stillness around me and the lulling melody of the storm.

At least until I hear the low mutter of an accented curse and the whip of the door flying open. Quinn. He must not see me at first as he stretches, bare-chested, with his shirt hanging in his hand and low-hanging black rugby shorts revealing a thick trail of hair below his navel. It's not until he has taken a few steps out onto the porch, throwing his shirt around his neck and pulling a cigarette from the pack in his pocket, that he notices me sitting on the swing watching him.

"Bollocks." The curse is whispered, but I don't care enough to pretend I hadn't heard him. By the casual glare he offers me, I get the impression that Quinn doesn't care either.

Another low grunt, another stretch and he glares at the sky and the dark clouds that loom above us. "Fecking rain."

"Well, good morning to you too, sunshine." It seems the only sound he'll make is that annoying grunt. Quinn holds the cigarette loosely between two fingers, moving his knuckles to twist it side to side as though he needs the distraction. As though the scent of rain and maybe my presence gives him something to consider, maybe something to glare at before he attempts smoking.

Feeling the smallest bit smug that my irritation at his smoking might be what keeps that cigarette unlit, I grin, stretching my legs out again. The small gesture moves the swing, makes the chains creak and moan and Quinn glances back at me. When I return his stare, he gives up, returning his attention to the black clouds.

A smart aleck part of me that hasn't had a lot of exercise of late gets ahold of me, and I casually say, "Isn't it a little early for you to be up?" Another glare, this one with a hint of offense and I shrug, harboring a hidden grin. "Don't you trust fund, party animal types sleep in until just before the midnight hour beckons?"

That doesn't even warrant a smirk. "Bit hard to get any sleep around here," he says, stretching his neck, "with all the yammering about and laughter."

Joe and I hadn't been that loud; he was just yanking my chain. I decide to yank back. "That must be horrible." He glances at me, eyebrows drawing together. "All that God awful laughing."

"It does wear me down a bit, if I'm being honest."

Quinn slips his gray t-shirt on and I try not to look, reminding myself that those beautiful eyes, that lithe, athletic frame doesn't excuse the attitude or his bothered, entitled manner. But I'm human. I'm a single woman in her twenties who hasn't had regular sex since the falling out with my ex Sam, a couple of years ago.

Quinn is beautiful and he damn well knows it so the small effort I make at not staring while he pulls on that shirt, is weak. And he catches me.

I don't need a mirror to know the look I'm giving him and I don't think I care much that subtlety is off the table at the moment.

He pauses just long enough for me to notice the lift of his eyebrows before he steps in front of me, kneeling next to the swing so that we are eye level.

"See something you like?" I do. I like that shape of his face, the soft contours of his eyes, how gentle they make him look, how they contrast to the angular cut of his jaw and the wide stretch of his mouth. Quinn stops the swing from moving by holding his leg against the underside of the seat and then he leans forward, his arm resting just inches from mine. "Do you then?"

How many seconds, I wonder, would it take him to have me in his room? How quickly, how thoroughly would he perform knowing that Joe is just a few feet away, that Declan and Autumn would be back soon? Quinn doesn't strike me as the sort to rush anything, least of all fucking. Certainly not fucking a girl he sees as a challenge. And that's what I am. I see that plainly in the way he stares at me, how he tries to appear so unaffected by my presence. Do I like what I see? Of course I do. Will I tell him that? Not ever in life.

It would be fun to play with him, to pass the time while I wait for Autumn. I even consider it—flirting a little, trying to remember what it is to laugh, to forget worry, but then Quinn shifts his legs, moving his weight from one foot to another and the pack of smokes in his pocket falls to the floor.

"No," I say glancing away from his pack to glare at him. "Not even remotely."

"What have I done now?" he says, with feigned injury, while swiping the cigarettes off the floor and replacing them into his pocket. I didn't even light the fecking fag."

"As if that makes one whit of difference."

He stands when I place my feet on the floor, readjusting on the swing, but Quinn doesn't keep clear of me. I can smell the masculine scent of his hair and the mint from his toothpaste. "Aren't you just in a grand mood this morning?"

I sip my coffee ignoring him. "How would you know? This is literally the second time you've seen me. And in case you're desperate, there's a back yard to this place, you know. You can go out there to slowly kill yourself with those things for all I care."

"You really are a fussy bit of stuff, aren't you?" He follows me away from the swing, right behind me as I lean against the brick column and will Autumn to drive up the street. "You really that put off by me smoking? Care that much, do you?" He stands directly behind me, as though he expects me to be affected by how close he is, by how his chest is at my shoulders. All Quinn has to do is take a step and I'd feel the firm outline of his body against my back. But he doesn't move. He only keeps a few inches between us as though waiting. As though he's certain I'll lean back just to press myself against him.

"What?" There is laughter in his voice that I've never heard from him before. It's casual and annoying. "Afraid I'll get cancer and die?" When I wince, straighten my shoulders, all the humor leaves his tone and I catch how quickly his smile fades from the corner of my eye. "What is it?" he asks, voice softer, but not sweet. When he gets nothing more, he steps in front of me, leaning his hand on the brick right next to my hip. I don't move back.

"Who is it?" And just like that, he knows, as though he can sense where my attitude, my anger comes from. There is a look in his eyes, that quick frustration and anger that I've seen a dozen times in my own mirror. I have no idea why it's there in Quinn's eyes, as well. "Who?" he says again, this time he sounds almost concerned.

I can't trust him. I'm aware of that. There is nothing remotely logical about telling Quinn O'Malley about Rhea. There is nothing that he can say or do that would give me even the remotest comfort. Yet, I tell him anyway. "My little cousin."

"She's ill?"

I stare at him, then down at the cigarette in his hand, reminding myself how cavalier he is about his own life. Wondering why he wants to know anything about mine. But I can't stop myself from speaking, from offering up information that is not mine to share.

"She's dying. Cancer. Bilateral optic glioma. She's had it for four years."

The news doesn't surprise him. Quinn, in fact, doesn't really react at all. Instead, he merely nods before looking out over my head, as though he needs to work out something for himself. Maybe there's some memory that he takes stock of, something that keeps him from shifting focus back to me and what I just revealed. After a moment, he clears his throat, staring back at me again. "In and out of hospital?" I nod. "How old?"

"Eight." Again, he looks away from me and I catch the small effort of his fingers, how he seems to subconsciously move the cigarette between his fingers.

"It's a rotten thing to have to be stuck in hospital, especially when you're a kid." He steps back, then up onto the porch, making for the front door. He seems to be trying to keep his expressions neutral and his tone light, but there is that look again—the same one I know from my own eyes. Quinn crumbles the cigarette into his fist before tossing it out onto the front lawn. "And you…" he says, staring at me.

But whatever about me that made him pause, he doesn't finish explaining as Declan and Autumn pull into the drive with their brakes squeaking in the damp. They are out of the car and racing through the weather and onto the porch before Quinn can disappear into Joe's house. One look at Quinn, his stare still fixed on my face, and Autumn moves next to me, as if to protect me from whatever is happening on the porch.

Declan watches his brother, then glances between us. "Alright then?"

"Fine," I say, watching Declan's frown as Quinn shoots him a fierce glare.

It's a tense moment, one that is too full of testosterone, but before I can call either of them out, Quinn rolls his eyes, opening the porch door. "Grand," he says, before he disappearing into the house without a backward glance, letting the screen door bang behind him.

THREE RINGS AT two a.m.

I'd gone through months waiting for this call.

"Hello?"

"Sweetie, it's Carol." There is a breath. I count the seconds. "Rhea's back in the hospital. That fever didn't lower. Her platelets have dipped."

"For how long?"

"Depends." Her voice is raspy, a deep sound that reminds me of mornings my mother just returned from her double shift at the hospital. She'd worked the ICU for decades and could never keep the tiredness from her voice when she woke us for school. "The doctors... hell, Sayo, they're saying it might be indefinitely. It might be until..." but Carol can't finish speaking. Her tone has become too weighted, the emotion, the desperation too heavy.

My room is pitch dark. The only light glows from my phone and even that bothers my eyes. I want darkness. I want silence. I want the nightmare to end. "Aunt Carol, what can I do?"

"Nothing." She doesn't hesitate and there is a second when her resolve falters. She is strong. She's had to be. She is Teflon and remarkable, trying like hell to pretend she can take on these monsters, fight this battle for her daughter and yet, with that one word, I hear how weary she is. "She's finally sleeping and I wanted you to know. I... oh God, honey, is that the time?" The rustle from the earpiece is dull, as though Carol has moved the phone. "I didn't realize."

"It's fine," I say, hoping she can't hear that half-asleep, exhausted tone in my voice. "It's fine... I'll... I can come right now."

"No, no get your rest. It's not like you'll be able to see her, anyway. Come tomorrow. After ten o'clock. She'll be awake then and she'll want more comics." It is a halfhearted joke, one that is forced and even that humorless laugh sounds weak.

"I'll pick some up," I tell her falling back against my pillow in the dark. "Anything else? Anything at all?"

"Sayo—I didn't want to say anything," she pauses, then seems to gain a bit of strength. "There's... there's nothing to be done really, but Doctor Simmons brought up that new experimental treatment again. The one that targets the mutation in the tumor." I knew what she was talking about; I'd done my research when the doctor first talked about it. But it was expensive, and insurance refused to cover it. It was a last resort. "Clay and I, we were talking to some of the nurses and they mentioned fundraising because... well."

"Where can we get it? Locally?"

"We can't. Not yet, Sayo. It's... without the insurance it'll cost eighty grand."

"I have thirty." I don't hesitate to offer up my savings. My job is decent. Our 401(k) is paltry but I'm a single woman with a rent controlled apartment and no bad habits other than Netflix binges. The money I have stored away has no purpose and retirement is a long ways away. This could help. This was almost half way to what they needed. "You can have all that I have, Aunt Carol."

"Sayo. No. I shouldn't have mentioned it. We'll do a fundraiser."

"I want to help. I have to."

"Oh, sweetheart..." I hear the defeat in her voice; she is utterly spent. I desperately want to help, but my offer is just one more weight around her neck. My heartbeat increases because I imagine my aunt there, in that damn hospital room again, the same one Rhea has lived in for four years. One step forward, ten back. It never seems to end and the good, the good is so fucking fleeting. But she rallies. She always rallies. "You help, honey. So much. You are such... Rhea loves you so much. You're everything she wants to be and I can't tell you how proud I am of you, how much we appreciate everything you do for her. We can't ask this of you, too. We won't allow it."

"It's selfish," I admit, frowning when my voice cracks. The moment is unguarded and Carol knows it.

"What, love?"

"Everything. I do it because I want... I don't want to miss anything, Aunt Carol." I should hang up. I should try to sleep and let her do the same, and my aunt already knows what I'm trying to say. She has to. Rhea is her child. I am only the cousin. Still, I can't help myself. "Oh, Carol, I don't want time to... to..."

"To run out."

"It will, though. It's coming."

"Sweetie, don't." She takes another breath, her resolve weakening. "Please don't."

I suddenly realize what I'm saying. I can't do that to her. Not Carol. Not that determined, strong woman battling for her child. My palms over my face, drying away the tears, I channel her, hope that I can absorb some of her strength.

"I'm sorry." I take another moment, clear my throat. Carol doesn't need this. It's late, she's worried, she needed an ear and I gave her nothing. "We'll talk about it, later." Another breath and I sit up, stretch out my shoulders so my voice will be clear, firm. "I'm fine and I'll be there in the morning. Give Rhea a kiss for me, okay, and try to sleep. You're... you're exhausted." We all were. We had been for years and as I disconnect the call and lay back on my bed, watching the darkness around me grow dimmer, I realize that we had only just begun to be exhausted.

We'd only just started.

FOUR

THERE IS MORE anonymity to be had as of late. I'm not really hiding, just preoccupied. Rhea rests, sleeps and struggles with the reaction to her meds most days. It's been weeks now that they've kept her in the hospital loaded up on pain meds, the poison of chemo keeping her tired, weak. The white blood cell count is so low now that they make us wear gloves and masks. They make no promises that the count will improve.

But that does not make up the anonymity. It's the way I guard myself, how closed off I am from the life I knew outside of the hospital. Rhea has become a planet I orbit around, where everything else is less import. Nothing compared to that child and what she requires.

Even the distraction of Declan and Donovan spotting me last week as I rushed into McKinney's to grab a bite to eat didn't rouse me. The only thing that registered was how low they spoke to each other, which meant that I had distracted them, hushed them, raised their pity. And then Sam, my ex-boyfriend who still ran the place, stared a bit too long at me with that same look of pity, and maybe the mildest hint of guilt about how we had ended. He'd wanted to say something. That was clear in his features, in the way his lips parted as if to say something.. But I didn't care what Sam had to say to me. I didn't care that my best friend's boyfriend and his teammate were gossiping about me, likely talking about how tired I looked, how disheveled, how worn.

I'd tossed the money on the counter and took the white bag stained with french fry grease and left McKinney's without a backward glance at anyone.

I feel that orbit, the one that keeps me tethered to my cousin as I walk toward a coffee shop, bone tired and weary from the worst nights Rhea has endured in four years. She is frustrated, she doesn't understand with the frustration of a child why her body refuses to behave the way she wants it to.

But tonight was the first I'd seen her argumentative. The first time she had retreated full into herself, not speaking to anyone, not wanting anyone's company. Not even mine.

That hospital, and the small, defeated girl is where my mind is now. It keeps my attention and I can do nothing to take in the town around me or the people I know who smile, who may or may not have asked after Rhea. I barely register anything as I walk to the coffee shop, focusing on the thought of caffeine to keep my eyes from slamming shut. The smell of dark roast, the sweet hint of sugar that wafts out of the shop as customers leave, none of it really distracts me. Nothing keeps my attention for long but Rhea… Rhea and the look she gave me. That look and the last thing she said to me before I left.

"Just leave, Sayo. I don't want you here."

She hadn't meant it. Logically, I know that. But the bite of her words sticks sharp. I feel wounded, feel the pain throbbing as I open the door, only to be assaulted with raised voices as I make my way inside. Even through my miasma, I recognize those voices.

"Layla, seriously?" Mollie is saying. "This shit has got to stop." The brunette's face is bunched and angry as she screams at her best friend. Layla's eyes are darting between Mollie and Donovan, who is looking both ridiculous and enraged as his skin has been stained a fantastic shade of pink. Without having to think about it, I know that Layla is responsible. She and Donovan have sparred ever since they were kids. They stayed away from each other for years, but when Autumn and Declan started dating, they were thrown back together again, and an increasingly obnoxious prank war had ratcheted up around them.

Normally we try to laugh it off, but this, this is ridiculous. This is pointless. For once, seeing them argue, seeing the result of their latent sexual tension, the anger they pretend keeps them apart, is so fucking juvenile and pointless that it becomes reprehensible.

"Then tell him to stay away from me. Tell him to not even look in my direction!" Layla's voice is pathetic, pleading though she is adamant, proud, growling at Donovan like this latest fiasco is his fault.

Autumn and Mollie step away from Layla, as if they know they cannot save her from herself. Normally, they'd find this funny. Normally, I would, but my friends are finishing their last semester. Soon they'll be out in the world and supposedly functioning as adults. They'll be leading lives that Rhea never will. The commotion around me is too much—Declan holding Donovan back, Mollie and Autumn alternating between yelling at Donovan and fussing at Layla, the balding shop manager screaming about the noise, demanding everyone leave and Quinn in his juvenile "Please Feck Off" shirt grinning around them all as though this latest debacle is the height of amusing.

"I didn't do a freakin' thing to you, you insane woman!"

"Really? Nothing at all? Do you know how long it took me to get the green dye out of my hair? You're about to find out, asshole."

It's too much, all of it. My anger rises, boiling until I cannot take the ire of those two idiots and their pointless fucking shouting a second longer, and I snap.

"That is enough!"

The quiet becomes a tangible thing. It seeps around the room, stilling everything, filling up the space with awkward tension my shout created. My hands shake and for the life of me I cannot keep my lips from trembling.

Layla, at least, is immediately repentant, stepping toward me, hand outstretched.

"Sayo…"

"No, Layla, this is bullshit." I can do nothing but glare at her. I know what I must look like, desperate and hopeless, with deep, dark circles around my eyes and a sallow color of my skin, but it doesn't matter for shit.

Layla lowers her head, ashamed, guilty, it's all there. "I come in here for caffeine because I haven't slept, I can't sleep, and this shit is still going on?"

"I didn't know…"

I silence her with a wave of my hand. "You will be finishing college next semester. Both of you," I glance at Donovan, taking no joy in how he frowns, in the way he lowers his gaze. "I don't give a shit what your problem is with each other. Grow. Up." They remind me of children uncomfortable about being caught in something stupid, embarrassed that they're getting a lecture and that just pisses me off even more. "I just came from an eight-year old's hospital bed. She's dying…" Something huge, something thick clots my throat and it takes me a moment before that word leaves my mouth. I haven't uttered it once, not about Rhea, not even when she asked me about Heaven and angels. The room has grown silent.

"My little cousin wanted to go to college." It's the only thing I can think to say. It's the only way to make them understand how precious time is and how recklessly they squander it. "Hell, she wanted to turn ten. She wanted to come to CU because she knows how much I love it here. She knows how much we all love it here."

Autumn is my best friend, but she reaches out to touch my shoulder, to offer me the comfort she always has in the past, I resent it, I resent her for no reason that makes any sense. I shake her off, not giving her more than a glance because my skin feels tight. Because my anger is a chain weighing me down. "But that's not going to happen for her. She's not going to get the chances that you both have. The opportunities that you are ignoring because you can't let go of whatever high school bullshit you both are still holding onto."

Donovan starts to protest but one flash of my glare and he backs down. "I'm sorry, Sayo. You're right. You're absolutely right." His mouth works for a moment, and then he stammers, "I'm sorry you had to see this."

"Sayo—" Layla tries but Mollie and Autumn are pulling me away, taking me through the door with Declan trailing behind.

"Sweetie, I'm sorry you heard that," Autumn says but I'm still angry. I don't want to hear her. I don't want her comfort.

"It's fine." My arms are tight around my waist and I want to shout, to rage some more, and I find Autumns attempt to tug me against her side extremely annoying. "Stop…" I manage, breathing through my nose when she doesn't hear me, when she tries patting my back. "Autumn, please." It comes out as a growl.

"Sayo?" Since we were kids Autumn has never looked at me the way she is looking at me now. Her eyes are round, her pale face flushed, her expression confused.

I step back, then another and they don't move, not my friends, not Declan or Quinn who stands behind him. I want to tell them I'm fine, but that would be a lie..

"Autumn, I just want…"

"What do you need, sweetie? I can help you." She moves forward, wanting to bridge the gap between us, ignoring Declan's hand on her elbow. "Sayo, we love you. We're all here to help you."

I know that. I honestly do, but I can't take their help. I can't take anything. I don't want to feel anything. It's too heavy—the frustration, the loss of hope, the emotion, the mother fucking emotion is choking me. And when I catch the glint of moisture in Autumn's eyes, when Mollie's normally stern, stoic expression slips into something softer, something that looks too much like sympathy, that emotion threatens to choke me completely.

"Just please, Autumn, please, all of you… I just want to be alone. Please, just let me be alone."

I don't look back, even though I hear footsteps behind me, even though I smell Autumn's faint perfume in the air, even when I hear Declan's voice, him telling her to leave me be. The humidity has thickened in the night around me and I walk right into it, seeking comfort that I can get from my friends, comfort that I refuse to take from any of them.

WHEN I WAS a kid, I got the strangest looks from people in town. Looking back, I understand it. I was one of the few non-Irish, non-redhead kids at my school or sitting in the pews at St. Theresa's Catholic Church. As time went on, the scrutiny lessened, especially when my parents filled their house with one child after another that looked even less like the good townsfolk of Cavanagh. We didn't mind it much and it became something we outright ignored. When our parents introduced rugby into our lives—which was impossible to avoid in this town—that scrutiny disappeared altogether.

Everyone was the same on the pitch. Every voice rooting for the Cavanagh Cocks in the stands, was a brother or sister in arms. Every shot of excitement, of joy at a try made, echoed in the stranger's voice next to you.

There is something that happens when CPU plays. The town goes still except for the activity on the pitch. Stores shut down, churches end Saturday mass early and only the bars open, and even those have a live feed of the matches for the poor sods not lucky enough to get a seat at the match.

It was here, right on this pitch that I spent most of my best teenage moments. Autumn, Mollie, Layla and I snuck our first sips of whiskey from Layla's older brother at the topmost bleachers. Autumn got Artie Jones' number for me right on the sidelines as we left a match our junior year of high school. Mollie got her first kiss from Tommy O'Claggin just below the seat I'm sitting on underneath the center row of bleachers.

Everything about the pitch reminded me of happier moments—those where I laughed the hardest and, later, when the performance of our squad mattered to me, screamed the loudest.

Tonight, the uprights sway slightly in the wind that has picked up, and the pitch itself is freshly mown, ready for the rugby season and the match tomorrow morning. All around campus and in town, there are crimson flags with our mascot and the university crest flapping along light poles and emblazoned across the windows of buildings. Cavanagh is prepared for another banner season and the town has been dressed for it.

I won't be there. I'll be back at that hospital, sitting outside of Rhea's room, waiting for Aunt Carol to tell me I can go back in. I won't push myself on her if she doesn't want me there, but I have no intention of doing anything but being there with her.

"Just leave, Sayo. I don't want you here."

It's stupid. Pointless to cry. Tears don't help. They are a useless waste. Yet I sit here, leaning on my knees, nudged between the end seats with the pitch looming massive in front of me, and the tears come. They cover my face. They frustrate me and as the wind continues and the moisture on my face makes me shiver, I curse my stupidity and pointless need to be left alone. I could have let Autumn hug me. I could have let Declan buy me a coffee and I wouldn't be wasting my tears. I wouldn't be alone.

I damn sure wouldn't be freezing.

Another whip of wind and I close my eyes, wiping my face dry against the sleeve of my dingy, thin sweater. The weather hasn't even turned cool yet but I haven't been able to shake the chill that has set in my bones. It's been months and months and nothing I do warms me up.

When my face is dry, I open my eyes blinking at the sudden appearance of a Styrofoam cup sitting on the bleacher in front of me. It's still warm, the heat from the coffee pipes small lines of steam from the opening in the lid. It smells like heaven.

"Think nothing of it. I was getting one for myself anyway."

Dammit, it's Quinn. I want to be angry at him for disrupting my pity party. I want to hate him and roll my eyes at him and tell him to piss off.

But, I want the coffee more.

In way of a thank you, I nod at Quinn because it's the only gratitude I'm willing to give. I am not one of the gold digging tarts he's used to. I suspect none of us are. Cavanagh is not the Dublin that Declan warned us Quinn was used to. The lavish parties, the easy drugs, the free-flowing drink, the lack of care or responsibility—that is a world away from life in Cavanagh and I suspect that Quinn is quickly discovering this.

So he gets a nod and to his credit, he seems satisfied by it.

"You hiding?" he asks, not looking at me as he leans his arms against the bleachers behind him. He is relaxed and his tone tells me he only asked to pass the time, maybe fill up the awkward silence that crowds around us.

"I'm not hiding." My voice is thin and rough.

"What is it, then?" When my only answer is to take a quick gulp from the warm cup, Quinn leans closer, this time shifting his leg to rest his foot on the bleacher in front of him. "Just now you looked like how I reckon I have every bleeding morning." When I frown, Quinn shrugs. "When I wake up and remember I'm in this shitehole."

"Shitehole?" At his flippant nod, I dump the coffee he brought me onto the ground and crush the cup in my furious fingers.

Brushing past him, I angrily stomp down the bleachers to fling the ruined cup into a trash can, not interested in spending another second with that asshole.

"Oi. Hold up." I don't do anything but along the sidelines, flipping my fading pink hair over my shoulder as Quinn trails after me. I hear his big boots clomping down the metal steps. Shitehole? This town? Really. What an insufferable…

He catches up to me, effortlessly. "Have I twisted your knickers in a knot or something?"

"Don't," I shout, turning in a flash to poke Quinn with my finger, "you ever, *ever* call this town a shithole. You're damn lucky Joe and Declan are letting you darken their door. This town? A shithole?" Winded by the quick release of my anger, I inhale, filling up my lungs just to give myself the capacity to continue yelling at him. "This *shitehole*, as you put it, has a university with sister programs all over the world including Trinity, Cambridge and Oxford. In this *shitehole* we have *five* New York Times best-selling authors, *two* Grammy-winning producers and *ten*, count them *ten* rugby players that went on to play in the international leagues, two of who landed on squads that won the World Cup. So we must be doing something right in this *shitehole*."

We'd drifted from the bleachers, just outside the edge of the pitch where the steps lowered further down onto the field. Quinn stares at me with his mouth slack and his gaze busy moving all over my face as though he'd caught sight of something he wasn't quite sure he knew how to process.

He keeps staring, even after I calm down, after the cool wind bristles against my hair and I wrap those faded pink locks around my fingers to keep them from flying in my face. Quinn's silence, the attention he gives me is unsettling, as though he needs time to sort out who I am and what he wants to do with me. But I am not a woman who waits for any man, no matter how pretty they are. "What the hell are you looking at?" I manage, pulling my wild hair around my shoulder while I lift my chin, expecting Quinn to say something insulting.

"Jaysus, are you gorgeous when you're angry."

Yep. I knew it. Leave it to an asshole to completely block out what I said and focus on how I look saying it. "And you are a misogynist pig."

He has the audacity to laugh. At me! And Quinn doesn't fight the fit of laughter or even pretend like he's the least bit remorseful. "Can't deny that."

"Get the hell away from me, Quinn."

I manage a step, but suddenly notice the form of a large man walking straight for the pitch. Dammit, it's Sam, my ex. He must have come looking for me after hearing about my blow up at the coffee shop—news and gossip goes light speed in this town. He'd given me a look the other night at McKinney's, one I thought had been pity, but him coming this way, looking the way he did—like a man on a mission—maybe he wanted to start something back up again, and thought finding me might give him the opening he was looking for. I wasn't eager to deal with that crap right now, so without thinking, I backtrack, grabbing hold of Quinn and using his large body as a meager shield.

"And what are we up to?"

"Quiet," I say, craning my head around him to spot Sam getting closer. I flash my eyes up at Quinn's face. "Ex-boyfriend that I really am in no mood to talk to right now."

The hesitation in his body lasts only a second and then Quinn nods, grabbing my face so that I am forced to look at him. "Relax, love. I'll handle it."

And then he is kissing me. Quinn is forceful, his tongue gliding along my mouth, insisting, expectant, then he pulls on my arm like he has the right to, moving us until I am against the wall of the restrooms, my back cold and scratching on the brick wall.

There are footsteps behind us, the crunch of gravel and the long, slow release of an exhale but all of that is secondary sensation, something that barely registers as Sam retreats. I am too caught up in Quinn's mouth, his touch, and why the hell I'm not tell him to piss off.

Finally, he pulls away, but Quinn is not smiling. There isn't the slightest hint of laughter on his face. There is only that tight, blazing glint in his eyes and his gaze burning over my features like he means to set my skin on fire.

He isn't aggressive, isn't hurting me, but the delicious musky smell of his skin and the cologne from his body is like a tranquilizer, as if the very scent of him is some numbing drug that keeps me paralyzed against the brick wall. Somewhere in the back of my mind I hear myself screaming, telling me to push him away, to escape. He isn't holding me there, in fact he is barely touching me at all, but still I am immobile and hate that nothing but the pull of his gaze and the whisper of his fingertip along my cheek is locking me in place.

"Was that sufficient?" I can barely hear him over the wind, and he pulls the hair from my face and keeps it still between his fingers with his hand cupping behind my ear. "You damn well kissed me back."

"No," I say weakly, trying to pretend that I am indifferent to the smell of him, the feel of those hands. "I didn't."

"Liar."

"I meant what I said. Get the hell away from me."

Instead Quinn steps so close that the smallest hairs on his chest tickle my collarbone and his wet bottom lip skims along my chin. "You like having me about, don't you, love, because I don't mince my words." I close my eyes, not wanting him to see anything there that he might take as longing. But Quinn is a bully, a beautiful, seductive bully, and he doesn't seem to like me not watching him. He doesn't seem to like not being able to read me. He curls his fingers, tightens my hair around them and my eyelids flutter open. I'm careful to glare at him, leaving nothing sweet or honest in my eyes. Still, he doesn't buy it. "Don't worry. I'll let you have your anger."

"That's because…"

He stops me with his thumb smoothing along my jaw. I am distracted by the sight of his face so close to mine, his dark eyes, and the smell of coffee and sugar lingering on his breath. If I move my head, pull my hair free from his fingers, then my mouth would be on his; our bodies would be pressed together. For a brief second, I wonder if his stomach is as firm as I thought it was that morning on Joe's porch. I wonder how far down that thin patch of dark hair goes, if it thickens further down his body. Just the thought of him, of that beautiful skin and those taut, lean muscles has me wanting to let him take me, right there against the wall. I'd defile the place that holds my sweetest memories if only to quell my curiosity.

If only to forget everything else.

Quinn drifts so close, holds my chin, keeping my head still with his free hand and I swallow back the knot of worry, the words I know will stop him from kissing me. He's so close, the airy breath from his mouth tickling down my nose… just a half an inch closer and I'll taste him again.

If I hadn't glanced at him, if I hadn't glimpsed that slowly creeping smirk—one that was all attitude, all smug triumph, then maybe I would have let Quinn kiss me, this time without the excuse of putting off my ex.

But I do glance at him.

I do see that smirk that every entitled asshole learns, it seems, before they utter their first "I said right now," and it is that smirk that totally snaps me back to reality.

"You let me have my anger, O'Malley," I pull his hand from my face and feel a stab of vindication as the smirk disappears, "because if you didn't then you'd have to apologize for once in your entitled, pampered life, wouldn't you?"

He jerks back, putting at least a foot of distance between the two of us. I can feel his anger spark against mine. "I apologize for nothing. Not one fecking thing."

"And that's your biggest damn problem, isn't it?" Quinn's body has gone stiff, his shoulders so straight I wonder how his muscles aren't cramping. "You are too proud. You have zero shame. You are nothing like Declan."

"Jaysus, I hope not." He laughs then, but there is no humor in the sound. Quinn sounds, in fact, mildly disgusted by the comparison, which only adds fuel to my anger.

"You could learn a lot from him, you know that? You could learn what it is to be generous and thoughtful. You could learn what it means to care for others before thinking only of yourself."

"Why in God's name would I want to do that shite?" His voice was flippant, but there was no humor left in him.

"You wouldn't. In order to do any of those things, Quinn, you'd have to have a freakin' heart."

It was a burn that I could not back up, but the insult made Quinn retreat, keeping him still as I walked away from the pitch oddly empty, and still cold, wondering if I'd ever be warm again.

FIVE

AUTUMN MCSHANE AND I have shared everything since we were little. She knew that I stole twenty bucks from my mother's purse in fifth grade because I wanted five books, not three at the school book fair. She knew that when Nicky Thompson pinched and fondled my boobs freshman year, I'd orgasmed in just under a minute. I knew that she snuck out to see Roger Smith our sophomore year because he was moving back to Houston the next day and Autumn wanted to see if *everything* from Texas really was bigger. I knew that she'd secretly wanted to say yes to Declan when he first proposed despite them only dating for a few months. He's asked every week since then, always with "Is it *sometime* yet?" and she always answered "no, not yet." I also knew that my best friend's refusals were getting less and less adamant.

We knew each other. We knew each other's faults and habits and we knew how to apologize, when that usually it only took a hug and a teary laugh to forgive and forget.

It's all it took now. One smile and my eyes a bit blurry, and Autumn was hugging me, the pair of us blocking the hallway leading to Rhea's room.

"I love you," she whispers, hugging me so tightly that my back popped.

"I love you."

"Jaysus," Quinn moans, earning a glare from me and a jerk of Declan's head, instructing his brother to sit on the benches at the end of the hall.

"Wanker," Declan mutters as his brother moves down the hall. It isn't until Quinn is nearing the benches that Declan loses his glare and his gaze passes back to us. "How is she?" the big Irishman says, letting Autumn slip to his side.

"Better. Much better." For the first time in weeks, I feel rested, not as down. Carol's phone call this morning had pulled me out of my funk.

"White blood cell count is inching toward normal. We still have to wear masks but she can have visitors again." I hadn't let Aunt Carol finish her explanation before I hopped in my car and made it to the hospital in less than fifteen minutes.

"Can we see her?" Autumn asks and her smile is so wide, so hopeful that I can only return it, feeling an uncommon swell of gratitude toward my best friend.

"Yeah, of course, but first I wanted to talk to you about the fundraiser."

"What are we raising funds for?"

"Um," I start, checking to make sure my family isn't there. "The experimental treatment for Rhea. Aunt Carol has been trying to organize something to raise the funds for it, but she's been so overwhelmed with taking care of Rhea that it hasn't gone anywhere. I thought since we've pulled together a massive book sale every year then maybe we can organize the fundraiser for her. You think perhaps Ava…"

"How much do they need?" Declan tilted his head, smiling easily to apologize for interrupting me.

"I know what you're thinking," I tell him. "But it won't work. I offered up my savings but they wouldn't take it." Declan opens his mouth, encouraged by the proud smile Autumn gives him, but stops when I shake my head. "Declan, whatever you're thinking, really, I so appreciate it, honestly, but it just won't do."

"I don't want that money, Sayo." His expression darkens when I continue to shake my head. Declan had never met his birth father, Quinn's father. But when Quinn's mother died, the inheritance she'd withheld from Declan went directly to him. I'd never asked how much money Declan had inherited but I did know he had no interest in that money just as his birth father had never had any interest in him.

"Deco, you're so sweet. Thank you," I say, meaning it. "It's too much. I… um…" I glanced back at Quinn then stepped closer to Autumn and Declan, not wanting to advertise my business. "I have thirty grand and they refused it."

"How much does the treatment cost?" Declan asks again, clearing his throat when I close my mouth.

"Eighty grand."

"Jaysus."

"Indeedy."

"Sayo?" Aunt Carol is walking toward us, looking rested. The dark circles around her eyes have dimmed, finally. "Oh, Autumn, sweetheart, Declan, so good of you both to come." Carol kisses Autumn and pats Declan's back as way of greeting.

"Carol, Sayo mentioned a fundraiser." Autumn's smile is still wide, still sweet and my aunt, being the well-mannered southern lady that she is, nods to my best friend, though I can see her discomfort. Autumn sees it to, but grabs Carol's hand and rubs it, like a mother comforting a nervous child. "Sayo and I organize the library book sale every year. We even put Declan to work, didn't we, sweetie?" She winks at Declan when he nods. "Anyway, well, we'd be happy to organize a fundraiser for Rhea. There's really nothing to it."

Aunt Carol seems a little overwhelmed by the way Autumn takes over, already offering up ideas and plans, whiffing on organizations that could donate and volunteers that we could pool from her freshman classes. As Autumn runs through a list of projects and chores we would need to tackle before the big day, "starting with the day of the event," I step back, glancing down the hall to see that Quinn is missing from the benches. I wave at Declan while Carol and Autumn improvise ideas about the fundraiser, and go to check if Rhea is finished with her lunch.

But as I inch closer to her open door, I hear unexpected laughter coming from her room. Rhea hasn't laughed once in months. No jokes, no shows, no films or comics have lifted her spirits since she landed back in the hospital. Until now.

"Do it again," I hear her say, that soft giggle getting louder. "Oh, that's so funny."

Nothing could surprise me more than what I see as I turn the corner and walk into Rhea's room. She's sitting up in her bed, as Quinn scribbles with a black marker over a green paper face mask. On his head he wears two more separate masks, both with oversized eyes drawn on their surfaces. When he pulls them down over his own eyes, they look ridiculous and crossed.

"Rhea?" I ask, stepping further into the room, but my little cousin ignores me in favor of the two new masks Quinn fastens over her eyes.

"There you are, love. Look, we'll have a photo." Completely ignoring me, Quinn leans next to Rhea and they move their heads together just as he snaps a selfie with his phone.

"What's going on in here?" I ask, stepping closer to the bed. "Rhea?"

"Quinn's making me faces with the stupid masks, Sayo." Her laugh is still blessedly light and buoyant. Although I cannot believe that asshole is being sweet to Rhea, I don't have the heart to kick him out.

"Is he?" I ask, leaning next to her on the bed.

"Yeah, do you want one?" She doesn't wait for me to answer before she hands a clean mask from the small pile in her lap to Quinn. "Make Sayo some, okay?"

It's only then, when Rhea prompts him, that Quinn finally looks at me, nodding in answer to her question with his attitude cool, unaffected by how stiffly I sit on the bed and how hard I glare at him.

"Hey, Sayo, Quinn says he has a Thor comic book signed by Stan Lee, isn't that right, Quinn?"

The smallest shift of his gaze in my direction and Quinn nods, focusing on the cross eyes he draws on the masks.

"Full of surprise, aren't you?" I say to Quinn when he hands me the masks. And I sit there with the verbal lashing of a lifetime pulsing on the tip of my tongue, slipping the masks over my eyes, earning a laugh first from Rhea and then from Autumn and Declan as they stand in the doorway.

When Carol announces that it's time for Rhea's nap, and I follow Autumn and Declan out of the hospital, with Quinn trailing behind, I glance over my shoulder, wondering what game he's playing. He catches my look, his face hard, his expression blank before he looks away from me.

O'Malley is a strange one. Entitled, absolutely. Arrogant? Definitely. So why am I not as uncomfortable as I should be that my little cousin likes him? A better question is how is Quinn able to be so nice and sweet to a kid when he has no evidence of an actual heart beating beneath his chest? As I drive away from the hospital, I promise myself that was a question I intend to find out for myself.

SIX

FIVE DAYS.

It's been that long since Quinn O'Malley decided to replace me. At least, when he's not being forced to help Joe with repairs to his house and Autumn and Declan with gathering supplies and commitments from the local businesses to donate to the fundraiser. When Quinn threatened to throw Sam, my ex and the night manager at McKinney's, through the front window for not giving him an immediate yes or no about donating soda for the fundraiser, Autumn relegated Quinn's chores to inventory and securing the folding tables.

But that asshole still thinks he can cut into my reading time with Rhea. A fact I plan on having words about with him the next time I see him. I purposefully arrive at the hospital a half an hour before his allotted time with my cousin was up. The idea of a schedule, ridiculous as it sounds, hadn't come from either of us. But when Aunt Carol saw us arguing, yet again, over time spent with Rhea, she decided a schedule would be in everyone's best interests.

"Quinn, it's only fair that Sayo get more time."

"That's bollocks."

"She's family. You're…"

"She can't do the voices like I can, can she, and she's crap at drawing. The sprog told me herself. 'Sayo sucks at the drawing.' Really I'm only trying to save you the embarrassment." Carol hadn't appreciated my flipping him off or either of us raising our voices twenty feet from a room full of pediatric patients getting chemo.

So I got three hours in the morning and Quinn got an hour and a half in the afternoon. Only, today I was cutting into his time so I could speak to him. He wasn't keeping to the schedule, anyway, coming in earlier and earlier for a week and it was starting to piss me off.

"Sayo, hey," Rhea says as I step into the room, passing my little cousin some comics that I had picked up that afternoon. "Quinn went to Marty's this morning while you were here with me. And look what we did!" My cousin pointed to the crumpled bag from Marty's that had been used as a page for her to doodle on. There were three fairies drawn across the backside of the paper and along the top.

"How sweet." Rhea doesn't notice that my voice is less than enthusiastic. If Quinn's eyes could have shot fire, half my face would have been melted. "I knew you were running low on paper, so I got you this." I handed her a new sketch pad, pleased by the small squeal she let out as she reached for it.

"Oh thank you! Thank you both!" Rhea says, pulling open a fresh box of colored pencils that I had not bought for her. One glance at Quinn's smug grin and I knew he'd beat me to the punch with that as well.

"No problem, kiddo," I tell her, taking the paper bag off her mattress.

It is ridiculous for either of us to act so possessively. Logically, I know that. But Quinn has crossed a line, infiltrating my family, wiggling his way into my little cousin's life, seemingly out of boredom. Autumn had mentioned that Declan had encouraged Quinn to volunteer at the hospital, thinking that his half-brother could use a lesson in perspective, not realizing that Quinn would use that as an excuse to show up at Rhea's room, and to keep her company when Carol was off with the doctors and my Uncle Clay was working or, wherever it was that kept him away from the hospital.

"That's fine," I'd said to my best friend, returning the smile she'd given me when she told me, and glaring at Quinn as he and Declan argued in Joe's backyard while stacking bricks for a new fire pit Joe wanted to build.

"It might humble him," Autumn had offered, nudging my elbow when I stared a bit too long at Quinn's shirtless chest.

"Maybe," I'd said, sipping from my beer. That day I'd been unable to keep my gaze from Quinn's body and had spoken the smallest prayer of relief when he turned his back on me. But the smug asshole that he is, he'd noticed my attention, throwing me a wink over his shoulder. "But I doubt Quinn has ever heard the word 'humility.'"

It was a notion I still held firm to, especially now as I caught Quinn's frown, and his barely-contained glare as Rhea flipped to a new page in her sketchbook and leaned against my shoulder. Her smile was infectious, but I couldn't enjoy it, not with the glare that Irish asshole shot my way.

"Sayo," Quinn starts, his voice even, calm. I answer with a shift of my eyebrow, distrustful of how polite he sounds. That asshat knows he sounds like a twit. In fact, he's likely getting a kick out of being sweet to Rhea, by the thick levels of metaphorical bullshit he piles into the room. "Give us a chat, yeah?"

"Of course," I say, stretching my lips in an overdone smile, not blinking once or letting that smile waver in the slightest until I am out of the room with Quinn trailing behind me. I don't, in fact, relax my mouth until we are nearly to the nurses' station and down the empty corridor on the far side of the desk. Then I drop all pretenses. "What the hell do you want?" I ask him, my voice like a hiss.

"What the bleeding hell do you think I want? You're well early, aren't you? Who the feck do you think you are, creeping in on my time?"

"Who am I?" He doesn't move when I step close to him, having to cross my arms to keep from smacking him. "You've got a lot damn nerve." When he only glares at me, the hiss turns into a snarl. "She's my damn cousin, Quinn. Besides, creeping on my time hasn't bothered you for a solid week."

None of that warrants his sympathy. Quinn simply rolls his eyes, grunting as though what he and Rhea do together is far more important than anything I choose to do to entertain her. "We're working on something. What we do whilst I'm here is a feck of a lot more important to her than reading bloody Potter books yet a-bloody-gain."

The grit in his tone and the contempt on his face has me stepping back, more wounded than I'd ever admit to him. "Did she... did she say that?"

Quinn's frown doesn't leave his face and he keeps his mouth and eyes tight. "She didn't have to. I've seen the way she carries on with you. I see how she is with me. She likes the drawing bit."

"That doesn't mean anything other than the fact that she has a crush on you."

"Does she now?" I hate the look he gives me. It's all amused and almost hopeful. It makes me hate him even more than I already do. "What's wrong love, you don't like me giving my attention to another girl?"

"Would you get over yourself, you asshole?" Quinn's attitude remains. He finds my upset funny, as though I'm beneath him and no insult I fling at him will even register. I don't care if it does. But I do know he's up to something, a fact he should know I'm onto. "And anyway I thought you were reading to her too! What project are you talking about?" When he doesn't answer, I step back, frustrated, worked up over the secrets Quinn keeps from me.. "I don't know what game you're playing, Quinn O'Malley but I swear to Christ if you fuck her over even once, one damn time, that's it. You're gone. You won't put a toe into that room. I can promise you that much."

His laugh is quick, a small sound that tells me he's insulted but pretends he isn't. "You think I'm plotting something?"

"Why else would you be here?"

Quinn moves his jaw, grinding his teeth as he stares down at me and I can't help but get the impression that I've somehow insulted him. But his attitude has always been biting and cruel. There is nothing I can do or say that would hurt his feelings. So why does he look a little off? Why isn't his glare quite so severe?

"Why indeed," he finally says, walking away, back toward Rhea's room. I catch up to him, intending to follow, but Quinn stops me, holding up his palm to keep me back. "I don't think so. I've another twenty minutes before you're due to start in with your boring books. Don't creep on my time and I'll stay clear of yours."

※

JOE PLAYS POKER with his friends in the campus square every Wednesday afternoon at two. It was perfect timing really. He'd would be out, Declan had class and Quinn would be visiting with Rhea. This afternoon was the only time I could investigate Quinn and the things I know he keeps hidden.

But I'd need a thief to get me inside.

At least, the daughter of a criminal.

Mollie jimmies the back lock with little effort. A credit card, a jiggle of the doorknob and the lock releases and no sound emits from the alarm. Mollie had bypassed that too.

"All in the wrist and the intimate knowledge of the mark," she'd told me as we leaned against the side of Joe's house, trying to figure out the code he'd use to secure his alarm.

Mollie had waited a full minute, thinking to herself, likely wondering what Joe would use as a password and then, a calculating, dangerous smile—one that reminded me a bit too much of Mojo, her former biker father—inched across her face as she punched in six numbers. The system disarmed and the back gate opened, letting us onto the property with little problem.

"Autumn's birthday," she'd said, opening the back gate for us to jimmy the lock on the back door. "Remind me to have a casual convo with Joe about passwords."

With Mollie's stealth and skill we are in the house in under five minutes.

It is Wednesday, a work day and even if Autumn wasn't in the thick of teaching class or holding office hours, the place would still be empty. We walk through the back door, past the kitchen and the clutter of dishes on the counter, thinking idly that the fundraiser and Quinn's invasive presence has kept Joe and Declan off their cleaning. With another glance into the kitchen, at the empty beer bottles and the disgusting smoked butts floating inside them, I'd guess that Quinn is at fault for the additional mess.

"He's a slob," Autumn had told me just two weeks after Declan and Quinn had returned from Ireland. Between her boyfriend and her father, Autumn had heard her fair share of complaining. "He smokes in the house when Dad or Declan's not there and leaves all his empties and old butts around the house.

"Joe needs a maid," I offered, understanding that Joe and Declan hadn't had to pick up much after themselves since Autumn's OCD prevented her from letting her father and boyfriend live in squalor. But with Quinn joining the fray, even Autumn's clean freak ways had been squashed.

"No," she's told me, frowning hard, "they need to teach Quinn how to clean up after himself."

"Teach him? You act as if he's a third grader."

"He may as well be. Declan said he doesn't even know how to work the washer or load the dishwasher. Until he came here, he'd never even seen a washer."

By the state of the place, I guess that Declan and Joe hadn't given Quinn the first lesson and my suggested maid service had yet to be obtained.

But it was the spare room, the one near the front porch where I knew Quinn slept, that had me covering my nose.

"Oh my God, this dude is nasty," Mollie says, pulling her t-shirt over her nose.

"Tell me about it."

The room was both foul and putrid with dirty socks and boxers crowded around the door. Leftover food, stained clothing, or other, um, mysterious items were strewn on every surface, both floor and mattress. Mollie kicks off a load of laundry from the bed, using her foot.

"I hope he doesn't bring girls back here."

"No decent girl would do him in that bed."

"Yeah," Mollie says, sidestepping around a stack of dirty dishes, "O'Malley doesn't strike me as the type that much cares for decent girls."

The mess was overwhelming, but, over the stench of dirty plates, and sweaty socks, was the hint of Quinn's cologne.

It takes several minutes of snooping but I finally find a small box among the empty suitcases at the top of Quinn's full closet. It is a solid cardboard box with old packing tape loosened around the edges and threads of loosened adhesive hanging from the opened center.

"Anything good?" Mollie asks, then we both freeze as we hear the noise of a car door slamming outside the window. "I'll go investigate," she says.

Once I kick aside some empty boxes that litter the floor and use my foot to shove off a stack of black t-shirts from Quinn's bed, I sit with the box in my lap, pulling open the folded tabs. Inside are photographs—most of Quinn with half-dressed girls, blondes, redheads, their arms draped around Quinn, their lips on his neck, his face. Those I set aside, not remotely curious about the partying Quinn had done back in Ireland or the girls he kept company with.

Behind the pictures are stacks of envelopes, some bills, some used airline tickets and then, in a leather satchel tied with a black, satin ribbon, is an official looking document that reminds me of the legal docs my dad sometimes brings home with him. It is very formal-looking, on expensive letterhead with a logo I know comes from an exclusive barrister group in Ireland. The dates and address on the thick paper tell me this has to do with Quinn's estate and I scan the document, my gaze catching here and there at Declan's name. It contains legal jargon that is familiar, but it wouldn't give me any information as to why Quinn was hanging out with my little cousin.

Digging deeper, shuffling through other papers and documents, I find a small leather bound photo album. It is red with gold edging, and has the O'Malley crest stamped on the front cover.

The cover creaks when I open it and the thick pages tend to stick together, so I have to proceed carefully. Flipping through the photographs, is see image after image of a kid, thin and very pale, but they are still undoubtedly Quinn's features. I go a bit further and come to the same boy, older, but even thinner, and in a hospital gown. At his side is a thin woman with dark hair and eyes that remind me of dimes—a little dull and very narrow. She has the look of a bird, underfed and unwanted, but she holds onto Quinn as though he were a lifeline. There is no smile on her thin face, but the expression of the man on Quinn's other side is friendly, a little flirty. The elder O'Malley had been handsome, his eyes bright, his expression open and I pull the album closer, scanning the man's features closely, seeing a thicker, broader version of Declan in those features. But where Declan's eyes, and Quinn's if I'm being honest, are bright and open, their father's seem guarded, and even a little weary as though his smile is forced and the welcome he projects is one that isn't sincere.

No doubt the elder O'Malley had been charming, that I could tell by that cheeky grin and the soft, gentle cast of his features. But it struck me as odd, not that Quinn's parents who seemed so different had been together, but that they had produced a son that was equally as unfriendly and as charming as the both of them had been. The oddest thing, though, was how different their expressions were—hers, haunted, his, wearily coy.

Quinn had clearly been very ill for quite a while, a few more flips of the pages tell me as much, with Quinn in one hospital room after another and his parents posing with him, their expressions unchanging from page to page.

And then, just like that, Mr. O'Malley no longer appears in the pictures. A few more flips and Quinn grows older in the photographs, healthier, and then the scenery changes. There are no more hospital beds, no more hospitals and only Quinn and his mother on the beach, then in the mountains, at the theater or in front of some monument or another, until I reach the end of album.

Is that all there is to it? Quinn had been a sick kid and likely had hated every second of it. From the pictures, I gathered that holidays, birthdays, at least until he was ten had been spent in a hospital bed. No wonder he seems partial to Rhea. He can relate. Oddly enough, his behavior and these photographs prove that there is, in fact, something other than venom beating beneath his chest.

But Quinn's motivations leap from my mind when I place the photo album into the box and my fingers brush across a thick sketch book. It is here where I discover who Quinn really is. It was all there in charcoal pencil. The paper is thick and the charcoal dust falls from the sketches when I move the book, when the pages turn from one image to another, each with his sloppy O'Malley signature at the bottom.

The sketches themselves are remarkable lines that arch and move into forms. Mountainsides, horizons that go on and on and then figures that become forms, forms that become women, lots and lots of women of all shapes and sizes. Women who are young, beautiful, stunning. Breasts that are imperfect, bodies full and voluptuous, some thin and waiflike. They all come to life on these pages, are so vivid and real that I find myself stopping on each one, looking into drawn eyes that should have been flat and crafted but were vibrant and almost alive. They are all drawn from life, all drawn with at least some small affection. Who knew? I didn't believe Quinn had it in him.

But what he was or who he'd been before he came to Cavanagh would be left for another day, another time when snooping could be more thorough. Joe's tires stop just outside of the sidewalk in front of his house and Mollie darts back in the doorway.

"Come on, Joe's back."

Joe jiggles his keys in the lock and I move as quickly and quietly as possible, stuffing the envelopes and album back into that box, forgetting for a second about the sketchbook, I pull on the corner and stuff it back into the box, then up onto the shelf and close the closet door with a small thump that I hope Joe doesn't hear.

It's only when I hear Joe's low, soft voice humming down the hall and then muffled by the shower running in his bathroom that I follow Mollie down the hall and out of the back door, locking it carefully behind us. And as we leave Joe's home, I try my best to put thoughts of Quinn and the kid he'd been out of my mind. That look in his young eyes had been too haunted. That expression too damn familiar. It matched the one Rhea had worn up until a few weeks ago, before her health had improved. Before Quinn had made his way into her life without permission, without invitation. But maybe, just maybe, for a good reason.

SEVEN

THERE IS ALWAYS chaos and activity at my parents' home. But Mom and Dad, if not my brothers and sisters, are, at least, well-meaning. For example, inviting everyone, including Joe (who declined) and Layla and Mollie (who conveniently found something else less embarrassing to do), to their house for Sunday lunch, had been born from a desire to catch up with my friends who hadn't been over for a visit in months. Joe, Autumn suspected, had a date he didn't want to mention to her. And so it was only Declan and Autumn and ~~Satan~~ Quinn, who rang my parents' doorbell precisely at twelve-thirty and as soon as they arrive, I grab her, greeting Declan with a kiss on the cheek and ignoring Quinn completely because he was a supreme asshat. Despite what I had learned about his childhood, my heart had not softened much to O'Malley.

It might have, had he not continued to greet me with an eye roll whenever our paths crossed at the hospital, and insist that whatever he was working on with Rhea stay a secret just between the two of them—not that I hadn't tried to get to the bottom of it (without being too obvious, of course).

"What's the project you and Quinn are working on?" I'd asked Rhea nonchalantly just a few days ago after she had hastily stuffed her sketch pad under her pillow as I walked into her room.

"Nothing," she'd answered just as offhandedly, too young, too inexperienced to understand that avoiding my gaze only made me more suspicious.

"Nothing?"

"Well, Quinn says it's no one's business."

"Not even mine, kiddo?"

She's glanced at me then, attempting a smile that was pathetic if she really thought it would charm me, and one that did nothing to hide her humor. "Quinn says, especially not your business."

Hence, my standing *O'Malley Can Suck It* attitude.

Not welcoming him into my folks' home ala the ingrained southern hospitality Mom had raised me on was highly immature. Still, it makes me feel better, especially since he hadn't missed the chance to call me a wanker yesterday when Rhea and I hadn't finished our reading of *The Forest Again* chapter in the final Potter book before Quinn came in for his time with her.

"Pathetic," he'd muttered as I'd left the hospital room. It was an insult I now returned when I saw him curiously scrutinizing the obscene amount of family photographs in the den. He kept poring over them, which gave me the perfect opportunity to be an asshat, too.

"We don't all have different fathers, in case you're wondering, O'Malley."

I shoot a grin at my brother, Booker, who laughs at the old family joke. Of course we have different fathers. Duh, adopted.

"Nope," Booker calls as he flops into the recliner in the living room. "But Mom swears the sperm bank screwed each one of her pregnancies. Except Carver. We got him from the Freak Show."

"Oh you mean your *identical* twin brother? What does that say about you?"

"I was the better looking one."

"You wouldn't say that if he was here." Booker's laugh is loud, welcoming as my friends and Satan follow me into the room and I kick his feet off the coffee table to make him sit up.

My brother completely ignores me, standing to greet Autumn when she reaches up to kiss his cheek. Booker sighs as if all his dreams have just come true, an exaggerated sound that I know he utters for Autumn's benefit and to annoy Declan, who stands right behind Autumn. "So, beautiful," my brother says, his dark eyes sparkling with mischief, "Not married yet, are you?"

"No, Booker, not yet." She is ever gracious with this running joke between them, tapping his shoulder to rustle his thick hair.

"Excellent," he tells her, stepping closer before Declan clears his throat.

"But still taken, mate." He offers Booker a hand to shake and my brother relents, laughing when Declan squeezes his fingers too hard.

"So you keep saying and yet," he glances at Autumn's hand, "no ring."

"Sorry, I was always partial to Carver," Autumn admits, laughing when my brother pratfalls onto the recliner. "He still in California?"

"Working, yes. He'll be home next Easter," I fill in, waving off my brother when he eyes Autumn with a mock expression of longing on his face. "Leave them alone, perv," I say, pushing him further down onto the sofa. "No one wants your stinky butt anyway."

Booker mocks offense, shooting me the bird just as my younger sister Alessandra walks in, pulling her thick, long hair into a bun at the back of her head. She's inching toward twenty, is obsessed with dance and it shows in those long, muscular legs that she shows off in shorts I'd never be caught dead wearing. Dad can't have seen those shorts yet, I think, squinting at her when she glances past Autumn and Declan and her attention hones directly in on Quinn.

"Who is this one?" Alessandra asks, showing her barely eighteen year old immaturity, her grin obvious.

"That one is a lot of piss and wind and way too much trouble to even consider." I push my sister out of the room, ignoring the grin on Quinn's face when he inches behind me.

"Worried I'll fancy your bitty sister?"

"No," I say, glaring at him over my shoulder. "Worried she'll catch your bastarditis."

"That I can offer for free," he says, standing close enough to bend next to my ear. "Care to have a nip?"

"Bugger off." Declan pulls his brother by the collar and away from me as we all move towards the kitchen.

"Oh, Autumn!" Mom squeals, rushing to Autumn and squeezing her tight. She returns that hug, smiling when Mom grabs her face, gaze working over her features as though she's checking for something to worry over.

"I'm fine," Autumn tells her indulgently, pulling Mom's hand from her face. "What I really need to know is—is there fudge?"

"Autumn," Mom says, frowning. "Are you trying to insult me?" Then she breaks into a laugh and nods toward the center island where a pan of homemade fudge sits waiting. Eagerly Autumn drags Declan, who had stopped to greet my mother with a kiss, towards the decadent treat, my siblings joining them in the now crowded kitchen.

"Who is this?" Mom asks me, stepping to my side as we both watch Quinn leaning against the doorway.

"This is Quinn, Mom. Declan's brother."

"Half-brother," he reiterates and I try not to laugh at my mother's humor or the way Quinn squirms under her scrutiny.

"So this is the one I've heard so much about," she tells him walking away from me to stand next to Quinn. "How are you liking Cavanagh, Quinn?" They both glance at me when I laugh and Quinn's glare almost dares me to rat him out. I could easily relate to Mom Quinn's attitude about being here, how he thinks we live in a *shitehole*, but that would be too rude, even for our dueling.

Still, the expression on his face is mildly worried and I get where that comes from. My mother. There's something about her, something that even as kids made us all vie for her approval, her affection. It is the same something that has my dad buying her flowers every week, even though she's told him not to waste the money. Mom is simply one of those women who effortlessly holds attention with her openness and her vivaciousness. Her features are still soft. Her skin only mildly wrinkled around her eyes and her hair still a vivid auburn. Her beauty, her kindness, has always endeared her to others, even those who aren't so used to being around women with such outgoing personalities. But even with as lively as she is, it is still in her nature to comfort, to make everyone feel welcomed and loved first and foremost.

But I wasn't quite so sure she could pull that off with Quinn. She tried, engaging him in conversation, laughing, smiling where appropriate, joking to put him at ease. And he did seem to soften. He didn't at least call her a wanker or ignore her when she spoke to him.

"Well," Mom says to Quinn, brushing her hands along his arm, an affectionate gesture I've seen her do a million times when my brother is upset about something. "My sister Carol has nothing but sweet things to say about you. Rhea adores you." Mom holds Quinn's hand and the frown leaves his face, as though just hearing that has somehow evaporated his attitude. "Anyone who treats our Rhea kindly, who makes her happy, is alright by my book."

"Aye, erm… well…" Quinn tries and my mom ends his suffering, guiding him further into the kitchen, to the center island. Strangely enough, he doesn't seem interested in Alessandra, or my sister Adriana, who walks in from the backyard with my dad. But he isn't frowning, even ignores Declan when he mutters something in his ear. For a brief few minutes, Quinn actually keeps his attitude in check, sparing it and his frown for quick glances at me, sometimes at Declan. Everyone else is ignored. Except Mom. Her, Quinn seems eager to impress, telling her jokes, asking her about the dishes she prepared.

It's damn weird to see him like this.

And then Dad says grace, holding Mom's hand as he speaks about family, about friends, and I watch Quinn, peeking at him behind my lashes, curious what his reaction to this familial moment will be. When Dad mentions Rhea, Quinn's expression changes completely.

"Father, we pray for a healing over Rhea, that you would cast away her illness and give her the strength to fight this battle. Lord, she's such a blessing to us all…" Dad pauses when his voice cracks, and I slip my gaze to his face, then down to my parents' hands held tightly together. Dad is an intimidating man—most litigators in this town are—tall, but not brawny with long legs, broad shoulders and a deep, barreling voice that carries, but he has always been sensitive, especially when he prays. Rhea has touched our lives, each one of us, and it no longer surprises me when one of us gets caught off guard, when the thought of her and the fight she's had to battle has emotion slipping to the surface.

It's a shock to Quinn as well, or so his reaction suggests. As my dad takes a few moments to compose himself and then continue with the prayer, Quinn looks at my father as if he's never seen anything like him before. His face reflects confusion, and what looks to me like sympathy. For once, there is no condescending attitude, no tense frown, and amazingly, he seems to actually relax.

Other than my irritation, and my curiosity at Quinn's motivations, I have no idea why it seems impossible for me not to watch him. Sure, he is very beautiful on the surface, anyone with a pulse would say that, but that attractiveness shouldn't hold my attention so long. Yet it has, for weeks, and today I've watched him interacting with my parents, even speaking with Booker when there's been a lull in the mad chaos that generally happens around my parents' home. Our family is a circus and sometimes, to outsiders, it's fun just to watch the madness unfold. Declan and Autumn are used to the chaos, but Quinn is not and he's been an active witness to the insanity all day.

Yet even today, he's watched me watching him, as though he senses when my gaze lands on him. Like right now, during the prayer as I observe him staring at my dad, Quinn glances at me, and that constant frown of his returns when our gazes meet. Normally, he'd do something foul like lick his lips or wink at me just to make me look away, but he doesn't do either of those things now. He waits, just for a beat, his eyes locked on mine, until with an infinitesimal shake of his head he disengages, returning to the prayer with closed eyes and bowed head.

For some reason, and I'll never be able to sort that reason out, this bothers me. For some reason I can't name, I don't want Quinn to frown at me anymore.

DECLAN AND MY father had argued both Autumn and I out of the kitchen to clean away the dishes. My siblings and mother headed up to the attic looking for the box of used Halloween costumes I'd stashed there when I moved into my own apartment a couple of years ago. Halloween had always been my favorite and the stuff of legend between me and my friends. We'd spent the past five years upping our cosplay in honor of the holiday, one of us winning the costume contest nearly every year at Fubar's, the pub we often frequented. But costumes and the holiday itself seemed less important to me now, not so much to my siblings who Mom directed to my stash just to shut them up.

Autumn and I take the quiet time to move outside, near the pool and back patio. We sit under a large grouping of pine trees along the backside of the fence, swinging on the wooden yard swing hanging from a large oak tree with limbs that stretch toward the pool. I'd found it a little weird, and even mildly suspicious when Dad asked Declan what his post-graduation plans were and the Irishman had glanced at Autumn, who quickly grabbed my hand and led me and my mom's two dogs, Georgina and Darcy out the backdoor. But, I let her weird behavior pass, for the moment, too full from lunch, too sated by the falling temperatures to think about much.

"Georgie, stop it," I call, clapping at the silly beagle puppy when she grips hold of one of the fallen deck chair cushions. The dog scampers away from me with only one quick bark in my direction when I pick up the cushion and replace it on the chair.

"She's getting big," Autumn says, laughing when Georgina jumps on Darcy's back, pulling at his ears. "That poor thing."

"He barely notices." and, sure enough, the big bullmastiff only gives the puppy a little grunt before he moves his ear out of Georgie's mouth.

"I feel like I haven't seen you in months," Autumn says, pulling my attention away from my fur siblings. She leans her head back against the back of the swing, smiling when I look at her.

"She takes all my time, sweetie." Of course, she knows who I'm talking about.

"I know she does. I'm not…" Autumn grins, looking around the yard, to the large crepe myrtles and magnolia that stretch above the garage roofline. There's a tone in her voice, maybe a little bit of worry, that has me frowning, but then Autumn grips my pinky as she moves the swing with her foot. "I hate that this is the hand you've all been dealt. It's like… well."

"What?"

She closes her eyes, taking in a breath through her nose. "I was going to say that it's like when Mom died." Autumn moves her head, a small roll to the left to stare at me. "But it's not. I don't guess it matters if it's the same. No matter how sudden or how expected, it comes and there's never enough time to prepare for it." She looks out at the yard again, watching Georgie as she chases a dragonfly along the pool's surface. "One day, one second, a million years, we're never really ready to say goodbye."

"No," I say, leaning back to rest my fingers on the braided rope holding the swing to the tree limbs above us. "We never are."

I hadn't been ready for the final countdown when Aunt Carol gave it to me last year. I'd hadn't expected the doctor's to be so certain that a "year, maybe two" was all they could foresee of Rhea's future. I only knew that the clock was ticking away and I had to do everything in my power to make time stretch. Autumn hadn't even gotten that. Her mother was taken in a blink of an eye. One rainy night, the screech of tires and Evelyn was stolen away from all of our lives. *No,* I think to myself, watching my best friend's expression shift, a smile, a frown and then finally nothing at all moving her mouth, *we are never ready to say goodbye.*

Autumn exhaled, taking a second before she sat up, stretching her long legs in front of her as though she wants to be rid of the sudden sadness that's come upon us like a raincloud. "I think something's up with Layla and Donovan."

A few blinks and I smile at Autumn's tone. "You think?"

"I do. She's being really secretive and Declan said Donovan was changing in the dressing room a few days ago and he spotted a hickey."

The image comes out of nowhere, unwelcome and unexpected and I fail at keeping my laughter quiet. "What? Is he fifteen?"

Autumn shrugs, moving her legs around to sit on them. "Usually when Donovan hooks up with someone, he tells Declan. That hasn't happened for months."

Donovan hasn't dated anyone as far as I've seen for at least a year, and Layla broke up with that rent a cop from campus security at the beginning of the semester. I manage a squint, watching my best friend, knowing with one look that she's serious. She might have the availability right, but I still think she's reaching. "That automatically means Layla gave up the ghost finally?"

"No. I'm just adding two and two."

"And getting five." No way it's that easy. There's just no way that after years and years of hating on each other they'd finally decide to move things forward without any provocation. "You're not going to win that bet, friend."

"I'd almost forgotten about that. Damn. You know I think I am."

We'd made that bet a year ago when Layla and Donovan had traded some particularly nasty pranks, the best of which was Layla filling the AC vents of Donovan's car with over a pound of glitter. The poor guy had looked like a severely pissed off Edward Cullen for at least a month. The sexual tension between them was palpable and Autumn had predicted that they'd end up naked in bed together before they graduated. I disagreed. Donovan's position on the rugby squad was too important to him, and with Layla being the coach's daughter, he'd make sure to keep his nose clean until then. The wager was a hundred bucks and I doubted, despite Autumn's little theory, that my bank account would be that much lighter any time soon. Especially not after that screaming match at the coffee shop.

"Keep telling yourself that, friend, but I don't think either of them will ever stop being pig headed."

"And blind," she offers, still smiling.

"Yep and blind."

The laughter is comforting, reminds me of a time when our lives were normal, when I didn't live in the constant worry that one phone call would change my life forever. I'm reminded of happier days with Autumn, when our lives were our own, when we didn't keep things from each other—like whatever it was she didn't want Declan telling my father about after they graduated.

I mean to ask her, since we're alone and in a decent mood, about what it is she's keeping to herself, but then Georgiana growls, running behind the swing and toward a retreating Quinn on the other side of the fence line. The dog's bark is so pronounced that even Darcy lifts his head, watching Quinn as he moves toward the back gate. When he steps through the gate and onto the property proper, Georgia attacks, yelping and growling as she latches onto Quinn's jeans.

"Piss off, you pouncy mutt." He jerks away from the small attack and I sigh, leaving the swing to grab the puppy.

"Not a mutt." Quinn ignores the growling dog and my frown.

"So you say."

"I do." There is an unlit cigarette behind his ear and I shake my head. But it's pointless to lecture and I don't want getting in a fight with him to ruin my day. "There's a bench and metal ashtray behind the garage. Dad likes to smoke Cubans sometimes."

"And do you give him fits for that then?"

"I do, actually, but like all the Irishmen in this town, he's a stubborn jackass." I wave my fingers, dismissing him. "The seat to kill yourself is that way. Off you go."

He doesn't seem to like my dismissal or the way that Georgie continues to growl at him, but Quinn walks off, toward the garage on the other side of the property. Autumn stops the swing from moving for me to sit and once Quinn is out of view, I set the dog on the ground.

"So damn bull headed."

"It's hereditary." Autumn shifts her gaze toward the house, right at Declan who smiles at her through the kitchen window where he is drying dishes. She gives him a thumbs up when he nods in the direction Quinn had disappeared to.

"No way is Declan's that bad."

"Honey," she says, looking at me again, "why do you think they argue so much?"

"Because Quinn is an entitled asshat?"

That earns me a laugh and Autumn nods, agreeing. "Well yes, but they have the same damn temper. I swear I think Dad has to refrain from throttling them on a daily basis."

"Poor Joe."

"Poor me!" Autumn lifts her eyebrows, eyes round as though she can't believe I didn't offer her my pity. "I have to be around them all the time."

"Yeah, but you get to go home. Sometimes take Declan with you."

"True, but not as often as I'd like." The sigh she releases sound a bit too much like frustration and I decide not to open the gate for that topic. I really didn't need to hear my best friend complain about lack of alone time with her man "Declan doesn't trust Quinn will stay put at Dad's if he's not there, so he rarely stays over anymore. Even when Quinn goes off to wherever the hell he goes when he's not with Declan, it's still not enough of a reprieve."

"Where does he go?"

Autumn shrugs. "Clemson Drive. Some warehouse. Declan found some papers but what Quinn would want with some abandoned building, I have no idea. Still, it's better when he's out and not at home with Dad and Declan."

"What will you do after graduation?"

Autumn's gaze jumps to my face, her eyebrows shooting up behind that long ginger fringe covering her forehead. "What do you mean?"

I debate making her sweat a little, make her think I want to know what she is keeping from me, but didn't have the energy. Instead, I shrug, letting her off without an interrogation. "You telling me Deco and Quinn are going to live with Joe forever?"

"Uh, no." She looks away from me, watching the plume of smoke that rises from behind the garage. "The estate trustees say that courts will only turn over Quinn's inheritance once he's been sober and out of trouble with the law for a year. But when he turns twenty-five there's nothing they can do. Until then, his behavior will determine his living allowance."

"I get the feeling that allowance is probably more than you and I see in a year."

"No doubt." Quinn coughs from behind the garage and Autumn shakes her head, rubbing the bridge of her nose, but then looks up when Declan emerges from the house with two steaming mugs in his hand.

"I love you," Autumn tells him, taking the kiss he offers as she grabs a cup of coffee.

"Me too," I tell Declan as I take the other mug. "What, no kiss for me?" I wink when he laughs, chucking my chin with his large finger.

Another hack from the other side of the yard and we all glance in Quinn's direction. "He really is stupid," Autumn starts between sips of coffee. "All the shit his folks did for him, all they sacrificed and he repays them by chain smoking, drinking and screwing tarts."

"McShane." Declan frowns at Autumn when she winces, but then shrugs, waving off her. "It's fine. Sayo's your best mate and I doubt she gives a duff what that wanker does."

The frown on Declan's face becomes more severe as that plume of smoke stretches above the garage and the coughing continues.

"What do you mean 'the shit his folks did for him'?" I ask Declan, bringing his attention back to me.

Declan leans against the tree, lowering his voice. "Heart defect. He was in the hospital for most of his childhood. He was quite sickly til about ten when he got a transplant."

"Wow."

"Yeah," Autumn offers, gripping Declan's hand when he touches her shoulder. "The trustee told Declan he believed the O'Malley's spent hundreds of thousands of pounds getting him a new heart." She shrugs, moving the swing again.

"But that arsehole spent most of his time as a kid in hospital. They'd been so worried about him getting better that they never even tried to have any more kids. They were older when he was born from what Joe says, anyway" Declan said. "Guess they just didn't want to try again."

Declan straightens, folding his arms when Quinn appears from behind the garage, stretching like he doesn't care about the glare his brother gives him. When Quinn flips Declan the bird, Declan rolls his eyes, tapping Autumn on the shoulder. "Mrs. McIntyre wants you to explain the sponsorship for the fundraiser. I've no buggering idea what she means."

"Okay." She shrugs at me, jumping up from the swing to follow Declan inside, pausing before she leaves me to glance at Quinn, who is eyeing Georgie as if waiting for her to attack again. "Hey, don't mention any of that stuff about Quinn, okay? Technically speaking, Declan wasn't supposed to mention it to anyone.".

"No problem." Autumn's hair slaps against her back as she makes for the back door and I wait for Georgie as she abandons her curiosity over Quinn to investigate a lizard running under the potted plants on the other side of the pool. I'm not really eager to engage in another sarcastic battle with the lanky Irishman, myself. "Come on, Georgiana. Let's go inside." I whistle to the dogs and Darcy stretches, walking toward me but Georgie keeps her snout buried behind one of Mom's plants. I whistle again, but the puppy ignores me completely. Then Quinn kneels, slipping his fingers between his lips and lets out a sharp, piercing whistle of his own, which is a little jarring, but at least gets Georgie's attention..

"Come. Now," he tells her, voice sharp, and the damn dog listens. Quinn looks like he'd rather pluck out his own nails than hold the dog, but he picks her up, barely blinking as she licks his chin.

"How the hell did you do that?"

He shrugs, moving Georgie out of my reach when I reach for her. I cock an eyebrow at him. "What?"

He nods toward the house. "The fundraiser. It's for the sprog?"

"Yes, it's for Rhea. An experimental treatment that my aunt and uncle's insurance won't cover."

"Haven't they the cash?" He frowns, as though a middle class bank account is something done intentionally. "Is begging necessary?"

"They aren't begging, asshole." I grab Georgie from him, turning quick just to get away from him. "God," I say glaring at him, "why do you always have to be such a jerk?" Quinn only watches me, expression bored, with one eyebrow arched as though my yelling is something he's already gotten used to. "I've seen you with Rhea. You like her. You make her laugh. You even manage to smile when you're around her. But the rest of the world? You act like everyone else is the enemy."

"She can't help her situation."

"And you think everyone else can?"

Quinn runs his fingers through his hair, rubbing his face as he walks toward me. "I think everyone else takes advantage. She's not like that. She's... different."

"My aunt and uncle pay their taxes and aren't trying to put anything over anyone. They have good insurance, but the insurance company has said no to the treatment because it's not on the approved list of procedures. So they're trying to do everything they can to save her, even if it does mean that they have to ask for help." Georgie wiggles in my arms and I drop her to the ground, not caring if she eats the damn lizard. "It's what any parent would do for their child, Quinn." I think he suspects I know about his childhood but he doesn't mention anything.

"I didn't... fecking hell..." he says waving me off.

"Not everyone was born with a silver spoon in their mouth. Most people in this world have to actually work for a living." I walk in front of him, blocking him from the door. "Not all of us can live off the hard work of our families."

"Oh and that's what I do?"

I grab his hand, holding his wrist firm when he tries jerking out of my touch. "These aren't the hands of a working man. These," I lift his wrist, "come from privilege."

"You done?" I drop his hand, turn to open the door but Quinn grabs the handle, making me stare back at him.

"How much do they need?"

"They won't take your money. They wouldn't even take mine and they've already caught on that Declan is willing to hand over his inheritance to help." Quinn's jaw tenses. "Your brother, Quinn, he has a good heart." He glares at me like I'm ridiculous. "You're both judging each other for shit neither one of you responsible for."

"His mum was a slag."

I step up, get eye level with him. "You want a broken jaw, maybe a bloody nose, say that to his face. Besides, she didn't do a damn thing by herself." He frowns at me hard, warning me away from the insult he thinks is coming. "Your father wasn't innocent."

"How *fecking* much?" he asks, jaw tense as he steps up, as he stands inches from me.

That isn't frustration on his face. That isn't even anger. A petty part of me thinks it would be funny to antagonize him right now, call him out again for being an asshole, but what good would that do? A few seconds of fleeting satisfaction is pointless.

But I don't give Quinn the answers he wants. If he wants to help, he's going to have to do his part like everyone else. "Come to the fundraiser and you'll find out."

EIGHT

APPARENTLY, QUINN HAS decided *not* to live like a monk. At least, that's what Autumn told me when I showed up at Joe's tonight and the Irishman wasn't there.

"Some girl from the art supply place asked him out for coffee." When I frowned at her—my thoughts alternating between why the hell she thought I cared and whether 'coffee' meant nakedness at some point—Autumn shrugged, waving off her explanation. "More liquor for us."

"I can't get drunk, friend. I have to be at the hospital early tomorrow."

"It'll be fine. Besides, if you get too shitty, you can just stay here. We'll kick Quinn out of his room and he can sleep on the sofa."

"No way in hell, lady. I've peeked in that room. It's nasty in there."

But, I had an ulterior motive. Seems like I always did where Quinn was concerned. I'd already snuck into his room once before and since that day I hadn't had a chance to go snooping again. When he wasn't at the hospital working on project with my cousin, Quinn was here at Joe's in that stinky room doing things, likely, that would have me turning my nose up, and whatever time he was spending at that abandoned building that Autumn had mentioned earlier wasn't consistent enough to count on.

Declan and Autumn hosting a Rugby Sevens watching party was the perfect opportunity to find out what Quinn was up to. Really, this was more about me uncovering whatever it was he'd been hiding yesterday when I waited outside Rhea's room for him to leave.

The new Ms. Marvel comic had come out yesterday afternoon, and I had taken the opportunity to pick up a copy for Rhea, as it had quickly become her favorite new series. I knew that technically it wasn't "my time" to stop in and see her, but I knew she'd be excited, so I didn't want to wait until the morning. That's when I'd heard Quinn talking to Rhea through the half opened door. That's when I'd decided more snooping was in order.

"Can she have a red cape?" Rhea had asked him as I listened from out in the hallway.

"Red? O'course, love. Red, purple, bloody pink if you'd like."

"I don't want pink. I want red."

"No pink?"

"Nah… unless… do you like pink?"

"Well, sometimes…"

"What about Doctor C? Can we make him really mean looking?"

"Of course, love. Meanest villain ever drawn."

It was then that I couldn't help myself. Quinn was working on something for Rhea. Something that meant a lot to her, that much I could tell from the tone of her voice. And when I inched toward the opening in the door for a peek at them, my chest tightened at what I saw, and I couldn't help but break into a smile.

Quinn sat with his back to the door, right next to the lamp on the bedside table and Rhea next to him, her legs dangling from the bed. They both focused on the sketchpad in his hand and the quick movement his fingers made with a charcoal pencil. He drew lines that were thin, forming something remarkable, bringing to life a character that looked like Rhea, one that gave her power and strength.

She soared. She flew and there was nothing tying her to that hospital bed, nothing keeping her ill, nothing that sunk in her cheeks or paled her skin. In one picture, Quinn had drawn Rhea as she wanted to be—he'd drawn her strong, fearless, he'd drawn her as a champion.

It was only when I stepped back, when I cleared my throat and knocked on the door that either of them seemed to know I'd stopped by. As predicted, the second I walked into the room, Quinn closed his sketch book and adopted that evasive, disconnected attitude he seemed to reserve for anyone who wasn't Rhea.

"So what are you guys up to?" I'd asked, wondering if Quinn would let me get a better look at the sketch, but he hurried to excuse himself from the room, giving me the time with Rhea I'd wanted without even a frown over his shoulder in my direction, even though I had protested that I was only there to drop off the comic book.

It was then I got it: Quinn O'Malley didn't want anyone to see him being sweet, because that meant he would be vulnerable. Instead, he expressed himself, his feelings in that sketch book, I'd seen that much in the brief glances I'd stolen in his room. His point of view was in every line, every curve of his pencil and he hid them all away from the world, away from anyone who might disagree with him. Anyone who might judge him. Rhea wouldn't do that. She was still a kid. She hadn't learned about judging others. She hadn't learned about differences. To her, we were all the same and everything was worthy of friendship.

It was then I resolved to understand Quinn better. I wanted to know what he saw. I wanted to know what he'd shown my little cousin. I wanted a glimpse into the world he hid from everyone else.

The day before, I'd been convinced Quinn was putting on an act. I'd been convinced that what he showed the world was a mask—the disguise he wore because he didn't want anyone to see the real him beneath it. That's where my thoughts had gone when I left Rhea's room. That's what occupied them as I made my way to the parking garage, huddling against the late October wind as it whipped across my face. It was Quinn and the façade he wore that kept me distracted so that I didn't pay attention to the footsteps that echoed behind me as I walked up to my car.

It wasn't until I was unlocking my Jetta that I heard a low breath right behind me. Defensively, my elbow went up and out, and Quinn, who had slipped up way too close sucked in a breath, leaning against my car, holding his stomach.

"Sodding bollocks," he'd said, groaning as I stepped back. He rested his forehead on his arm, breath rough, labored as he moved his head to bring his gaze to me. "What the fecking hell…"

"Don't you know better than to sneak up on someone in a damn parking garage?"

"I bleeding well do now."

I gave him the pause he needed, but still kept my keys in my hand. I'd seen a glimpse at his softer side. That didn't mean I'd let my guard down around him.

"What the hell are you doing here?"

"I wanted…" he grunted, clearing his throat as he straightened, as though the pain in his stomach still smarted. Damn. Didn't realize how bony my elbows were. "I wanted to know," he said again, "what the hell you were doing lurking in the hallway." He stepped forward, that ever-present glare making him look less and less like he'd just got jabbed in the gut. "What are you on about?"

It would have been easy to goad him, to lie because he expected it. But I had convinced myself that I wanted answers. If I could get them from him, then there'd be no need for me to go snooping again. I knew that would probably be like expecting to win the Lotto without even buying a ticket, but I still gave it a shot.

Quinn stood in front of me, his back and shoulders rigid and straight. He looked very much like he expected a fight. He didn't move his body when I stepped forward, when I tilted my head, narrowing my gaze to really look at his face, examine those highborn features. He remained cool and didn't flinch until I spoke.

"I don't buy the bullshit, not like everyone else does."

There wasn't surprise, exactly, on his face, but his eyebrow did lift even as his frown relaxed. "You've no bleeding clue about me. None of you." Quinn laughed, once, bitter. "You lot think you know me, but you don't, do you? None of you…"

"You're good to Rhea." That quieted him, but it also made him nervous, had him taking a step away from me. "You're sweet to her. You speak to her with a kindness that no one else gets. Why is that?"

"No one else deserves it."

I licked my lips, continuing to look at him, see how close to the edge I could take him before he walked away. That seemed to be Quinn's M.O. He jetted when things got to be too much. Still, I went for it anyway, my curiosity greater than my worry that he'd turn his back on me. "You relate to her, I get that."

He dropped his arms, letting them hang at his side. "What?"

Several cars passed us; their taillights blinking colors over Quinn's face. Still he remained motionless, shocked, but unflinching. "I… I know about your childhood. I know that you…"

In a second his calm fractured and for the first time, I saw something real from Quinn O'Malley. Two quick steps and we were nearly nose to nose. "Fraser and his woman need to keep their fecking mouths shut." I suppose he thought his height, the reach of his shoulders would somehow intimidate me. It didn't. I'd grown up around rugby players my entire life. I was small, but I wasn't skittish.

"They didn't tell me," I lie. "I... I found out... another way." He glares at me, opened his mouth as though there was another insult queuing up to level at me. I stopped it before it came. "It doesn't matter. You know what Rhea's going through. You know what it's like to be stuck in a hospital, to be poked and prodded." Quinn worked his jaw, teeth grinding together and the anger brimmed close to the surface, pulling the muscles of his face tight. His nostrils flared and the top of his cheek twitched, but still, I continued, now too curious with what my accusations would force him to say. "You understand what she's going through and so you are nice to her, but why just her, Quinn? Why not everyone?"

"Because..." his voice was rough, as though the rage bubbling in his gut threatened to burst free. "Because she's the only one..."

"Everyone is struggling with something, Quinn." He stepped back, but I grabbed his arm, pulling him toward me. "Every single one of us."

"Bollocks." Quinn jerked from my touch, but didn't leave. "You're full of shite, the lot of you..."

"You have no reason to be angry." He stepped closer. "You lost your parents..."

"You don't know what you're talking about."

"Autumn, Declan, they both lost their moms."

That brimming anger surfaced, and he slammed his fist onto the trunk of my car. "They bloody well have each other; they have all of you…"

"You could too." My voice carried, lifted above the noise of engines and braking cars and the thump of his fist against my car. Quinn looked at me as though he didn't quite catch what I had said. Eyes blinking, his mouth opened, slowly. I took the advantage, wondering what he'd do if I kept at him, wondering if he'd show me a small peek of what Rhea saw every day. "We aren't hard people to get along with. We aren't closed off, none of us. You open up to us a little and maybe you won't be so miserable."

"I don't need anyone. Not a fecking soul."

"Is that how you get through the day? Lying to yourself?" When his top lip curled, I shook my head. "How's that working out for you?"

That barb hit the target. Quinn's frustration turned to rage, and he grunted, a loud, desperate sound I'd never expected him to make. Before I could react, he charged forward, and grabbing me by the shoulders, backed me up against the concrete column I had parked next to.

His fingers dug into my shoulders. I expected him to shout. I expected him to get right in my face and make threats. I expected him to curse at me, rail against me, say things I'd likely never be able to repeat to any of my friends.

I did not expect Quinn O'Malley to grab my chin.

I did not expect for him to stare down at me, gaze on my mouth, his tongue wetting his lips.

I did not expect him to kiss me.

And I damn well didn't expect to like it.

There was so much anger in his touch. Fingers gripping tight, breath fanning from his nostrils, warming my cheek; his angry, desperate movement against my body—it should have insulted me. It should have hurt. But Quinn's angry kiss changed when I didn't struggle, when I took what he gave me, when I welcomed it with a return of my lips against his, my fingernails running up his scalp, pulling him forward.

I forgot who I was, who was touching me. Quinn's anger turned into something that ebbed against the cool temperatures around us. He warmed me, lit me up from the inside with his tongue intruding, commanding inside my mouth, with his teeth against my bottom lip and his fingers tightening against my hip, pulling me toward him.

It only lasted a moment, but it was a moment that stretched, one that seemed to slow into forever until I suddenly remembered who had hold of my mouth. It was a realization that Quinn seemed to have at the same time and he pushed away from me, grunting again before wiping his mouth with the back of his hand as though my taste insulted him.

I barely noticed when he walked away. The shock that came into me then, wasn't from the sting on my lips left by Quinn's kiss. It wasn't the anger that left me speechless. It was the fact that I had liked it. His kiss has set something loose in my brain, and, various other tantalized body parts. And as his footsteps clicked against the concrete as he retreated, a singular agenda pulsed in my brain like a neon sign: Get him to do it again.

NINE

DEAR GOD, DECLAN Fraser was a ridiculous drunk.

This entire night would have been more enjoyable had we been watching a real rugby match and not just the local feed for regional semi-pro squads playing the Rugby Sevens.

"Ridiculous fecks." That's what Declan decides is the appropriate insult to sling at the two squads in the last match he actually watched. This, according to the Irishman, was nothing like "real" Sevens competition. "Not even playing in the right bleeding month, for feck's sake!" The Sevens were usually held later in the year for the international squads, two teams pitted against each other for quick fourteen-minute matches. It's the roughest, quickest matches you can watch and is a true display of real athleticism and teamwork.

The squad from Jefferson County and the pathetic redneck squad from Mississippi weren't performing up to Declan's liking and so the cable access feed got muted in exchange for beer pong. Joe's house had been taken over by the CPU rugby squad and it was well past eleven when the squad's captain, Declan, decided he needed several shots to erase the piss poor playing he'd just watched.

"Tequila?" Donovan asks, fighting both Declan and Vaughn for the bottle—it seems like the entire squad had ended up in the kitchen, where the entire center island was covered with bottles and plastic cups.

"Who's up then?" Declan asks, tilting it toward Mollie and Autumn.

I bypass the offered shot glass, handing it over to my best friend. Seeing his girlfriend down the drink then quickly suck on the lime, Declan forgets he is hosting his squad in the eager hurry to have a go at Autumn's neck.

"Fecking hell, love, you're sexy."

And... that little praise and the Irishman's mouth descending on Autumn's neck is enough to make Joe retreat to his bedroom and the entire squad to leave the kitchen.

Mollie crinkled her nose and the way Vaughn tugs her out of the room, tells me I'll likely not be seeing them the rest of the night, not if the Marine's groping hands are a clue to his plans.

Across the kitchen island, Donovan glances at me, rolling his eyes at how Declan and Autumn carry on before he snags the tequila. "Later, Sayo. I'm going to crash in the den."

And then I'm alone with the happy couple, itching to be rid of them as well. I have plans for that spare bedroom that won't stay empty all night.

"Um, guys?" I say, looking away from the couple as they block my exit from the kitchen. Declan fondles Autumn, hands firmly on her ass and she returns the attention, shoving her hand under his shirt, raking her nails across his chest before she uses her free hand to flirt her fingers against his waist. She is at his zipper before I can clear my throat.

"Autumn!" I shout, breaking their contact with my sharp yell.

"Oh, Sayo, sweetie, I'm sorry," she says, doing a poor job of getting Declan's lips from her neck. "Do you… you want something to…"

"Ugh, Autumn, take it to his room. The crowd is thinning and you guys are blocking my escape."

"Autumn my love, is it *sometime* yet?" Declan whispers against Autumn's skin and I roll my eyes, pushing them aside when Autumn giggles at him.

I wait for Declan's bedroom door to close, and move purposefully towards Quinn's empty bedroom, only to find a couple making out in the hallway. I tap the guy on his massive shoulder. It's Sona Pulu, a new Wing recruit from Samoa who is sweet if not a little thick, especially when it comes to girls. He's not yet cottoned on to the notion of rugby groupies and is currently tangled up with Lizzie Hamilton, a sophomore Cockie, (Cavanagh Cocks groupie), who spent all of last semester trying to get into Donovan's bed.

"Sorry Sona, party's over," I tell him, shrugging when Lizzie frowns at me.

"We can't just borrow…" Lizzie nods toward Quinn's room and I laugh.

"Not unless you want a very grumpy Irishman kicking you out when he gets home. I nod toward the door and Sona smiles as Lizzie pulls him out of the house.

Not including Donovan, only two players are left from the party, both passed out in the den. Joe slips back into the kitchen, but only to retrieve a bottle of bourbon that he tucks under his arm. I watch him from the dining room entrance and wait to hear his bedroom door shut before I beeline toward Quinn's bedroom.

It takes more effort than I'd like to admit, but I manage not to wonder why his date is going on so long. I feel like a hypocrite. I know damn well Quinn's date isn't my business, but neither is anything in his room. The guilt is a small burn against my conscience, one that I try to ignore right along with the assumptions of what Quinn is doing on his date as I slip into his room, a little surprised that it was tidier than it had been the first time I snuck in here. There is still a mound of dirty clothes near the window, but the bed is made and there aren't any half-eaten meals or empty bottles of beer with floating cigarette butts next to the bed.

A few errant pieces of clothing litter the floor, near the closet. I open the closet door and suddenly discover where all the previous mess has gone. Bypassing the clutter that falls from the open closet door, I reach up, feeling for the box on the top shelf I know holds his sketch book. When I find nothing but empty boxes again and a small, empty duffle bag, I step away, standing on the balls of my feet to see if anything else has been stuffed in the back of that shelf. But it is empty and a quick inspection of the floor under the bed and Quinn's bedside table provides no sketchbook. I think about leaving. It is a risk snooping in here when he can return at any second, when Joe can walk in at any time, but I want to see what he is hiding. I need to see the sketches he's kept from me. I have no real reason, nothing that makes any sense other than blind curiosity, but I suspect my motivations are twisted, a little unsettled from that kiss.

Just the thought of that kiss makes my bottom lip throb and I shake myself, squashing the memory before it can rise up properly and stuff the rubbish and clutter back into the closet before I start for the door. One look at the dresser, though, and the open bottom drawer on the left side stops my exit.

Listening for any noise down the hallway, I kneel in front of the dresser, pulling open the drawer and there it is, the sketch book, looking just as it had the day before. But it holds so much more than the first time I found it. Now it holds all those sketches he's been creating for Rhea, and I waste no time flipping open the pages, smiling when I spot the picture I glimpsed yesterday—my beautiful baby cousin looking fierce, strong. The glint of health, of power in her eyes is enough to blur my vision with unshed tears and I push them back, sniffling as I turn the page. There are more variations of the same sketch, Rhea soaring through the night, her zipping among the stars, past clusters of galaxies, then more of

Rhea, as she is now, only without the pale skin and bags under her eyes.

This is Quinn's version of my cousin—strong, beautiful, timeless. The image is so detailed, so real that I find myself touching it, absently believing that I will get some sort of spark from one graze of my fingers on the page.

But it is the next page that staggers me, leaves me unable to do anything other than stare unblinking.

Quinn has never struck me as anything other than crass and unaffected. He has never looked at me with anything similar to longing or respect. He's only ever made me feel anger, rage, like I am someone to toy with, not anyone he'd love.

Yet the face staring back at me was drawn with emotion. It's right there, me, through a mirror distorted, altered by whatever filled Quinn's mind when he drew it. It's a picture that is both totally me and not me at all. That face is beautiful, if not a little sad. There is strength behind those eyes and vulnerability in that expression.

Unable to move, I can only look at myself as Quinn sees me. The movement of the image, the wave in my hair, the flawless shape of my features, all tell me one thing: Quinn O'Malley is capable of emotion. He's capable of a lot of emotion and all of what he feels for me, what opinions he has of me outside of the public bluster, are reflected in the paper and lines, shading and shadows that stare back at me.

"What the fecking hell are you doing in my room?"

My heart jumps to my mouth and pounds wildly. I've been caught. I was so wrapped up in staring at his sketch of me that I didn't hear him come in.

"Quinn…" I stop, but can go no farther. I have no excuse. There's nothing I can say that would make that anger leave his face. Me, here, among his things, it's a betrayal, an offense that I have no way of justifying.

He kicks the door open all the way open, charging at me as I jump to my feet, retreating. "Find everything you want, did you?" He jerks the book out of my hands, and rips out the drawing that had stunned me into silence. "Here, have it then, you nosey bitch."

"Don't you dare…"

"And don't go thinking me drawing you means a fecking thing." His voice is low, so quiet that I feel the sting of each word as though he's funneled them directly into my veins. "This," he says, jerking the torn picture between his fingers, "is nothing more than bleeding wank material I might use when I'm too fecking pie eyed to remember that pretty face of yours." Quinn grabs my arm, pulling me across his room, too angry for me to make much of an effort of prying his fingers off me. The doorknob slams against the wall when he opens the door and pushes me harshly across the threshold. "I don't think I'll be needed to remember what you look like anymore, now will I?"

"If you'd shut up for a second..."

"No, I bloody well won't." His frown pinches his mouth tight and Quinn stares at me, disgusted, his nostrils flaring. After a second of scrutiny, his grip on my arm eases and he tilts his head, pulling me close to whisper in my ear. "Did you think this sketch and that snog last night meant something, Sayo?" When I only manage to swallow, trying to wake myself out of whatever trance his touch, the smell of his skin is doing to me, Quinn touches my face, his fingertips barely against my skin. "Because it didn't mean a fecking thing." He tones is light, soft but it belies the mix of emotions in his eyes. There is a twist of something I don't recognize in his expression. "It won't mean a thing, but if you're so damn curious, I'll take you right here, just feet from my brother and your best mate. We can see just how loud you get, see if we can't be louder than them going at each other like it's the end of the fecking world. You want that?"

"I..." Clearing my throat, jarring away the knot there, doesn't help. Quinn's closeness is too much, the rude invitation that I know is supposed to offend me only twists up my logic, has my heart pounding.

"I didn't bleeding think so," he says, shoving me into the hall and just before he slams the door in my face, Quinn throws the sketch at me. It flutters to my feet, and I am left alone in the hallway with my own face staring up at me.

TEN

QUINN DOESN'T CARE about anyone.

At least, that was my thought as I left Joe's house, still reeling, livid that I hadn't given him much of a fight. Outside my small apartment, the early November wind moves the small planter hanging from my balcony against the sliding door and I watch the ivy leaves tangle and break in the wrought iron light fixture above the door frame. It's a mesmerizing sight and it takes my mind from the tangle of emotions that keep me from moving off my sofa. I haven't even bothered to take off my coat or drop my purse on the coffee table.

I am numb. Still.

Part of me understands the reaction. That vapid, young girl part was transfixed by Quinn's temper, by the sliver of idea that he was capable of real emotion; that the façade he forces on the world is just a mantel he wears. He is a scared little boy broken down by tragedy and loss.

But he is still an asshat.

That ivy limb continues to move and I give fleeting thoughts to the speed of the wind and the storm that approaches. There are lawn chairs in the back that need moving. Mrs. Walters in 2C has a cat that likes to go hunting mice in the wooded area behind our complex. There are newspapers stacked up in the recycle bin right outside my door that I haven't found time to get rid of... all these thoughts compete for attention right alongside the memory of Quinn's mouth and the steely strength of his hands. It's those hands, that mouth, that flicker in and out of my recall when I realize someone is pounding on my door.

It takes two loud bangs to get me up and off the sofa and when I open the door, I don't think of anything—not how I'm still wearing my coat, how my purse is still over my shoulder or why my keys are still in my hand. I can only stare stupidly at Quinn on the other side of that door.

"Are you off then?" When I frown at him, confused, Quinn nods at my keys threaded between my fingers.

"Uh, no. I just..." I exhale, standing straighter, bothered with myself that I thought to answer him. "What are you doing here?"

Once again Quinn's features tighten and those bright, clear eyes become hard. "You've something of mine."

"No," I say, stepping away from the door, not bothering to close it. I know that wouldn't keep him out. "I don't have anything of yours." When he steps inside I pull the sketch from my purse, smoothing it out on top of the coffee table. "You gave it to me."

"That's not what I'd call it."

"You're right, Quinn." I wave the sketch between my fingers. "You threw it at me swearing it didn't mean a damn thing."

"It still doesn't." He moves to stand the table from me, eyes still burning fire as though he wants to lash out, to scream and yell. "But it's a good piece and I want it back."

"That's not why you're here." One slip of my gaze down his body and I catch the tight fist he makes and his whitened knuckles.

He's holding back, shooting for patience, something I've never seen from him in the few brief months I've known him. "Say what you need to and get out." Finally, I slip off my coat, throwing it across the sofa. The day, the weariness, hits me at once and all I crave is a dreamless night and my comfortable bed.

He moves around the room like a fighter preparing for a match, hands massaging the back of his neck, jaw working behind whatever he tries to keep from speaking. It would be funny if he wasn't so angry.

"Quinn…"

"Tell me why you were in my room." It isn't a request. Quinn demands and though I know I should feel guilt, at least a little shame for snooping, his attitude has me wanting to lash out.

"Oh now you want to know?" I drop the sketch on the table and walk around it, needing to see his expression close up. "Before you didn't give me time to explain."

"Well I am now."

My temper loosens, I block out what he says, too amped up to make him feel as shitty as I have since I left Joe's. "All you could do is scream at me like a crazy man."

"I'm a bit calmer now, am I not?"

He steps closer and the heavy scent of hard liquor and male skin permeates in the room. "And then you made lewd offers to me like I'm some common…"

Quinn stands right in front of me, the twitch across his lips stilling. "There isn't a bleeding common thing about you, you mad woman."

Rare moments come, like this one, where I'm not certain of my next step. Warring thoughts still consume me, taking up space along with the shape of Quinn's mouth and the small pulse that moves the pale skin along his neck. "I…" He's rendered me speechless and if I'm not careful, my inability to form coherent sentences will give him the upper hand. "I… I'm not crazy, I just…"

"Sayo," he says coming so close that his fingers graze my wrist and the scent of liquor moistens my face as he watches me. "Why were you in my room?" When I only stare back at him, Quinn's shoulders lower and any softness that made him look less livid, disappears. "Why the hell am I here?"

"I… I…" My throat tightens when he glares at me and once again I retreat within myself, frustrated that plausible excuses won't leave my mouth. Quinn is the only person I know that has me reverting back to the emotional range of a teenager. "I didn't ask you to come here."

"No," he says, following me when I return to the table to grab the sketch, "but you damn well invaded my space. You stuck your buggering nose where it doesn't belong." He ignores the sketch when I offer it to him. "Fecking ridiculous. You really are mad, aren't you?"

"No, I'm not." The sketch falls to the floor when I drop it, coming back again to him, wanting nothing more than to yank him out of my apartment. The next ridiculous thought I have involves him and those lips and the disturbing things I wish he'd do with them. "Nothing hurts you, does it? Right, Quinn?" I move my head, gaze following him when he stares at the floor, out the window, anywhere but at me. "You are unaffected, unable to feel any damn thing, right? That's what you want everyone to see."

Quinn's gaze jerks to mine. When he speaks, his voice is deep, bordering on threatening. "You don't know me."

"No? And you think you do?"

"I don't want to know you."

"That's not what I mean." He starts to retreat, but I follow. He wanted a fight, I'll give him one if only to avoid apologizing. Yes, I snooped. Yes, I had no right, and I do feel guilty, but my need for answers is just as important. "You don't know yourself. All you know is what feels good, right? All you know is indulgence. You only know pleasure, whatever gets you off. What a pathetic life that is never understanding anything more than what feels good. Never seeing anything beyond the surface."

Quinn grabs the sketch from the floor, waving it at me like a threat. "This? This proves that I see beyond the surface otherwise you wouldn't have sat there staring at it for ages, would you?"

Some of my anger eases, dips down in the pit of my stomach as I watch him. He'd just revealed more of himself, unintentionally, than he ever had before, and there was no way I'd let that bit of information go without comment. "How do you know how long I looked at it?" He walks away, stepping backward, like he's only just realized what a slip he made, but I follow, edging him toward the door. "Is that what you're always going to do, Quinn?" He is almost gone. "Run away because you're scared?"

"I'm not scared of anything." He takes a step, shoulders back, ready for a fight. "Not a fecking thing."

"Yeah? Then why are you leaving? Because I upset you?" I grab his arm when he turns, making him face me. "Because I made you admit how empty your life is?"

Quinn won't look at me, seems to prefer to keep as much distance between us as possible and I almost let him leave, figuring that he'll argue with me all night if I allow it. But the emptiness, the need to seek out what is missing in his life from my little cousin, is a warning sign, a flag of caution that tells me he is hurting, far more than he lets on. It's not unusual, something that everyone else on the planet is going through, but Quinn is the one around Rhea. Quinn is the one that has opened a chasm in our lives just by being here.

When I step forward, he retreats further until he is against the door. His swagger is gone. His attitude missing. Standing before me is a scared boy, one who swallows thickly, who blinks as though he isn't sure what's about to happen. I've never seen Quinn like this. I've never seen him as open, as raw as when I reach for him, extending my fingers so that they hoover next to his cheek.

"What are you doing?" He grabs my wrist, but his grip, his defense is weak.

"Seeing how scared I can make you."

He doesn't move when I touch him. Quinn holds his breath when I move my fingers across his face. His cheeks are arched, the bones long and supple and he shakes, the tips of his hair moving the closer I get to him. He doesn't resist me, but his back stiffens when I kiss him, barely putting any pressure at all against his mouth. It's only when I move his face, when I slip the slightest hint of tongue against his mouth that Quinn makes a sound at all. And then, he responds, like someone has turned a switch in his brain, given him permission to respond. Quinn moves his hands up my back, threading his fingers in my hair, yanking so that my head comes back, but our mouths stay connected. He towers over me, his body moving, grazing against mine.

We become motion, heat. I sink further and further into the abyss, forgetting who I am, what I'm supposed to be. There is only Quinn's mouth against mine and those low, primal sounds that lift from his throat. His breath coats my neck, his fingers dip, they spread against my skin, down the slope of my back, up to tweak and cup my breast.

Against my hip, I feel the thick outline of his dick and shudder against him, tightening my fingers into his shirt as Quinn grinds, pushes himself into me harder and harder. He doesn't stop, isn't cautious or kind and pushes me up, holding my ass against his squeezing fingers, our bodies coming together, needy, gripping like something desperate, something inevitable.

"Feck," he mutters so low that I barely make out the curse. He is breathless, desperate and I feel it in every swipe of his mouth, his tongue along my skin and the gripping possession of his hands pulling my leg up to his hip, settling me so close that our centers meet over and over, teasing, promising.

My thoughts are clearer now. There is only sensation and that drive to complete, to finish, a will older than any of us and it is this Quinn who matches me. Quinn who helps me loosen the tight hold I have on everything weighing me down. There is no logic to this. There is only need and that ancient inclination to fill it.

It's only then, right at that moment, that I realize the past few hours, fighting with him, insulting each other, was the first time in two years Rhea didn't consume my thoughts and the smallest hint of suggestion flirts in my mind. Quinn had done that, his words, his anger, then his touch, had all numbed me to the sense of loss, to the one thing I prayed every day I could avoid.

I break the kiss, pushing on his chest to catch my breath. "You... you let me forget," I tell him, a little out of my mind with lust, then stoned completely when Quinn moves his tongue across my neck, biting gently against my collarbone.

"I can make you forget, Sayo... we can forget together."

But I can't forget, not completely. Quinn is a bully, a liar unwilling to share who he is with anyone but a dying girl. This thing between us, whatever it is, is a Band Aid, not a fix and no matter how good he feels, no matter how strong that drive is, it will not answer my questions or keep the nightmare that approaches at bay. But maybe, just maybe, it will be enough.

"Tell me," I say, holding him back when he presses forward, needy for my mouth, anxious to taste my skin again. "Why did you draw that?"

Quinn stops, staring down at me, watching my face closely for something he doesn't mention. "Why does it matter?"

"I need to know."

Nodding once, Quinn drops my legs, pushes off from the door, and moves away from my body with a only a brief touch of his fingertips on my face before he jerks his hand away and moves me aside to open the door. "Get used to disappointment." And then, he slams the door behind him as he leaves, taking the warmth of his body and the promise of what he could give me.

ELEVEN

I HAVE MISSED my friends. Autumn, of course has stayed front and center. She is my best friend. I could no more be rid of her than I could the blackness of the hair that overtakes the pink dye since there has been no time for girly maintenance. But Layla and Mollie, I have not seen in weeks. Texts and Facebook posts don't count. So when Layla calls to ask if I'd meet her for coffee, I eagerly agreed.

I had no idea our little friend date would turn into something else entirely.

The confession came wordless, a reaction to my stupid joke and I knew what Layla had kept from us for months. "What? Finally getting hot and heavy with Donovan?" When that fear crowded around her features, my mouth fell open and I reached for her. "Oh my God. I was joking. I was... I mean, *are you*?"

She and Donovan were sleeping together. Really together. Gone was the Rent-a-Cop boyfriend that no one liked, (not even Layla) and in his place, had been Donovan.

Who we thought Layla hated.

Who we thought hated Layla.

And then, Walter, the aforementioned Rent-a-Cop tracked Layla down and got a bit too insistent that she take him back.

Now Donovan is playing the hero. The happy melody of "The Gypsy Rover" plays like a backtrack in my mind as Donovan pummels Layla's ex-boyfriend, Walter. To be fair, he had threatened us both. So maybe he deserves it, but hearing that tune—one that Layla and I stopped to listen to as a small street band started up the impromptu concert happened just outside of McKinney's—is like some sort of weird soundtrack to the pummeling, maybe our on Irish brawl where we watch and make snap judgments.

"Dude. Two guys are fighting over you." The comment is stupid, but I can't help myself and by Layla's smile and quick blush, I get that she appreciates it. Still, looking at her, seeing how she watches Donovan come to her aid, how her entire face flushes, lights up with longing and pride, well. If she hadn't inadvertently admitted that she and Donovan have been sleeping together, then one look at her would have given their little secret away.

"See that woman, Rent-a-Cop?" Walter ignored Donovan's question, either due to blind stupidity, or his being a simpleton. When he finally relents, half-heartedly acknowledges the question, then Donovan continues, his voice sharp and damn scary. "She's off limits to you. You see her on campus, in town, any fucking where and you so much as look in her direction, I will fucking end you. You feel me?"

Next to me, Layla makes the strangest, pleased sound, something that reminds me of cotton candy and a free turn on the Ferris wheel. She is next to Donovan the second he leaves Walter on the street. Their touches are frequent, tender, and watching one of my oldest friends and the man she's pretended to hate for decades finally come together, finally treat each other with something other than cruelty, does something to me. They aren't playing games anymore, not that I can see. At least, they don't seem to be. And when Donovan touches Layla's face, when he looks to be suffering from the scrape with the rent a cop and the urgency to touch Layla, I figure it's time to bail out.

It's only when I touch Layla's back that she remembers me, but I dismiss the apologetic way she frowns and stop her excuses before they come. "Get him home, Layla, before the real cops show up." My friend hesitates, but only for a moment, as though she's only just remembering that I know her dirty little secret and that she'll get zero judgment from me. A glance at Donovan's wincing face and I shrug, kissing Layla's cheek. "Patch him up, make sure he gets home okay."

I could say something to her, maybe tease her for abandoning me to be the last remaining singleton in our circle, but I don't. I'm not remotely bitter about that. My friends are growing. They are setting upon lives that will likely lead them away from Cavanagh, away from everything that we've ever known. It is not something that I haven't considered over the years, but it was bound to happen. It's not like I haven't prepared, but as Layla and Donovan walk away, with her nestled under his arm and that worried, anxious expression on her face, the realization comes to me that no amount of preparation will ready me for the ends that are approaching. And there are many of them—Rhea, Autumn and Declan, Mollie and Vaughn— too many to list. The loneliness that settles in my chest is cold and mildly sharp, and no matter how many of the CU rugby players call after me as I walk back through town, no matter how many open, genuine smiles greet me as I head back toward my car, that loneliness will not lessen.

Maybe it's because those players, those sweet, flirty faces, aren't the one that's taken root in my brain. The one I want to throttle and kiss equally.

Shit. Did I just think that?

All through town, driving, not paying much attention to my surroundings, the image of Layla and Donovan, the look between them, keeps me from focusing. I might want that one day. Maybe. When my life is less chaotic. When I'm not needed as much.

Hell, I'm the oldest of five siblings. There will likely never be a time when I'm not needed. And with Rhea…

Coming to the intersection that crosses the campus and Old Cavanagh, my gaze unfocuses as I stare blindly into the street lights, watching the wind zip CPU flags and holiday decorations against the light poles and street signs. There is a light drizzle frosting the air with the approach of Christmas and the promise of more time slipping. Without really meaning to, I think of Quinn, his touch, the severe way he handled me last week in my apartment and how much I liked it.

Because he made me forget.

Only a second, a pause between his lips and mine—in that instance there was nothing but him, the taste of his mouth and the feel of his breath.

"Clemson Drive. Some warehouse." Autumn's voice floats around like an echo, a nudge I know she'd never inch me toward if she realized it was there. I was three blocks from the warehouses on Clemson Drive. I was lonely. Quinn O'Malley didn't do anything for anyone without getting something in return and I have no idea what I'd have to offer. I only know that Layla and Donovan are changing. My guess is that Autumn and Declan will likely leave. Mollie will probably end up with Vaughn in Maryville. Rhea is… slipping.

I am being left behind.

My blinker is on before I stop myself, my wheels turning, and I'm coasting down Clemson Drive. Then I'm pulling over and putting the gear in park. Across the street, despite the soft, dwindling drizzle and the cold, Quinn stands in front of a large brown brick building, a scatter of spray paint cans at his feet.

Reason tells me to only watch. It tells me that voyeurism is all I should allow myself. It's all I should give Quinn. But his hands are uncovered and paint wets the back of his fingers. The leather jacket he wears isn't zipped and the beanie on the ground should be on his head.

Without really considering it, I am out of my car and across the street within seconds. Just standing, watching, observing from the corner of the building, hidden between shadow and the dull, yellow street light. The large, beaming handheld flashlight shines onto the building's surface and the sketchy form of what I know will be Rhea flying through space.

A quick shiver breaks across Quinn's broad shoulders but he doesn't move; simply steps back, lowering the paint can as he looks over the work he's started.

"Come to give me company?" he asks, keeping his gaze on that wall, as though I don't warrant even a single glance over his shoulder. He shakes the paint can so that the marble inside clicks against the metal, his movements easy, light. He doesn't wait for me to answer. His attention is on the long, solid lines that will make up something I can't see yet. It's while he is distracted that I move, inching closer, unsure why I am here at all.

"Her top lip is fuller," I offer coming to stand next to him, looking up at the face I've memorized since she was a baby. "There's a bigger dip in her top lip. It... makes her mouth heart shaped."

For some reason, my throat catches and just for a blink, I don't care that Quinn hears me upset, that this depiction of my little cousin has my eyes getting misty.

If he wants to insult me, maybe yell at me for correcting his artwork, Quinn retains the smallest semblance of decorum and only nods, stretching his arms before he stops to watch my profile.

"It's not done. Not even close."

"Is this..." I wave at the building, the large stretch of the scene, reaching nearly the entire surface, "What is this for?"

But as always, Quinn keeps his business to himself, offering me nothing more than a turn of his head and a long, slow glance as though I'd insulted him.

"She's my cousin, you know." He remains silent, tossing the can on the ground next to a canvas bag holding the others. "Aunt Carol, she might not like…"

"Why are you here?" Quinn steps in front of me, keeping my gaze from the mural, from everything but the backlit highlights of his face. "You want…" he steps closer, so that I straighten forgetting for a second that he shouldn't be touching me, that his hands don't belong on my hip, that his fingers shouldn't be resting on my lower back, pulling me forward. "You want me, love?" Another pull and our chests connect. "Want my mouth again? Want to feel everything I've got to give you, Sayo?"

That bravado is like a sheen. Something that mars the surface, something that covers whatever is real, whatever is true. It's a shame, really. He is beautiful, has been given so much because of that beauty. And yet he uses that to distract from who he really is, from the kindness that seems hidden beneath all that attitude and innuendo.

"Can you ever stop putting on a front?"

He doesn't seem to like my question. Quinn drops his hand and I feel the cool wind that his arms, his fingers had blocked. But he doesn't step back. When I inch close to touch his face, Quinn grabs my wrist. "Don't touch me."

"Always hiding, aren't you?" My step is quiet as my boot pops a small piece of gravel under the heel. "Still running?"

"What do you want from me?" He jerks me toward him, his hand jumping back to my hip. "Hmm? Is it not enough that I keep away from your schedule at hospital? Or is it something else?"

Quinn walks forward, making me step backward. "Do you want to finish the business from last week? I have to warn you, love, you've no idea what you're getting yourself into. I'm not sweet. I'm no gentle lover. I take and I give and there are no fecking apologies." I don't stop him when he leans us against the back building, picking me up by the hips. "It's a bit cold here, but the building is mine. So long as you understand what I offer, we can keep ourselves warm… somehow."

He doesn't mean it. Quinn might want me, but he is only acting on that drive because he refuses to explain himself. He's deflecting. He wouldn't tell me why he drew my sketch. He won't explain what he has planned for the mural. Most of all, I doubt he'd ever give any of us a why for any of it.

When I don't react the way he expects, when I push him away from my neck Quinn frowns, staring at me with more confusion than irritation.

"Can you give me something real?"

He waits, the grip on my thighs, the tension in his fingers tighten for a second before he relaxes. He is fighting with himself. There is something skirting around his tongue, as though there is something he wants to say but pride, ego prevents him from uttering a sound.

The truth would cost him too much.

Being real is too high a price.

"This is me, love. This is as real as I ever am."

The truth is a blade Quinn keeps hidden. That edge is too sharp and lowering it would leave him unprotected. He is a fog to me, something that covers, something that can be easily brushed aside.

The paint fumes linger on the wind, mix with peppermint that hits my senses when Quinn sighs. It's an odd mix that is intoxicating, just as he is. But it's not enough. He's not enough. Not the partial person he wants me to see.

"You're a liar," I tell him, pushing back so he will release me. "You'll show me the real you or nothing at all, O'Malley."

It's hard, so very hard, but when he doesn't respond, merely keeps looking at me as if his stare could change my mind, I turn and walk back to my car. Part of me—the selfish part—wants him to follow, but he doesn't. I force myself to not look around, but I listen for any indication of what he might be doing.

The sound is faint, but clear—the spray can, the marble moving as he shakes it again and, I swear the low mutter of his cursing as he watches me walk away.

TWELVE

THERE IS NOTHING worse in life than waiting for news you know is coming. Births, deaths, dreams snatched out of your future—all keep you in limbo. They keep you waiting. Like now, sitting on the crowded bench next to boxes of latex gloves and paper masks the nurses haven't had a chance to bring to the supply room with my ear close to Rhea's door. I can almost make out the muddle of voices. I can almost hear the news I hope will get me through the door.

While it's only been about twenty minutes, it feels much longer, and I have nothing to do but bite on my thumb nail and try to keep the promise I made to Rhea—that I wouldn't look inside the sketch book she asked me to hold. The sketch book Quinn left with her for safe keeping, after he caught me snooping. It holds another clue in the great secret he doesn't want me to know about. He doesn't know I have it. I should maintain the higher ground, be the bigger person.

But I suck. I betrayed my little cousin and had a look.

Just one.

Only one.

What the hell is taking so long in there?

When a chair on the other side of the door slides against the floor, I stretch out my legs, drumming my nails against the sketch book because there is nothing else I can do. My mostly black hair is braided. All the purple polish has been chipped from my nails. I have discovered there are two hundred and thirty-five tiles along the ceiling of this hallway. And still, no answer, no explanation.

Ah hell, Rhea probably suspected I'd peek.

There's no need to be quiet opening the book. No one can hear me and my gaze instantly catches on the same drawing I saw before, the hasty sketch of a scene, the battle of our two heroic champions against a sinister foe.

The book rests against my knees as I adjust my legs, then I run the tip of my index finger along the thick pencil marks Quinn made—the power behind Rhea's kick, the strong set of Quinn's jaw. The entire scene has me smiling, staring so that I no longer hear the noises inside that room or the footsteps that approach.

"Jaysus, you must be the most nosey little shite I have ever come across in my bleeding life." Quinn's tone is low, as though he's only pretending he's annoyed with me. I let his insult slide, not caring if he is and close the book, fold my arms over the top of it just as he comes to stand next to me, that familiar look of disappointment on his face. "Why do you have that?"

"Relax. Rhea knew I'd look when she asked me to hold it." When Quinn only glares at me I nod at the space at my side, thinking he might want to hear the voices beyond the closed door too.

Apparently not. Quinn sits across from me, arms on his knees. "Why aren't you in there?"

"One of the night nurses has the flu and didn't tell anyone. She's new and now she's without a job." There is movement in the room behind me and I lean my ear against the door, squinting as I concentrate, as though that will help me hear a damn thing. A minute of silence and I lean back against the wall. "Two of the kids on the floor have tested positive for the flu." My wool pea coat gets caught on the metal back of the seat when I scoot closer to the door trying to hear. "They want to make sure Rhea doesn't have it either."

"If she does?" This time, Quinn does a poor job of hiding his worry. There is a rasp to his tone, something that tells me there is more fear than I'd expect from him at his question.

No need in sugar coating anything for him. "There might be a quarantine, but I'm not sure."

"That's bollocks," he says, voice high and cracking. "I'm not bleeding sick." Quinn ignores my frown, covering yet again with a glance over my face, down my body, not hiding the slow slip of his tongue along his bottom lip. "Are you fit to see her?"

"There's nothing wrong with me."

"That's debatable," he says, leaning his head back against the wall just as Doctor Allen barks at one of the nurses trailing behind him at the end of the hall.

"The other file, Nurse Billings. Didn't I say that twice already?" He doesn't acknowledge either me or Quinn as the pair passes us.

"Fecking wanker," Quinn offers, following the doctor's hurried walk to the last room at the end of the hall. "Rhea hates that arsehole."

"Yeah, I know." I hold the sketch book up, giving it a small wave. "I see you don't like him either."

He peers at me hard, before easing off and Quinn shrugs, as though explaining anything to me is somehow both funny and irritating. "I'm only drawing what she wanted.

"Gave yourself some bulk, didn't you?"

"I did not!" He lifts his eyebrows when I slide across the hall to sit next to him and open the sketch book to the piece in question. Quinn doesn't bother looking down at it. "That's an accurate depiction."

"Is it?" I can't help laughing, pointing at the sketch Quinn had done as *Omnigirl* and *Sovereign Smash* attack the villainous *Death Doctor C* who has the same build and shaggy hair as the curt, unfriendly oncologist down the hall.

"I'm not slight," Quinn says, defending his sketch. I don't miss the way he rubs his arms, as though he needs to double check that he hasn't gotten scrawny since arriving in Cavanagh.

"Your jaw is not that square and perfect."

"Oh," he leans close on the pretense of looking down at the sketch, but Quinn's mouth lingers a bit too close to my ear. "But you're saying it is somewhat perfect."

"I'm definitely not."

"You know, I think you are, in fact," he says, knocking his shoulder next to mine, just like a normal human. Someone who isn't all venom and anger, or put upon bravado meant to offend.

"Well," I begin, liking the small glimpse of what I believe is the real Quinn peeking out behind the almost smile on his mouth. "I wouldn't say perfect at all." That exaggerated glare he gives me doesn't break my humor and I manage to pretend I'm not looking him over. "I mean, you're okay to look at if you're into that sort of thing."

"What? Devilishly handsome blokes? Utterly shagable men that will make you see heaven?"

"And there's the asshole we all know and love."

There's a moment when Quinn's expression shifts, as though he might have enjoyed me saying that. It only lasts a few small seconds and then the Irishman's body goes rigid and the pleased, the happy set of his mouth tightening as though he can't give in to two friends joking, or the idea that I might have acted remotely kind to him.

I recover as quickly as I can, shaking my head, adding an exaggerated eye roll to make him see I wasn't serious. "Figure of speech, O'Malley." I don't bother looking at him when I speak, keeping my attention on the sketch book, nearly getting the page turned when the door to Rhea's room finally opens.

"Sayo... Quinn." Aunt Carol emerges, followed by two nurses and a doctor I don't recognize. I can just make out Uncle Clay's feet as he sits next to Rhea on the bed before one of the nurses pulls the door shut. Odd that he'd be here when Carol swore he'd been called in to work and couldn't be here when the labs came back. Quinn and I are on are feet when Carol crosses the threshold. "You're both so sweet to wait."

"Well?" I ask, noticing how tired Carol looks, how the faint lines around her eyes and mouth have somehow gotten deeper in a matter of months.

"She doesn't have it, fortunately. But since the wing was exposed, I... well..." Carol dismisses the head shake one of the nurses gives her as she passes, then lifts her chin, looking determined, confident. "Look, I realize it may seem a bit of an overreaction, but I still want her quarantined. Clay is staying with her for a little while and then I want everyone else to clear out for at least five days."

"Five days?" Quinn clears his throat, looking sheepish that he'd lost his composure again. "Well what's to be done until then?"

"Nothing. I..." My aunt eyes me, looking for sympathy she know I'll give her.

"This happened before, when Rhea was younger. One of the kids got sick and the staff weren't that concerned." I push my hair behind my ear, lowering my voice as one of the doctors passes by us. "Well, it took Rhea a month to get over the flu that time."

"I won't have that happen again.." Carol rubs her neck, groaning when it pops.

Next to me Quinn opens his mouth and I can see by the way one vein on his neck pops that he's gearing up for an argument. One that Carol doesn't need. Before he opens his mouth, I jab him in the ribs, hoping he will keep silent.

"Won't she be lonely?" Quinn offers, not bothering to look at me.

"The nurses will read to her. They'll make sure she isn't on her own too much."

My aunt looks behind her to the closed door and between that worried, anxious expression and Quinn's brewing anger, I offer a suggestion that I hope will alleviate the issue of Rhea being on her own.

"What about her laptop or iPad?"

"I don't want anything from home in there. The contamination…"

"For feck's sake," Quinn says, voice a little loud.

"It's not her fault, asshole," I tell him, lifting a finger to shut him up when he looks as though he wants to argue with me. "What about a new iPad? We can at least chat with her, read to her and Quinn can do…" Quinn's grunt is low, but I ignore it with another hand wave, "whatever drawing things he does with her."

"That's not a bad idea. At least she'll have a way to pass the time."

Carol reaches into her purse, pulls out her wallet, but Quinn shakes his head, stopping her. "Leave it to me." And he is down the hall and away from us before Carol can stop him.

We pass the time like this: Rhea looking more like herself, but somehow stronger, happier via the small screen on my laptop. She seemed so much stronger that I went back part time to the library. Aunt Carol even decided to pick up a few massage therapy clients while Rhea was quarantined. Between my work at the library and Aunt Carol getting back into the swing of a light work week, we had time to organize the final details of the fundraiser with Autumn's help. Uncle Clay too seemed to be keeping more work hours which seemed to annoy Carol but when I asked her about it, she changed the subject.

Quinn and I keep to our schedule, me in the morning chatting with and reading to my little cousin from my library office and Quinn in the afternoons drawing at Rhea's direction from his phone wherever it is he spends his day. This Rhea relates to me, though she's still very vague about what it is exactly Quinn draws for her. I do not speak to him or see him but every afternoon when I pass the warehouse on Clemson Drive, that mural gets larger, more detailed.

Then, around the end of the second week in December, Rhea tells me that Quinn's attitude had surfaced again, this time in front of her.

"Did you and Quinn have a fight, Sayo?"

"I'd have to see or speak to him for that to happen, kiddo." I move closer to the laptop screen, worried when Rhea's mouth stretches into a purse. "Why? What happened?"

I don't buy the shrug or way my cousin exhales like she's worn out. "I don't know. He got all funny when I told him they're letting me come home for Christmas since my quarantine will be over. He just, I don't know, got really quiet and didn't talk too much." She leans in, tilting her head. "Why would that make him mad?"

"I'm sure it didn't, sweetie. Maybe he's just a little bummed he can't see you for the holidays."

"But he can. I'll ask Mama."

I couldn't tell her that Quinn wouldn't likely be welcomed. Aunt Carol was particular about Christmas Day. She and my mother had always kept to their husbands and kids the day of Christmas and reserved the day before or the day after for dinner with the rest of the family. I couldn't see Carol changing that tradition just for O'Malley. Besides, my aunt and uncle knew how precious Rhea's time was. I suspect they'd want to keep her to themselves for that day at least.

"You do that and I'll be sure to ask him why he's mad tomorrow at the fundraiser."

"Okay, Sayo. Tell him not be so fussy next time. He's never like that and it sort of hurt my feelings."

A smile is all I manage to give her. Hurt like hell biting my tongue, but Rhea didn't need to know that the sweet, funny man drawing for her is not the same person he is to everyone else in the world. She'd never seen the asshole Quinn O'Malley generally is and if I had my way, she never would.

THIRTEEN

NOTHING IN CAVANAGH was subtle. Not our rugby matches, not our St. Paddy's Day celebrations and definitely not fundraising, especially for an eight-year-old cancer patient. Autumn, with some help, has utterly out done herself.

The main courtyard on campus has become something of a winter wonderland. Cobbled sidewalks and pathways have been transformed with faux snow and the glittering brilliance of fairy lights, streamers and Christmas trees of every conceivable size and color on each corner of the two block area. There are swags of white lights streaming from four large temporary poles and draped in several rows to the crown of a large tent covering a carousel in the center of the court yard. Carnival rides and games, Santa Claus taking pictures with kids, raffles and live bands all make up the cacophony of sound and chaos as I walk through the court yard unable to keep my gaze from all the lights and activity.

"My God," I say to myself, mesmerized by the magnitude of the miracle Autumn has conjured for my little cousin. I knew she'd taken care to facilitate her charm, garnering the support of nearly every shop and business in the downtown district. I knew there had been donations of cash and necessities required to pull this off. I just had no idea of how capable Autumn actually was.

The weather has turned and I huddle against my leather jacket, tucking my scarf beneath the collar as I nod greetings and smiles at people I know in the crowd, some that know me. The air fills with the smell of ozone burning off all the white lights and the deep fried scent of funnel cakes and donuts, while kids run all over the place, cotton candy and lollipops in hand, stuffed elves and reindeers dragging behind them as they make a beeline for the carrousel in the center of the courtyard.

It is remarkable.

I only wish Rhea could see it, that the doctors had been convinced the danger of her getting sick has passed. But I understand why they are overcautious. Stage four cancer, for anyone, is no joke. It's especially not something to take for granted with an eight-year-old.

Overhead a streamer catches my attention, swaying against the breeze that ruffles my hair. Glitter from its the oversized lettering cascades around me, showering me in gold and silver. For just a second, I revert to who I once was, to who I believe Rhea would have been had her childhood been happier, freer of worry and fear. With the wind brushing around me and glitter dusting my face, I close my eyes, wanting to keep myself in the wonderland around me. For a moment I am a kid again. I have no fears, no worries that weigh me down. There is no illness, no need for fundraising because everyone I love is happy, healthy. Everyone is free. My heart fills, expands and I breathe in the scents around me, overcome by the generosity of my hometown, But in the next moment I realize that I would trade a million wonderful moments for one great one, one impossible one. That one I'd gladly hand over to Rhea.

It's her face I think of, that beautiful smile, the hope in her eyes, the laugh that I don't hear often enough. But then, as I open my eyes and am thrown back into reality, what do I see across the court yard but, Quinn's focused gaze staring directly at me.

But I quickly forget about him and his brooding looks when I spot Aunt Carol standing next to Autumn, wiping her face dry.

"What is it?" I say, running toward her, my stomach twisting like a spring. "What's wrong?"

"Nothing, dear." Carol pats my hand, smooths her fingers over my face as I reach for her. "Autumn and your friends, oh Sayo, they're just too much." And then Carol can no longer speak, too taken by her tears and the emotion behind them.

"What is going on?" I ask Autumn when she steps next to my side. "What the hell happened?"

"The fundraiser," my best friend says, shrugging like all the magic she worked had been simple and hardly a bother at all. "Carol's just very pleased."

"You raised enough for the treatment?"

"Oh, we raised plenty, but the thing is, Carol told me this morning when we first got here to set up, that her bank had called yesterday afternoon about an anonymous donation to the benefit account."

"And?" I hate when Autumn goes all cryptic. It's annoying.

"And..." she says, walking with her arm locked with mine as she guides me toward the tent that houses the carousel. Under that tent Mollie, Layla and Vaughn are huddled in front of a portable heater and Layla waves to me, tipping her large cup of something that pushes out steam in the cold air.

"Technically speaking," Autumn continues, "the fundraiser wasn't necessary—the donation was that big. At first she thought Declan and I had done it, but it wasn't us."

"Then who was it?"

Autumn shrugs. There would be no one else that I could think of that would be willing to part with that much cash. Ava and her academic friends could have raised some of the cash, but eighty thousand dollars was pretty much out of most folks' price range.

As I walk towards my friends, I get the sense that I'm missing something, something niggles at the back of my mind; something that tells me I wasn't seeing the whole picture.

But before I could figure it out, and before I reached the welcoming crowd of friends and rugby players, I see Quinn standing on the other side of the courtyard, watching me as though he wants my attention. I return his gaze, wondering which Quinn I'd get this time. Would he be combative as usual? Would the days away from Rhea, forced to visit with her from the tiny screen on his phone, somehow have made him more appreciative? Kinder?

Nah. I doubted that was possible.

Still, I walk toward him, staring at his face, thinking that maybe he'll be nice. We are in this together, regardless of whether we like each other or not. Rhea has connected us and as I walk toward him, it's her, the connection, that I keep in mind.

Then an idea comes to me—maybe the big picture hasn't made sense yet because I haven't factored Quinn into it. Maybe his fondness for Rhea is more than skin deep. Suddenly, I have questions I need him to answer, and my steps toward him become more purposeful. But before I can reach him, Sam, my ex, steps into my path.

"Sayo. Hi. Um... hi. Wait, I said that." Autumn had given Sam the nickname Thor because he was so large, and because his complexion and hair reminded her of a Viking. That hasn't changed much in two years since we stopped dating. Neither has those sharp blue eyes or the dimple in his left cheek when he smiles. For a second, I forget that we'd broken up because of my loyalty to Autumn and his to her ex, Tucker. We couldn't accept the other's friendship with either. Sam thought Autumn was spoiled and selfish. I knew Tucker was an asshole who liked to manipulate people to get what he wanted.

I was right and gave Sam the toss.

But that had been two years ago. So why is he stopping me now? Why is he so nervous, repeating himself and rubbing his neck like he can't quite figure out what to do with himself as he waits for me to speak?

"Hi." The word comes out bland, a little curt, but I don't much care. "Something I can help you with?"

"Ah, no. Not really." Another side step and Sam starts looking over my head, to the crowd, then back to me. "I just wanted... *shit.*" He exhales, stretching his neck once before he keeps still and looks right in my eyes. "I realize I was a shit to you with the whole Tucker thing. He showed his true colors just like you said." Sam waits, I guess to see if I'd act smug and pat myself on the back for being right. When I don't, he continues. "I just wanted to say that I'm sorry for how everything went down." He steps closer and I'm too shocked to move away when he reaches out to take my hand. "I'm also damn sorry to hear about Rhea. I know how close you two have always been. I just wanted to let you know that if there is anything at all I can do for you, just say the word."

Sam hadn't been the love of my life, I hadn't gone into a spiral of depression once we ended things. But I'm pretty sure everyone wants our exes to feel remorse, shame and guilt for letting us slip away. Still, I am more than surprised by Sam's sudden apology—so much so that I'm not prepared when he bends and kisses my cheek.

"Take care, Sayo," he says, squeezing my hand once before he walks away.

Twice I look over my shoulder as I resume walking toward Quinn. And twice I see Sam still staring after me. It's a weird sensation, being looked at like you are something remarkable. But once I reached Quinn his ever present frown drove all thoughts of Sam and his out-of-nowhere apology from my mind.

"O'Malley," I say. In response, I get a grunt, dismissive and a little irritating, but I wasn't going to let his sullenness keep me from getting to the bottom of my suspicions. "So, Carol told Autumn the fundraiser was a success."

"That right?" he says, pulling a cigarette from inside of his jacket. When I eye the smoke, then raise an eyebrow in an unasked question, Quinn stares back, his face blank.

"It is." I step beside him, crossing my arms so I mimic his stance and the way he watches the crowd. "Funny thing is, there was a substantial donation made before the fundraiser even started."

"Hmmm." Quinn twirls the unlit cigarette between his fingers and I decide that the drop in temperature I feel standing next to him has nothing to do with the weather.

"So, I started to think of who might have the funds to make that kind of donation."

"There are fair amount of well off folk in this…" I glare at him, warning him not to insult Cavanagh and he shrugs. "This *town*. Could have been a great number of people." Quinn pushes the smoke between his lips, eyes low lidded but staring as several people walk by us.

Quinn pulls out his lighter, flicking it twice but not lighting anything, and nods with his chin noncommittally toward someone in the crowd. I turn to look over my shoulder and see Sam standing in Quinn's line of sight. "Take this pouncy wanker with the blonde hair. That's the same one you wanted to hide from that night I first kissed you. Could have been him. He seems keen on impressing you."

"It wasn't Sam." There would be no way. Sam doesn't come from a well off family and he is a shift manager at McKinney's. No way he has that kind of cash. But that isn't why Quinn had pointed him out—he wasn't being subtle at all about hunting for information, and it was pretty obvious that my brief conversation with Sam had unnerved him a little.

"Sure he's not wanting back in?"

"None of your business." I say, mainly to annoy Quinn. His glare becomes intense, and almost angry at my cavalier attitude, but I'm not going to let him off the hook that easily. "So what you're saying is that it wasn't you?"

There is the smallest bent of bitterness in his laugh before Quinn lights his cigarette, watching as I step away from him. "Do I really look like the sort to be that fecking selfless?"

No, he didn't. We both knew it, but as Quinn walked away, chucking his cigarette after just two drags, I thought maybe he was. At least, I thought he damn well could be.

IF I EVER want to be put off relationships forever, then spending a day Christmas shopping with Autumn and Declan will do the job. They are ridiculous—holding hands, always touching, peppering kisses on each other, recalling pet names and inside jokes that are likely ridiculously perverse. Although I love them and appreciate the ride into Knoxville because I hate driving in icy weather, half an hour in, I'd determined that I never wanted a repeat experience with those two.

Ridiculous.

But at least I now had most of the presents I needed for the holidays. The following night, even the roads in Cavanagh have gone slick and wet so I'm extra careful to take the corners slow as I head toward Aunt Carol and Uncle Clay's. Despite the weather, there's no way I'm going to keep from driving to their house; Rhea has been home for two days and, from the tone of her voice when I spoke to her this morning, she is feeling elated to be out of the hospital and back in her own home.

"Shit," I mutter when a squirrel darts in front of my car, sending the tires slipping across the pavement before I right the wheel and slow down even further. Christmas is only days away and my car is loaded with gifts I can't wait to wrap, tons of comics and games Rhea has missed during her quarantine. It's her and those packages on my mind when I pull down my aunt and uncle's street, my tires still slipping a bit on the thin layer of ice.

It's a good thing I'm driving so slow, because all of sudden I realize with a shock that the idiot Irishman is standing right there in the middle of fucking street! I slam on my brakes, and jerk the steering wheel, jumping the curb and coming to stop at the sidewalk. What the hell?

Through my windshield I spot his rounded eyes and the way he holds his hands on top of his head like he's trying to keep his brain from bursting out of his skull. "Are you mad?" he yells, darting to the passenger side of my car before he flings open the door. "Have you absolutely bloody lost your bleeding mind?"

"What the hell do you mean? You were the one in the middle of the damn road at eight at night! What the hell were you thinking, you stupid idiot?"

When he shivers, brushing off the movement by stretching his shoulders, I relent, spotting the red mark that looks suspiciously like a hand print on his cheek. "Get in the car before you freeze to death."

He issues his usual grunt of displeasure and then drops into the seat next to me. "Happy, are you then?"

"No, I'm not." I turn up the heat, moving the vent toward him, ease the car back onto the pavement, but then just sit there with the motor running. "Why were you out there in the middle of the street, anyway?"

Quinn looks out the window, his elbow on the door and his fingers over his mouth. "Fraser said I wouldn't be welcomed to see the sprog during the hols."

"I can't disagree with him."

"Especially after that business with your uncle."

"What?"

"I thought… bollocks." When Quinn leans against the headrest, rubbing the bridge of his nose, I jab him in the rib, making him jerk away from me. "What it…"

"What business with my uncle?"

He exhales, scrubbing his face. "Feck, I thought Autumn would have mentioned it. It's why I'm not welcome here, I imagine. Clay… that pouncy…" he pauses when I glare at him. "He was at McKinney's getting pissed when he told Carol he had work and couldn't stay with Rhea."

"You caught him?" I turn in my seat, folding my arms over my chest.

"Eh, no. Not exactly. I may have made a passing comment to Carol about seeing him pie eyed at the pub. She went a bit mad, to be honest."

"Quinn…"

"Shite, how was I to know?" He reaches for me, cursing when I jerk out of his grip. "Sayo, be wary. That bloke's about to check right out. I know a runner when I see one."

"Why? You spot your own kind?"

Quinn darts a glare at me and when he looks away and I see the red mark on his face up close, I actually feel bad for him. "I had a gift for Rhea." He speaks so low that I can barely make out what he is saying. Then Quinn opens his coat and pulls out a small box. The paper is Tiffany blue, but I know he hasn't bought her jewelry—he knew her better than that. She is eight and definitely not a jewelry kind of kid. "Give it to her for me, will you?"

The box is no bigger than a stack of cards and I slip it into my coat pocket. "No problem," I tell him, glancing up at the mark on his cheek, and before I realize I'm doing anything at all, I hold his face in one hand, scrutinizing it. "Autumn told me that Layla clocked you good."

Apparently, Quinn had tried to kiss Layla. At least that's what Autumn mentioned on the pitch that afternoon when she and I waited for Declan to finish running drills with his squad. It was more of Quinn acting like an idiot, trying to shock people with his ridiculous flirting, with the smug attitude, than anything he might have actually felt for my friend. More deflection, no doubt, to hide who he really is. Autumn had asked how I felt about Quinn trying to kiss Layla and when I thought about it, I told her - and myself—that it didn't matter to me at all. I'd kissed Quinn. He'd kissed me, but that didn't mean a thing. Not really.

"She's a mean right hook," he admits, pulling out of my touch.

"When are you going to learn?" If I was honest, really honest with myself, I'd examine that small ache in the pit of my stomach that had developed the moment Autumn told me what Quinn had attempted.

"And what exactly is it I should be learning?" His voice was no longer soft or low. Quinn looked in fact like he'd decided to do away with the niceties of polite conversation and let just a smidgeon of the real him slip to the surface. Those tight muscles around his mouth, the quick curl of his top lip, I wasn't sure I knew what to make of any of it. But if a small break down would show me who he really was, I'd take the insulted attitude.

"Should I learn not to act as I am? Should I learn to conform to whatever shite you lot tell each other is normal just to fit right in? Bleeding hell, do you think I should learn to get along with Fraser and his woman and the whole rest of you just to keep the peace?"

"Yes. You should."

"Well I won't do it."

I cross my arms, glaring right back at him when he stops speaking, and a small hint of surprise slips into his tone. It's almost funny. "Why the bleeding hell should I? I'm meant to keep my nose clean, stay well clear of trouble. I do that for another year and my money is my own again and I can go home."

"Home to what, Quinn?" I don't give him time to respond beyond the small bob of his mouth he makes, like he can't quite believe I've called him on his bullshit. "Women and liquor and the constant party?"

"Damn right."

"And that made you happy? Drinking yourself into oblivion?"

"Yes." There a small laugh that follows his answer, one that sounds like disbelief and arrogance.

"Sleeping with whatever gold digger was the most enthusiastic?"

"Yeah…"

He's lying.

"Waking up not knowing who was in the bed with you? Being so sick from drinking and drugs and whatever else you'd prefer to die? Feeling like that day in and day out? Thinking that no one in your life really gave a shit about you? Oh, right, that's *soooo* much better than what you could have here."

So much passes over his face. Expressions that could mean a good number of things: doubt, surprise, some latent need for me to understand. But like always, Quinn doesn't let that mask slip. Not in front of me especially. He will always deflect. He will always defend even when no one is threatening him. "What do you know of it?"

"More than you think."

For several seconds, he pauses, looking for a break, maybe hoping I'm trying to pull something over on him. Then the defensiveness and the deflection starts up again. "You don't know shite about me, woman. You don't know who I am or what's been my lot in life."

"Trust fund kid on a constant party?" I wave my hand, laughing at the idea. "Yeah, O'Malley, you're right. You've had it freakin rough, haven't you?"

"It hasn't damn well been easy." He sits up straighter, palm against the dash.

"Yeah?" I say, surprised that he could forget so easily how blessed he is. How he could disregard that our problems are meaningless to others. "Go talk to Rhea about a hard lived life, you selfish prick."

He stares at me, eyes round, fury simmering beneath he glassy surface of his iris. "I never fecking said I had it the worst. I never said she didn't…" He takes a breath and I can see his frustration, his anger welling. "I've been alone. I learned how to be alone. And a few months in this god-forsaken shitehole with my arsehole half-brother and his meddlesome woman and her friends isn't going to make things… this won't just… fecking, bothersome, bollocking bastards…"

Just then, despite what I know of him, what I've been warned, I truly feel sorry for Quinn. He doesn't deserve me brow beating him, not here, not now. It's not his fault that he doesn't understand about the real hardships in life, not like most of the rest of us do. And he's absolutely right: I *don't* know what he's undergone. I *don't* know what it is to feel the double loss of losing your parents, of being stripped away from your home.

I do know, though, that he is truly faltering, that the slip of his control is great and I want to help him, to catch him before he slips too far away. So I do the only thing that feels natural. I kiss him.

Quinn is momentarily shocked, but then he moves his hands on either side of my face, taking me deeper into the kiss, stealing all control from me and my aggressive charge.

It's only seconds before the windows around us fog up as we battle each other with our lips, teeth pulling, nibbling, tongues slipping back and forth against each other and then I shudder, overcome, overwhelmed that I had kissed him again and had liked it so much.

He moves away slowly, still holding my face, still close enough that his breath lingers on my bottom lip. Then, another shudder and Quinn sits back looking me over like he isn't sure what to make of me.

"What?" I say when he shakes his head.

"You're quite a quandary." He looks out the window again, rubbing his thumb along his mouth.

"I don't know why I did that." There's no need to hide the frustration in my tone or shy away from Quinn's touch when he moves his fingers through my hair. "I should never kiss you. Not once."

"No," he says, his mouth quirking. "You shouldn't a'tall." Another glance at me and he looks to his right, watching the neighbor's youngest son walking their Dachshunds. "It's because you think I don't see anything."

"What do you mean?"

Quinn shakes his head, scratching at the scruff on his chin. "Everyone thinks I don't see what's right in front of my nose. But I do. I see the truth of things. I see it all. It's in every fighting couple on the sidewalk, every ridiculous discussion. People fight, they row and scream because they are desperate." The way Quinn speaks, the listless defeat in his tone reminds me of someone doubting the existence of God. Someone so desperate not to believe for fear they'd have to atone for their sins.

Quinn doesn't want connections. I get it. It's no wonder with the childhood he had, with the apparent contentious relationship between his parents, his father's philandering, all the money given to him but no moral compass, his father's defection, his mother's death. It's likely why he's become so close to a little girl who may not have long to live. Relationships are complications he finds distasteful, still, none of us get through life without having them. No matter how hard we try to avoid them.

His voice sounds lost. "They do all that—fight and row and scream—because they are clinging to the last bit of passion left inside them, because they feel it draining away."

"That's life, Quinn."

"No, love, that's begging. That's pleading that the end won't come. But it always does, doesn't it? Declan, Autumn, all your barmy mates and the blokes they try to wrangle down, it's all fecking fiction. None if lasts. Not any of it."

"So why bother trying? You believe it's bullshit and you still keep at it, you still try to bed as many women as you can. It's why Layla smacked you."

"Who's trying? I'm just *trying* to have a good time, and there's not much trying to it, girls fall all over me. But you make it sound like I'm not fussed who I shag. That's your hypocritical assumption. I am. When you get right to it, I'm damn well picky over who I let in my bed. You're right on one thing, though. I don't *try*, not anymore. I haven't tried in ages and ages. I've seen where trying takes you and it's not worth the bother. But I'm a bloke, aren't I? I have needs. And I'm not particularly shameful about saying what I want. Like you."

"Me?"

"Aye, you. I won't lie about it. Twice now you've kissed me." He pauses, daring to deny it with one glance and when I only met his stare, when I lifted my eyebrow in my own small challenge, Quinn smiles. "Twice it never went further than that." He moves his gaze over my lips, a slow, steady glance that tells me all I need to know about where his thoughts have drifted to. "I'm saying that I'm not shameful about liking your mouth on me. You are. You're fussed what the others will think of you should you let yourself give in to me. You needn't be. It's not as if there's a soul here I'd brag to about bedding you. I only care that I do."

"You're a pig, O'Malley."

"That may be true, love, but you're the one who keeps coming back to this pig." Quinn reaches out to grab the back of my neck to pull me close to his mouth, and dammit, I let him. "You're the one pretending you don't like me a'tall." He takes a kiss then, fierce, firm, one that makes a quick moan slip from my throat.

And then he leaves me. Again. Sitting alone in that car, my lips throbbing, my mind twisted with the realization that he'd just shown me exactly who he was. And I didn't know if I hated him for it, or wanted him more desperately than before.

FOURTEEN

THE COLD SNAP came in between the beginning of mass on Sunday and my mother's peach cobbler that afternoon. There had been no warning. My father said it was one of those freak occurrences—the quick whip of cold, the hint of a storm that no radar predicted, like the rumble of something in the distance you aren't certain is thunder of a canon.

The cold, the light flurries that caked on the sidewalk and wetted the ground should have been warning enough. Cavanagh has not seen snow in ages. The cold and winter weather we usually get comes and is over before anyone can bring their snow shovels from the garage. But this storm, with the slowness of the falling flurries and the ache of cold that settled into my joints wasn't like the storms of past years.

It was harsher.

It was colder.

Much like the day itself.

It is two a.m. before Quinn shows in the waiting room. He bypasses my parents, my brother and sisters as they wait for news on the other side of the room. I have chosen the farthest corner near the bay window that looks out onto the small man-made lake in front of the hospital. The tall column of brick next to me hides me from those worried, anxious gazes my parents and siblings have sent my way in the two hours since Rhea was rushed to the ER.

It doesn't keep Quinn away.

How he found out, I have no clue. I certainly didn't call him. I could think of a dozen people I'd rather see, a dozen more that I'd want sitting next to me, watching the slow fall of flurries out of that cold window.

"How long?" he asks, and I realize he's been staring at me, maybe watching for a slip in my expression, maybe wondering why I haven't asked why he came at all. Of course, Autumn knows I'd be here, I'd texted her around midnight, just after I got here. There's no doubt she and Declan would have told Quinn to leave us be until there was news.

I'm not surprised he ignored them.

"Too long," I tell him closing my eyes, not wanting to see that constant frown on his face. I am some weird paradox—waiting in limbo for news that will either prolong my grief or force it forward. I want numbess. I want reality.

But as I'm sitting there with my eyes closed, he blurts out "Layla is pregnant," and it shocks me, not just because of what it is, but at who is the one to break it to me. Really, with the way that Layla and Donovan have been carrying on, the news shouldn't shock me. It does, but I can't seem to react. And Quinn speaks so blatantly, like this news is nothing, like it's at all appropriate to announce in the middle of my limbo.

He glances at me, eyebrows bunching together like he can't make any sense of my stoic, bland reaction. "Her father found out, forced her hand," he continues, ignoring the way my jaw finally drops, not picking up on how I really don't want to be hearing this right now. "Only found out cuz the mad bint tried blaming it on me. Didn't want her da knowing it was that Donovan bloke that got her up the pole."

Autumn surely would have mentioned it when I spoke to her earlier, when I gave her the news of… but I'd been brief, anxious, refusing her comfort when she offered it. She would have thought it wasn't the time to tell me.

"You slept with her?" I ask him, knowing his answer didn't matter to me, at least not right now, not here. It was just something to say.

"Think so little of me?"

"You tried kissing her."

He doesn't react. He doesn't bother denying his actions, but then I don't care as Aunt Carol walks into the waiting room. Nothing matters to me then, except that devestated expression on her face. Not Quinn or Autumn or my friends being pregnant. Nothing.

We converge, all of us, and Carol leans against my mother, like a sponge absorbing strength, solidity. "The tests were… fast tracked. They've…" Her breath rattles, weakens as she watches each face around her, finally stopping on my mother's. "Clay should be here," she tells Mama, frowning as though she isn't sure if she should mourn or rage against her husband leaving. It happened yesterday, just as Rhea stopped breathing. Quinn had been right. Clay had checked out. "They've given her a month at the most."

Someone unplugs me then. It's the only way I can explain the sensation that comes over me. Worse than having my feet kicked out from underneath me. Worse that the feel of my blood slipping right out of my veins. I am not prepared for the news, even though I knew it would come someday. Hadn't we waited for it? Didn't we know a timeline would be given eventually? But knowing and accepting are two very different things.

Around me, my family weakens until they fall back, separate, leaving me staring at my aunt as my mom steps forward and allows her sister to crumble against her. I can barely stand, myself, and am grateful when Booker leads me to a chair and lets me hold on to him as I slowly sit. Quinn has vanished. He was there, standing behind me. I smelled his cologne, felt the tremble of his hands and then he was missing. This is too much reality for him. Somehow I understand that.

"She stopped breathing and the doctor said it was because…"

"The experiemental treatment though…" my mother sounds hopeful, confident but one shake of Carol's head and we all know the truth. There is no more time. There is no more hope.

Idly, I stare around the room, waste time watching the lights outside the window, then for no other reason than distraction, I call Layla, leaving a message that I'm at the hospital.

Then, I block out everything—the explanation of Rhea's condition that doesn't matter, the lost hope and defeat that colors my aunt's tone. I'm uncertain how long we sit there with the low refrain of sorrow moving around us like a fog. It's only until Booker nudges me, nods toward the door at the end of the corridor that I move, standing up and walking to meet Layla at the edge of the waiting room.

"Sayo. Sayo, oh God," she says. Her emotion does something to me. It turns off my grief, the weight of agony that threatens to choke me.

My friend's face is so pale. Layla's flushed and looks tired. I know I should ask her how she feels. I should find out the details, how she let this *thing* that happened to her happen, what her plans are, but none of that matters really. All I know is that Layla is as scared as I am of the future, and we cling to each other, our tears flowing.

"I'm so sorry," she says, sniffling when I pull her into a hug.

"Me too, sweetie."

And we don't say anything else. We watch, take comfort in each other. Layla holds my hand and holds me much the same way that my mother holds Aunt Carol. Mama holds her sister and takes into herself that well of grief because she loves Carol. Because that is what sisters do for each other.

"What am I going to do?" Carol whispers to my mother, but her voice is harsh and ragged. The anguish pours from her, the fear moves her limbs like an exposed wire flickering electricity. "My baby. My poor baby. Oh, God, my poor baby." And then Carol cannot stop crying and because she can't, no one can.

THE MURAL IS incomplete. Skies have been left blank, stars undrawn. There are no billowing clouds on the left side of the mural and only one side of Rhea's face is finished.

It's the completed side, that round cheek, the bright, brilliant dark iris that I watch, sitting in my car with the engine off. The cold barely registers because that mural fills me up, warms me. Yet in the next second I am cold again, colder than I was walking away from the hospital, refusing my brother's invite for a drink, waving off my father when he suggested I stay with them tonight.

I didn't want their comfort or company. It would keep me too warm, too alive. Now I embrace the numbness.

I only want to forget.

Someone inside can help with that.

I'd found out that Quinn had actually bought the warehouse a month before. Declan told Autumn the trustee thought it was Quinn wanting to set roots in Cavanagh so they did not reject his request to buy it. But he has done nothing to set up anything more than a place to escape from his brother and Joe. The power and water have been turned on, but the elevator doesn't work. When I walk up the steps, the scent of vanilla candles and a musty, closed hallway greets me. I should worry about it being a fire trap, but I don't. I just don't care.

He has done nothing to make the building habitable. There are still tarps covering what looks to be old textiles factory equipment. The front offices are empty with only a few overturned desks and a reception area taking up much of the first floor. There is a staircase that looks equally old, its banister a dark stain of oak that swirls and curves up with a heavy coat of dust muting its color.

The vanilla I smell grows stronger as I make it to the second floor and the scent actually overwhelms me as I walk through an open door with light bending shadows from the cracks in the glass transom.

My footfalls are quieted by the ragged carpet lining the hallway and are only disrupted when that hallway opens into one large room, something that must have been a design studio at one point, with it's drafting tables and fallen sketches littering the floor. There are metal racks along the exposed brick walls, three spaced ten feet apart, each shelf full of crates of molding fabric, leather-bound record books and spools of thread in bins. On the far wall two large boards are bent backward on their sides, the wheels from their feet clogged with dirt and dust and what looks like years of knotted thread. There is a mid-century feel to the broken furniture and the large work table at the back of the room, which is made mostly of cast iron with a solid wood top and two swiveling seats that can be pushed underneath. On top of this table Quinn has stuffed a bundle of sketch pads, loose papers, paints, brushes and several cups of colored pencils.

Quinn is sitting on the floor next to that array of organized mess, a bottle of Black Bush between his feet. My gaze moves to the bottle when he lifts it, and the stretch of his neck when he swallows deep.

"*Uisce Beatha*" he says, wiping his mouth on the back of his hand. When I don't respond, Quinn smiles, making the expression fall from his mouth as he lifts the bottle, swishing the whiskey around. "Gaelic, love." He lifts the bottle by the neck, offering it to me. "It means 'water of life.'"

"I'm not thirsty."

Quinn's gaze is careful, scrutinizing as I walk further into the room, as I keep my distance from him. But the expression on his face is more open than I've ever seen from him. It burgeons on real, as though the mask is slipping and he can't be bothered to care that it is.

"I bloody well am."

Quinn takes another drink and I don't stop him. Why would I? I came here to add to the numbness I already feel. He's started without me. Behind me the whiskey sloshes against the glass as he drinks and I move to the window, looking out on old Cavanagh stretching below me. There is nothing stirring. No cars, no people. The town sleeps while I watch and I wonder if it would be different if those folk who had given so generously on Rhea's behalf would be so still, so silent if they knew her life has a deadline now.

With nothing left to do, no way to keep myself from feeling all that threatens to weigh me down, I lean my forehead on the glass, willing away my tears, not eager to let Quinn see me break down.

"Sayo," he says, getting up to stand behind me. The liquor sloshes again as he holds that bottle between his fingers. The scent of whiskey isn't so strong, but I smell it on his breath as he moves to my side. "What are you doing here?"

He knows. Why does he ask? And when I look up at him, my forehead cold from the frigid glass, I'm sure my expression confirms it. But he is not easily swayed. Hadn't he told me that he's particular about who he lets into his bed?

"You should go to your family." There's a warning in his voice, one I know I should heed.

"I know why you do it."

"Do what?"

In front of me the outline of the cityscape shines like fairy lights and I can just make out the mountains and the starless night beyond it.

"Never show anyone the real you."

He follows when I step closer to the window ledge. Quinn puts a one hand on that ledge when I lean against the glass.

"Why do you think that is?"

"Because… reality, it's too much." One deep breath and I move my gaze up to Quinn's face. "I don't want to feel anything anymore. I… I want to forget." Quinn lifts the bottle, offering it again but I keep my gaze on his face. "That's not what I want to be drunk on."

Quinn's shown me enough over the past months for me to know when he's weighing things in his mind, so when he hesitates, like he is now, I know it means he's being cautious. It means he's waiting for caveats. But I have none. What I offer now is what he wants. We both know that.

And still he wavers, his jaw working, his eyes squinting as he looks me over. "Careful now. The numbness won't last. Sometimes, just like reality, that numbness fucks you over."

Gazing back out the window, I slip the bottle from his fingers to drink, hurrying to coat my throat with the whiskey's bite. "Not sometimes, Quinn," I tell him, knowing that he is watching me, not caring that it's careful, that it's predatory. "Every damn time."

Quinn moves behind me. I can feel the bend of his legs, the thick muscle of his thighs and the sharp points of his hips. He doesn't make a sound behind me and I don't move, not when his hot breath falls on my scalp, not when Quinn weaves his fingers through my hair, moving my head so that my neck is exposed to him. He doesn't kiss my skin, doesn't do anything but wait, as though he expects me to stop him. As though he thinks I don't really want this.

"Don't talk unless it's to tell me what you like, what you want me to do."

"Aye."

I shut my eyes when Quinn moves his free hand to my stomach, curling his fingers to move my jacket and shirt away from my skin, his breath moving down my neck. When I speak, my voice sounds breathless, winded. "Don't read anything into this. I don't love you. I never will."

The press of his fingers on my stomach sharpens and Quinn pulls me even closer, so that I can feel his dick against my back. "Fine."

"This... with Rhea... this will take all that I am. There won't be much left afterward, but you can take the remains."

A small grunt, and the brief hesitation where his hold on me eases and then Quinn presses his mouth to my neck, sucking on the skin before he moves his hand, snaking those long fingers down my stomach. "Let me take it, then."

A slip of his fingers and Quinn opens the button of my jeans and those fingers shift lower, fanning over the fabric of my thong, moving down to cup me. My nipples rub against my thin shirt and I try to keep my breath even, but Quinn tightens his grip, the friction against my clit sharpens. "We'll sort out the fecking rules later."

"Late... later."

It takes an effort I don't have to keep upright and so I lean back, Quinn holding me up with one hand cupping me as I stretch my neck against him.

"You're wet, love. But you're not ready, not yet you aren't." Then Quinn sets about making me ready, moving his mouth along my neck, taking the skin between his teeth as he moves his fingers to slip them underneath my thong to slide them inside me.

"There she is." Just the sound of his deep, low voice next to my ear makes me wetter.

He winds me tight, seeming to have too many hands, making me pant. Two fingers, three, inside me, his free hand shedding me of my coat, my scarf and shirt. My skin is flushed, feels tight and all that sensation is coiled hot in Quinn's hands, his fingers on me, in me, picking me up, turning us so that now he leans on the window ledge with his fingers still inside me.

"God… harder, Quinn, go harder."

"Show me… show me what you want." And I do, inching my fingers into myself, laying them over his, working them, guiding them so he knows what I like, how I want to be touched. "That's fecking sexy, love." He withdraws his fingers, holding my wrist still when I try to withdraw as well and Quinn kneels down in front of me. "Keep touching yourself. I want to see it all."

I barely notice him lowering my jeans, the quick tug of the fabric down my legs, my thong going along with them, electrifying my skin. Quinn bends over, mouth licking up along my knee, inside my thigh, hands cupping my ass, inhaling deep, as though he wants all his senses to engage, as though the sight, smell and feel of me is stronger than the whiskey, will make him drunker.

Then Quinn covers my clit with his mouth, sliding his hands up my torso, to fish under my bra and tweak my nipple, to twist, the sensation shooting fire across my chest as he licks up my pussy, as the low grunts of his voice vibrate against my skin.

And suddenly something possesses him, and he shoots up, stripping off his shirt with one hand, unzipping his jeans, exposing the defined ridges of his stomach, the deep, deep dents of his hips, kicking off his boots until he stands in front of me. Those eyes are so dark, hungry and he fists his cock, stroking, watching me.

"I can't wait." Another stroke, another step and Quinn is so close that the head of his dick rubs against my stomach. "If you're not sure you want this, say so now. Otherwise," one long arm shoots out and Quinn wraps his arm around my waist. His long, thick cock pulses against my stomach. "Otherwise, love, I'm going to take you right bloody now."

He doesn't wait for me to answer, but then Quinn has never struck me as the type that waits for anything. In a matter of moments, he has me on the floor, on top of our discarded clothes, pushing apart my knees, slipping on a condom before he rubs his dick against my pussy.

"This... this means nothing," I tell him shuddering, shaking when he leans over me, palm next to my head and his other hand guiding him inside me.

"This," he says, slowing himself as he slides inside of me, cracking apart my composure with the steady throb of his cock, "this means bloody everything." And then Quinn sets about showing me how much he can give, how much I can take.

He fills me completely. That thick weight on top of me, inside me, is too much and I arch, craving more of it, wanting Quinn to go deep, fill me more.

"Gods above..." he whines when I grip his shoulders, when I pull him closer. "You... you feel..."

"Stop," I say, moving us over to straddle him. "Stop talking O'Malley." He listens, following my lead, touching, pulling and my skin feels electrified, sensitive to the air around us and when Quinn sits up, when he cradles my back, bends to kiss my shoulder, to guide me faster on top of him, then my skin becomes explosive.

We move quicker now and I forget that I want to control this. I forget everything but the hum of my skin and the way Quinn takes over, how he maneuvers us, how he hovers over me, pulls my leg over his shoulder to surge in deeper.

"I... I don't love you," I remind him, moaning when Quinn thrusts hard, loving how completely he fills me up.

"I don't bloody care."

And then, Quinn lowers, taking my nipple between his teeth, pulling another quick gasp from me, sending my shoulders back as he quickens his thrusts, and I clamp around him, my orgasm hitting from nowhere, from everywhere at once.

Blinking, I rub my fingers along his back, unable to keep still, to stop touching him as he leans his forehead against mine, hips moving in a frantic, uneven rhythm as Quinn comes, eyes wide, unblinking, gaze focused on my face until he shudders, is spent and kisses me lazily, over my face, hand holding my cheek.

"Jaysus," he whispers, sliding away from me with his hand moving across my body.

Had I imagined that moment, the need for touch, the slip of his mask when Quinn watched me, when he fell apart and used me as his focus? I can't be sure, am certain it didn't matter and I turn away from him, enjoying the buzz that still lingers on my skin.

Later, when he lays next to me with his arm draped across my stomach and the heady scent of vanilla and sex perfuming the air, Quinn turns toward me, pulling me close.

"Don't get fussed," he says when I stiffen at his lips on my temple. "I'll stick to your rules."

"Do that." I glance at him, smiling, staring up at the ceiling, at the broken tiles and dusty corners. "Do that and we'll both forget."

And for a moment, we get what we want, we take what is given and forget what lies ahead.

It's only later when Quinn has dozed off from too much whiskey, too much exertion that I find more sketches. These are more detailed, less of a sketch and more like a final draft.

It takes me a moment to understand who the new villain is—he is large and his skin is decorated in drawings, tattoos that connect. It is what Declan is to Quinn—the half-family who has had to abide by his brother's rules, who has been forced from his home supposedly for his own good—Declan would be the villain.

The second picture leaves me breathless, has my fingers shaking.

Rhea the fairy emerges with wings that stretch and curl, and a smile that seems to light her from within. There is a thick tangle of hair cascading down her neck and her eyes are brilliant and round.

This is no sick child. This is not the shadow girl that lays in wait for death. This is how Quinn sees Rhea, away from the hospital, away from the tubes and needles that mar her laugh.

As my vision blurs from the tears, as I study the sketch, I realize something that Quinn likely wants no one to ever know. He speaks through this art. This one sketch he tells me everything. It tells me how much he loves Rhea.

One glance in his direction, at the long planes of his beautiful body and the lean muscles that define his wide arms, and I crawl over him, kissing each ridge, sliding my mouth over his chest, down to that flat stomach.

Because he is my balm.

Because, one more time, I need us both to forget.

FIFTEEN

RHEA WANTED US together. Both Quinn and I next to her. He paints scrolling loops of filigree around her eyes because she has asked him to. Because today she wants to be a fairy. I read from Harry Potter, *The Mirror of Erised*, because it is her favorite chapter.

"What would you see in the Mirror, Sayo?" It's a question she's asked more than once. My answer has never changed.

"You know what I'd see," I tell her leaning on the railing of her hospital bed as Rhea closes her eyes. Quinn finishes the last embellishment around her temple, adding accents of gold and silver on the colorful loops. When her eyes stay closed, Quinn and I exchange a look. There is a glassy sheen in his eyes. "Rhea?" My voice has her blinking and a small flush of color warms her cheeks. "Did you fall asleep?"

She nods, shooting a half smile at Quinn when he packs away the paint. "What would you see in the Mirror, Quinn?"

At first he doesn't acknowledge her, deflecting the question by busying himself with his brushes and small tubes of paint, but then Rhea slips her fingers over his hand and the Irishman stills, blinking before he clears his throat. "You, love, flying like a proper superhero." He leans against the railing letting Rhea hold his hand, letting her draw an invisible sketch against his palm.

"That would be nice. I'd love…" The medicine has drained her and Rhea has spent the past couple of weeks unable to stay awake for more than an hour at a time. We are inching close to that now. "I'd love to fly," she tells Quinn and just like that, she is asleep, those small fingers stopping, that invisible sketch unfinished.

"Shite," Quinn mumbles to himself and I think for a second he forgets I am there. His expression is raw, open and that glassy sheen floods so that he dips his head, keeping his face hidden on the mattress.

Rhea has lost all of her hair. She has no eyebrows, no lashes, and she has grown so pale that the deep blue of her veins around her neck and temple stand out against her fair complexion. To me, she is a fairy—delicate and ethereal, and I let the silence, the stillness in the room fill me as I watch her. I have forgotten Quinn, too, but still we share this pain. We never speak of it, even when we try to ease it with the comfort of our bodies together, but it is still there. It births a breech between us. We can touch and taste each other, set fire to our skin, to our bodies, but we cannot talk about Rhea fading and what that reality does to our souls.

As though remembering where he is and who he is with, Quinn grunts, that same indistinguishable sound that alerts the world to his frustration, and then he kisses Rhea's forehead softly and leaves the room in a rush.

"Boys are stupid," Rhea says, eyes still closed, but a growing smile twitches her mouth.

"You think so, kiddo?"

A slow blink and she moves her head, reaching for me when I set the book on the bedside table. "Mama told me that once when Chris Larson called me ugly in second grade."

"Did she try to tell you that he said that because he liked you?" The idea had me frowning. That was the biggest load of shit mothers could ever tell their daughters.

"No," Rhea says, that smile widening. "She told me he was a jerk and I should ignore him. Then she said boys are usually stupid."

"She's not wrong."

"But Quinn…"

I lean on my elbows, holding her fingers against my face. "What about Quinn?"

For the longest moment Rhea just watches me. "Mama… mama said when boys are scared, they act mad."

"You think Quinn acts mad because he's scared?"

"I think he's the scaredest boy ever. You can't forget that, Sayo. Don't… don't forget how stupid boys are. Don't." She yawns, snuggling against the pillow. "Don't let him stay scared."

INTERLUDE

RICKY TIBBIT HELD a post-match party that Autumn made me swear I'd attend. I did, with the intention of ditching everyone when the drinks started flowing. Declan holds court, telling a joke, earning laughs from Ricky and Vaughn while Autumn and Mollie try to outdo each other with shots of Patrón.

There's nothing to celebrate but the win over Cameron.

Autumn had tried to get me to drink, so did Mollie. They'd given me three shots. I only took one but they are too drunk, too happy in their normal lives to pick up on what I was keeping from them. We are young. We are meant to be impulsive, immature. We should be drinking and road-tripping and doing things that we'll regret when we're forty and be grateful for when we're on our death beds.

But I don't feel young. Not tonight. I feel tense and tired and worn from circumstance.

When Autumn pours another round for her boyfriend and the rest of the squad, I leave the kitchen, itching for some fresh air, the smallest reprieve from my friends' good intentions.

Ricky's parents own every lumber yard in a twenty mile radius. In East Tennessee, that means ample supply and plenty of business. It's the reason they have this cabin in the mountains. There are stairs that curve up to the main house some thirty feet off the ground with a porch that wraps the entire structure. It's a typical mountain retreat—three story square log cabin with views of Smoky Mountain National Park, stack stone and slate fireplaces, floor to ceiling windows to take advantage of those majestic views.

I step out onto the deck because it's the only quiet place available. Ahead lies Chilhowee Mountain and the cut of a wide brook that runs the length of the property. The stars are brightest out here, shining so clearly that I think of reaching for them, to see if they will catapult me off of this planet, free me from reality.

But that doesn't happen.

My reality is sick and dying.

My reality edges out of the sliding glass door and stands behind me.

Quinn doesn't speak and I don't ask any questions. I only follow, let him lead me down the long hallway, away from the drunk crowd in the den.

The coats and scarves littered across the camp bed get pushed to the floor with one sweep of Quinn's arm. One nod for me to lay down and I oblige, too tired, too broken to refuse. Besides, I want this. So does he.

It had been a bad morning.

Why he's here, I don't know. Why Declan would let him tag along, why Autumn wouldn't have mentioned it on the ride over...

Then I don't care why Quinn is at a party where he isn't welcome.

I only care that his mouth is on my skin, that my fingers fit perfectly in his hair, that the way he moves us, the way we move together is like a dance—a sweaty, thundering naked dance that makes my stomach tighten and my thighs clench.

His mouth on my ribs, down my stomach.

My tongue in the hollow of his neck.

His cock in my mouth.

My pussy on his face.

In this room, in any room where we come together, there is only the music of our bodies and the low, constant refrain of pleasure moving like lyric and rhyme around us.

Quinn slides over me, inside me and I crave the what his body provides. I don't see anything in the shadow of the room but the shape of his shoulders, the outline of his hair, his arms as he works over me.

I don't hear anything but our breaths labored, pleased, exhausted.

I don't hear Rhea upset, apologizing, scared.

I don't see blood in the bin when she threw up this morning.

But I do…

Quinn stops moving when a low sob leaves my mouth. That gaze is focused on my face, on my reaction and I think he might stop, that he might take away my balm, but then I stuff my hand over my mouth and pull him close.

Needing.

Wanting.

Desperate for him to take everything from me and put himself in its place.

The tears still come, still flow but Quinn does not stop, will not stop, not until we are depleted from the effort. Not until the room goes still and silent.

SIXTEEN

RHEA SLEEPS NEARLY all the time now and when she isn't sleeping, she's barely lucid. I miss my little cousin. I miss the way she smiles, how she mouths the words when I read the books she's read a thousand times. I miss the secret way she and Quinn whisper, how they plan and scheme to make a wonderful comic, how Rhea planned to send it to Dark Horse, betting that they'd love the novelty of publishing a comic that came from the mind of a cancer kid.

We have not had more than ten minutes of conversation with her in weeks. We knew this would happen. We'd been warned. But sometimes we tell ourselves that the inevitable will not happen. We convince ourselves that life will move forward even when it isn't meant to.

We live in denial because it comforts us.

For weeks, without Rhea, watching her slowly fade, I have occupied myself with Quinn O'Malley. Taking from him what he offers. Giving only my body back in return.

Tonight he paints me, laying on his back as I straddle him, his thin brush dipped in red. He draws lines and circles, characters across the planes of my stomach, circling my nipples.

"Sayo, love, slip onto my cock."

I do. My pussy throbs when he directs me, when Quinn makes demands, probably because it's the only time I'll listen and so I do what he tells me, holding his hand smudged with red paint, hovering over his beautiful, long dick as he holds it up for me, then slipping down slowly, sheathing him deep inside me, feeling him, and then moving, moving, until we are both hissing, working against each other, racing toward that final finish.

Quinn holds my waist, directing me and I arch back, loving how tight his grip is, how he lets those fingers rest on my lower back, guiding me, and at my hip, moving, leading my body at the right angle.

"So fecking perfect, love. You're so fecking tight, so wet…"

I lean over him, moving my weight to the balls of my feet, hovering over him, covering his mouth with my hand. We've discussed this. So many times. No talking unless it's a demand, no compliments or excess words, and still Quinn cannot seem to help himself.

He nibbles at my palm and I straighten, lower back on my knees as Quinn dips red paint onto his hands, finger-painting across my nipples, tweaking one between his fingers as we continue to fuck, our pace easy, practiced, comfortable. Then he shifts his hands up my neck, coming to cup my face, sticking his thumb between my teeth.

"Fecking… shite…" he groans when I suck on his thumb, licking the bottom, and then Quinn moves quickly, sitting up, taking one nipple into his mouth, sucking and sucking, pushing me down on his dick until I feel the swell of my orgasm, until his dick and mouth and grip all level up the sensation, until Quinn pulls on my hair, tugging it because he knows I like it and I come and come and come until he joins me, until he fills me.

It is nearly an hour before I realize that he has abandoned our make-shift bed of clothes for his sketch pad. The red paint flakes when I touch it idly, staring again at the ceiling, thinking of everything and nothing. My friends are leaving me, abandoning the life they've always known for one that will become their future without me in it.

Declan has been offered a spot on The Blues rugby team. It's a start to the All Blacks, a promising beginning for him. But the team is in New Zealand. No one is supposed to know, but Cavanagh is a small town and gossip is a commodity most use to get what they want. Sam wanted to see me smile last week, so he told me. He thought I'd be happy for my best friend, for Declan and the life they'd build together. He'd heard the rumors from Declan's teammates, from the casual bar conversations Coach Mullens had with Declan when they thought no one was listening.

But Sam didn't get that smile he was hoping for, and I left McKinney's feeling sad, wondering when Autumn would tell me her plans. She can't deny it, not to me. Autumn will follow him. She'll follow Declan anywhere. Just like I know Mollie will move in with Vaughn in Maryville and Layla and Donovan will have their baby, maybe stick to the plan to give it away. Maybe move onward separately. But move on.

This is what clouds my head as Quinn sketches in his book. Because it keeps my thoughts from Rhea.

A turn of my head and I watch him sketching, his arms moving, his muscles flexing as he works, as he huddles close over that tabletop, naked, breathless.

He is beautiful. I think that often enough, but never tell him. That is not why we come together. That isn't who we are. But the strong stretch of his back, the narrow dip of his waist, the lean muscles of his thighs reminds me that he is delicious. If I had to fall apart with someone, I am glad it's Quinn. That's what I think when I leave the huddle of clothes to watch him.

"You can stop staring, love." Am I staring? I hadn't realized I was. My mind is a muddle of thoughts—thoughts of what this has been, Quinn and me, his accent, his body and what we are doing. Why? What had driven us here. But that is a reality I won't allow myself to think of. In this place with this man, there is only us, together, and the urgency I feel to have him back inside me. "O'course were you to keep staring, maybe step a bit closer, I could paint you again."

I let him touch me because it feels good when nothing else does. I let him take me because only Quinn knows the sharpness of this ache. He speaks and I feel, taste, touch. "You're smooth, love. But you burn." That makes two of us. It isn't a slight he makes. Quinn doesn't want to insult me, but he knows, like I do, what this is between us. "You're like something I know I shouldn't want. A habit I can't bleeding stay clear of." He holds my face, as though he can't believe how effortlessly he can control me. How quickly I surrender my body to him. "I could paint you all day." I'd promised myself he'd never get more from me than a look. I promised myself there would be no surrender.

I am a liar.

"Look at you, beautiful. So small, so fragile. I could touch you, never stop touching you, but not how I want. Not as I'd like." A tug on my hair and his mouth on my ribs, easy comfort, numbing blindness that I welcome. "I don't want to break you, love"

The pending loss.

The unknown past.

An uncertain future.

I am not the woman I once was. I am fractured, frayed. My spirit has been split and rendered useless. It has become something that feels like can never be mended.

"Nothing left to break."

Even to my own ears I sound pathetic and I know Quinn thinks so too, I can see it in the way he looks at me, in how his voice softens. "Sayo. Love."

"Don't, O'Malley."

I can't have that. I don't want him to comfort me. I only want to be numb to all but his touch, yet I answer him. I explain when he asks, "How broken are you?"

"Enough that there is nothing left for anyone else."

This isn't who we are. We will never be a couple. We will never have more than this ache in common and so I remind him. I remind myself. "Take what you want, remember? Take what's left."

"Aye, I remember." Back again is that frown, that protective expression I've come to rely on. He tastes me, touches me and my mind is no longer muddled. There is only sensation. For a moment, there is only this. "I could taste you, always. Sometimes I think I could never stop tasting you, don't I?"

Then that look, the possessive expression that Quinn has only let me see sometimes. It shifts something inside my chest. It breaks apart my guard, the same resolve I have asked him to loosen. And I do. I let it slip, my nails running across his forehead, his scalp, and it has him pausing, giving me that amazed, astonished look as though he cannot breathe, cannot move until I explain myself.

"Sayo…"

But he won't finish. He won't ask me what this small, insignificant gesture means. I won't let him. "Make me forget for just a little while longer."

Quinn has his entire mouth over my pussy, he opens me wide, licks and teases with his tongue, with his fingers until I cannot breathe, until I flood his mouth, grip his hair, ride my orgasms so hard that I do not feel him turning me, do not realize that my cheek is against the floor, until Quinn's soft, easy grips against my body have turned aggressive, commanding. He is behind me, moving me, filling me so completely, so surely that I come again, an effortless feat that only Quinn has been able to manage.

Sweat and dried paint clings to our bodies and afterward, our hearts settle. I let him touch me softly, kiss me. It is bliss, for just that slip of time while Quinn's delicious kisses, his drugging grunts against my skin again take me completely from the building, from the town.

I am free then.

We are free together. For a while I displace the knowledge of what connected us in the first place.

Quinn's hands down my back, rubbing, touching in a sweet, absentminded gesture is soothing, has me smiling, nearly drifting asleep. Each of his touches makes my skin buzz, makes my heart hum.

When the sharp ring of my cell phone sounds, I push him away, ignoring his sleepy admonishments that I let my voice mail pick up.

My mother's name and number fill the screen and the quiet bliss Quinn worked in my body disappears the moment I hear my mother's voice.

"Mama?"

"Sweetie," she says, her voice cracking. "Rhea is going. Get to the hospital."

He knows. With just a glance in my direction Quinn's face loses the pleased, contented expression. One look at me and his mask slips back on. As it always does. Sometimes when we are together, I let myself dream a little. I let myself think of a life with Quinn when things are settled, when the future is certain. He smiles, honestly smiles at me and I think that one thread could be pulled, that it would stretch and loosen until there is nothing Quinn can keep to himself. No more masks at all to hide him. But it's just a fantasy. This is all too real.

I think maybe he'll reach for me, hold me because he knows what lies ahead for us. I even tense, hold my breath waiting for his touch, telling myself it's okay to feel anything for him, that maybe he's capable of feeling something too.

But Quinn trusts no one. Let's no one see his real face. Not even me.

That mask remains in place as he walks to the pile of clothes, dressing mechanically. I can only watch him, sitting naked on the floor with that stupid phone resting in my hand.

"Come on then," he finally says, nodding toward my jeans and shirt on the floor next to him. "Let's get this over with."

SEVENTEEN

LOVE IS A vibrant, living thing. It starts small, a faint heartbeat, the idea that becomes thought, the thought that becomes feeling. Then, comes the breath of beginning, the form and mass of that small creature beginning to grow. Love is a creature that only grows when it is nurtured, when it is given limitless cultivation. When it is permitted the infinite possibility of hope.

It exists inside us all. We hold it, cradle it, until it is time to fly. That small love can soar, fly into the ether, become part of the great cosmic well that connects us all. Or it can fester, rot and not move an inch from that first idea to the last hope.

What love—thriving, living love—can never do, is die. That is the truth of this moment. That is the reality that I will cling to.

Rhea is surrounded by family. Cousins, parents, her sister, all of us watching her take in every farewell. She gives, receives kisses that linger, holds tight as she can to necks as she is hugged. It must be chaos for her. It must make her dizzy, all that filter of comfort, of love and fleetingly, I wonder what this would be like, this dying moment, had she never been taken from that orphanage. I know my life, all of our lives would have been duller, the color of our world paler without her in it.

Booker, Adriana, Alessandra, join Claire in their goodbyes, followed by the sweet tears my mother and father leave on Rhea's pillow. Then there is only my aunt and uncle waiting for Quinn to say whatever it is he needs. He is silent, brief, one hand against her face, his gentle kiss on her forehead and he whispers to her, something that makes her smile, something that gives her peace.

And then, just like that, he walks away. No backward glance. No look at me to see if I want him at my side.

"Sayo?" Rhea asks and I go to her, nestle at her side so that she rests against my chest, like she did when she was two. Like she did when she was still a baby, still willing to let me hold her. "I hear your heartbeat," she says, rubbing her ear against my chest.

A glance at the monitor, that slow beep that only grows dimmer and I squeeze her. "I hear yours."

"Can I ask you something?" Her voice has grown thin as though the rasp in her tone has weakened her right along with the cancer and the treatment.

"Sure," I say, more confident than I feel. Rhea's breathing quickens, but she still manages to lean back, looking up at me as though she'll find the truth. As though I have the answers she needs. "Mama cried when I asked her," she whispers, like she doesn't want Carol to hear her. "She still thinks I'm a baby, but you Sayo... Sayo, you don't lie to me."

"Never." We turn toward each other, face to face, hands held together and I block out the sounds around me, my uncle's low crying, Carol's litany of a soft prayer and the constant beep of the monitor. I only see this beautiful face, look at every curve, every dip, every shadow. I want them inside my mind, living there so Rhea will never die. "What... what do you want to know?"

Her eyes are the color of chocolate, the exactly hue of the most decadent dark chocolate, but she is sweeter. "All this," Rhea tugs at the IV connected to her arm, points to the oxygen tube resting in her nostrils. "I won't need any of this soon."

"No, baby. No, you won't."

It was a slip she doesn't call me on. She isn't a baby, not really and I haven't called her that in years, but this isn't a moment for saving face. She's my baby, our baby. Always will be.

"Well, what I want to know is… is… where? Where do I go, Sayo? When I leave, when it's… time… where do I go?"

I want to tell her the truth. I want to tell her I'm not sure. I can't be sure. I want to tell her she would be safe. She would be warm. She would be finished, but I just don't know.

"Sayo?" Rhea touches my face, clearing the tears from my cheek. "Where do I go?"

I try like hell to remember precisely how her small hand feels against my cheek and the smell of strawberry lotion on her fingers. Her skin shines luminous against the fluorescent light. "Oh, Kiddo," I say, unable to keep my voice from shaking or tears from building in my eyes. Rhea doesn't seem to notice either. "Everywhere. You go everywhere."

One smile. The brief twitch of her mouth moving up and the shudder of her breath as it weakens.

I kiss her then, put everything I cannot say into that soft touch. It will be the last. My sweet girl. My little kiddo.

The monitor dips, the peeps slowing and I leave the bed so that Carol can hold her daughter, cradle her tight. My aunt's sobs are quiet, but still sound to me like thunder across a still sky. They breech the quiet of the moment and pierce my chest.

"Everywhere, baby," I say, words muffled by the thickness clogging my throat. And then, the beep flat lines and there is no noise. There is nothing in that room at all except for goodbye.

INTERLUDE

QUINN LAYS ON the cluttered wood floor of the warehouse. Around him are sketches—drawings of Rhea that are a cruel reminder. Images that I will not see, that force my eyes close as I lean over him.

I told him not to move.

I want to take this time. I want to take and vanish and diminish everything.

He lets me.

We are naked and wet, from our sweat, from our tears and I do not feel pleasure in this.

There is only the sound of our bodies, the low grunts, the heady call of need and desire.

There is no love here because it has been stolen from us.

She took it with her.

And so I sob, taking him inside me, straddled across him, not asking permission.

I take.

He lets me.

EIGHTEEN

THERE IS A mirror hanging above the table that holds the guest sign-in book. It's the first time I've bothered to look at myself in two days. My hair is completely black now. Not even the smallest hint of pink can be found among all that straight, thick hair. Autumn offered to braid it for me this morning. My friends had barged into my apartment because I hadn't bothered to charge my cell. Because when your world has fallen apart around you, it is your friends, your family, that keep you from slipping between the broken crevices. Autumn is that for me, she and Mollie and Layla.

"Leave it," I'd told her, too exhausted to care that I look a mess. Layla, wobbling toward me, dared me with a glare to reject the simple black dress and heels she'd held in front of me.

"Put this on. No arguments."

Pregnancy has made her assertive.

"You ready?" Autumn asks, holding my hand to pull me away from the mirror, to allow the long line of guests to write their names in a book Aunt Carol will likely never read. I had not wanted to be with the family when they viewed the body. I hadn't been ready, but now with Autumn, Mollie and Layla standing sentry, my legs don't wobble quite as much and the fierce tremble in my fingers isn't quite as bad.

Still, as my friends lead the way into the nearly empty room with low lights and muted swags, that nervous feeling takes hold and something burns and coils in the pit of my stomach. Declan, Donovan, Vaughn and Joe stand when we walk in and I barely notice those somber expressions, the worry and concern that pulls their mouths down.

"You can do this," Autumn whispers and for a second I believe her. For a second more I want to believe her.

"Okay." Only Autumn hears me and as we step closer, I tighten my hold on her fingers. "Okay," I say again, coming closer to Rhea.

Nothing could have made me ready for the sight of her in that coffin.

Autumn catches me when my knees give and Layla and Mollie stand at my back and side as I stare down at the little girl I still love.

Carol had done as Rhea wished. She is finally the fairy she'd dreamt of being. Vivid colors cascade around the room, the coffin. The entire space has been transformed into a Technicolor vision—blues and greens, purples, all so brilliant they reminded me of a sunrise in spring, the backdrop of a vibrant field of lavender. And in the center, surrounded by all that color, by of flowers and cards, sprays that carry images of fairies and superheroes and versions of comic book characters, rests Rhea in a silver coffin.

She is dressed in a beautiful fairy costume of soft blue with a green tutu skirt, a flowing cascade of matching ribbons that fall around her from waist and to hem. On her face is the mirror image of the make-up Quinn had given her just days ago—swirls and loops of white, blue and green, accented in silver and gold, arching around her pink dusted eyelids and gemstones near the corner of her eyes with a flare of colored glitter sparkling around her eyebrows and across her forehead.

Rhea is an ethereal character out of one of her more creative comics—both woodland nymph and powerful sorceress. She would have found herself beautiful, just as I always had.

"You're colored up, kiddo." She always wanted to be. She wanted wings that stretched and grew. She wanted lights and colors and the brilliance of magic to pump from her veins. She had that now. She had it all.

My friends hold me up as I cry. The tears come uninhibited. They should. We are in the midst of our grief, surrounded by the warmth of love. Now is the time for tears. I watch Rhea through the blur of moisture with my best friends tending to me, making certain that I feel every emotion this day requires. Today, I will not allow myself to be numb. I will not allow myself to forget.

After a time, with the strength I borrow from my friends holding me, I notice the book next to Rhea in the coffin. It lays by her hand, between her body and the padded fabric; a thin, colorful book that I know. I take it, flip through the pages as *Omnigirl* and *Sovereign Smash* battle *Death Doctor C* and his engine of darkness. Rhea flies, fights alongside Quinn, a powerful team ridding the world of those who would see the cloud of illness come to children—those who would fill small veins and bodies with medicine that harms, not heals. This was their work. This was their legacy. Partners in crime working to make this small dream Rhea dreamt a reality.

"It was here when they opened the coffin," Carol says, standing behind me with her arms around my waist. "I don't know how he got it in there."

"He has ways," I offer, rubbing my thumb across the glossy pages. "He has so many ways." I slip the sketch book back into the coffin, making sure it is at Rhea's side, so she can have it with her, always.

Carol's attention is divided by her friends and those that have come to pay their respects. Cavanagh is a small town with a generous heart and it seems that all of those generous hearts have come to say goodbye to a sweet girl they didn't know. The crowd increases and I reluctantly leave Rhea's side, to get lost in the shuffle of well-wishers, in the mass and ceremony meant to send her onward.

Before I know it, I'm standing at the graveside. Around me, the crowd is silent, heads bowed as the priest offers final prayers, but I do not follow the others. My gaze slips around the solemn faces, searching, greedy for a glimpse of his features. But Quinn isn't here. I stand alone as we leave Rhea behind.

DARCY AND GEORGIE are at my feet as though they know there has been a great loss. I don't move them when I lean back on the swing and the huge bullmastiff lifts his head, moving on his belly to rest his chin on my bare feet when Autumn comes outside to join me.

It is nearly ten at night. Inside my parents' home my family recalls the short lived, precious life we celebrated today. Mom has brought out pictures. Carol has allowed this, letting her big sister tend to her, reminding her that she is not the only one feeling this loss, even though hers is the keenest. I suspect that is why Autumn has followed me out here as well.

Well. That and the bottle of Jameson's she hands off to me.

"It's yours. Your dad thought maybe you'd like one of your own."

"Thanks," I say, scooting over when Autumn sits next to me. Darcy doesn't move from my feet and my best friend picks up Georgie, scratching on the bridge of her nose until the dog collapses on her lap.

"Declan says Quinn has gone AWOL." My face nearly buzzes from the stare Autumn gives me. The way she watches, how closely she monitors my reaction tells me all I need to know about why she mentioned Quinn. She knows. And she's known me long enough to understand when things are being bottled up tight.

The whiskey is smooth, holds a bite when I swallow and as I pass the bottle to Autumn, I half expect her to refuse the drink. But then I glance at her, nodding once and she takes two gulps, one right after another.

"How long?" she asks, resting the bottle on her knee.

She should run a booth at a fucking carnival, I swear. Ten bucks to slip past the well layered walls I constructed to keep the world out of my head. Autumn navigates them with little effort. "A few weeks, but even before then there was… something."

My best friend leans on her side, watching and the guilt I feel for not relying on her is heavy on my chest. "You didn't tell me." Autumn brushes my hair off my shoulder, looking past the fence line as we swing.

"Did you really want to know?" Darcy grumbles when I turn. His whines are low when I pull my feet from under him and onto the swing in front of me. "Me? And Quinn? I got the feeling he was the last person you thought I should end up with."

Autumn doesn't abandon her long stare beyond the fence, remains calm, cool. "I make no judgments, friend." She lets Georgie jump down, finally handing the bottle back to me. "Am I to take it that he showed you a side no one gets to see?"

"Oh I imagine a lot of people, a lot of women, have seen that side."

"And?"

I take a drink, sinking further against the back of the swing. "We both wanted to forget ourselves. It hurt too much... Rhea..."

Autumn pulls on my wrist to hold my hand. "And he helped you forget?"

"For a little while."

"And now?"

The day, the raw emotion that keeps me open and exposed only intensifies when Autumn's hold on my fingers tightens, as she watches me as though expecting me to fall apart completely. She won't let me, pulls me toward her to rest my head on her shoulder so my tears are hidden.

"Don't tell Declan," I say when enough emotion has clogged my sinuses. "He wouldn't understand."

"You're right. He'd only see it as Quinn taking advantage." Autumn's nails against my scalp are soothing, lulling. "Seems hard not to given what he's shown us of who he is."

"He's scared," I say, wiping my face dry. "Even Rhea knew that, but I think he loved her. I know she loved him and he made her happy. At least for a little while."

"Did he make you happy, friend?"

I can't look at her directly. Autumn has a way of seeing the things I keep hidden from the world. With one glance she could pull all of my secrets to the surface. The silence deepens between us, and like the friend she is, she lets it. Moves on.

"There's something I need to tell you," she says, voice dropping.

"Does this have anything to do with New Zealand?"

She sits up, taking the bottle from me when I try to take a sip. "How did you know about that?"

"Sweetie, seriously? Where are we?" When she refuses to give me the bottle, I sit back, waving off her surprise. "People talk at McKinney's, especially when they think no one is listening, and you know Sam hears everything." When Autumn looks as though she might lose her temper, I shrug, stopping her with a shake of my head. "Tell me what this means."

"Declan and I... well, probably Dad as well... well, we..." She picks up the bottle, polishing off a quarter before she finishes. "We're going with him."

"I figured as much."

"I wasn't going to tell you."

"Why not?" I grab her hand, squeezing it. "You and Declan, friend, from day one I knew you'd follow him anywhere, and players like him don't stay stuck in small towns. Not this small town, anyway."

"You don't have to stay either. You can come with us."

"That's your dream, sweetie. He's your tomorrow." I nestle next to her, letting my best friend hold me. "I need to find my own."

NINETEEN

MIDNIGHT IN CAVANAGH is louder than usual. Sunday night, the new year bringing in the cold, taking away the last vestiges of the rugby season and the holidays. It has been two days since Rhea's funeral. Four since I've heard anything of Quinn.

"He stays in his room all day. Da says he's only seen him once and that was when Quinn got sick and passed out near the toilet." Autumn felt it necessary to let me know that he hadn't completely abandoned life. He was drinking at least.

Quinn is the least of my worries. With Rhea gone, I am expected to get back to the business of living my life. Ava came to the services, told me to take as much time as I needed before I return to the library. But there is no real sense staying away. It's what everyone expects of me. It's what happens. Life moves forward. I'm supposed to as well.

But I can't shake the feeling that moving forward, picking up where I left things when Rhea entered the hospital is some sort of betrayal to her. Am I supposed to live a normal life when my little cousin never could?

Outside, I hear the ending revelry of the weekend. Soon McKinney's will close down. The bars and clubs, like Fubar, will ask for last call and cut the lights. Quinn might be there, maybe alone, likely not, out in the freezing cold, perhaps in the dim light of a closing pub. I've passed his warehouse twice in two days. The mural has been surrendered in a half-finished state and the lights on the second floor have been dark.

When a siren echoes through my apartment, followed by another, I leave my bed, pulling my terrycloth robe on for a quick peek outside my balcony. The brick tile underfoot is frigid, so cold that my toes feel burnt and, after a glance at the wreck some two blocks from my apartment that has caused all the commotion, I turn to hurry back inside, stopping short when I spot the figure huddled against the railing on the other side of my balcony. It is Quinn.

"God!" I shout, ignoring my freezing feet to pull him up by his collar. "What are you doing, you idiot?" He smells of whiskey, reeks so bad that I have pull my nose away from his mouth when he starts laughing. "Oh, you are nasty, O'Malley."

"You like me nasty, don't you love?"

"Not tonight I don't." It's a struggle, pushing him inside my apartment, holding his large frame to keep him upright but I manage, slumping him onto my sofa with a whoosh. "How much have you been drinking?"

"All of it. The whole buggering lot." From the inside of his half buttoned coat, Quinn lifts out a nearly empty bottle, head swimming as he tries to make his mouth center on the opening.

"No. I don't think so." He is too drunk to fight me when I reach for the bottle, but not so drunk that he misses grabbing me by the waist to pull me onto the sofa. "Will you stop?"

"Fecking shite, Sayo, I've missed you, haven't I? C'mere. Give us your mouth…"

"No, Quinn. I don't think so…" He struggles with me, gripping as I lean away, groping along my chest, at my waist but he is too drunk to do much more than groan when I push him back. "Sleep it off, why don't you? Unless you want me to call Declan?"

"Fraser can piss off," he starts, sitting up, acting as though the only thing he wants is to make for my door. When he has to hang on to the wall for traction, I don't bother trying to help him. "You can piss off too." Quinn worries the deadbolt, cursing, swaying as he fights against the lock, then jerking out of my reach when I try bringing him back to the sofa. "Don't bloody well want to be here, do I? Leave off." He is a fussy drunk but as I grab his arm, pull him away from the door, Quinn leans into me, resting his forehead on my shoulder. "What… what have you done to me… what have you made me?"

"Quinn?"

He jerks up, ignoring how my voice has softened, how my touches aren't demanding. "Fuck you, Sayo." He pulls me forward, fingers digging into my arms. "Fuck me, yeah?" And when his open mouth darts forward, seeming with the intent on landing against my lips, I react defensively, knocking him once in the stomach, not meaning to smack him right on the cheek when he begins to fall.

"Shit!" He is swaying worse than before and I think fleetingly of maybe calling Declan, have him fetch his brother, but that would likely lead to more bother for my best friend's fella than is really worth the effort. "Ah hell, O'Malley," I tell him scooting him back onto the sofa as he grumbles, fading sleepily as I cover him with a throw, making sure he's upright and won't be able to fall over.

He is snoring in less than a minute and I move around him, taking off his boots, grabbing a bin from the half bath to set right next to his head. I take a moment to brush the hair from his eyes, run my nails over his scalp until his breathing levels out and those snores are constant. Despite the mess he is now, Quinn is still beautiful. He is lost. He is suffering and, I suspect, he believes I am too. That grief brought us together. Maybe tonight he thought it would have us back again.

There is a small tremor moving his left eyebrow, the smallest twitch that seems to disturb him as he sleeps. Otherwise, that face is flawless; when he sleeps, there is no tension around his mouth, no lines that make him look frightening or severe. Those soft features, the plump mouth are temptations I cannot resist and I lean forward, holding his face to kiss him once, ignoring the strong scent of whiskey.

"God, Quinn," I whisper, knowing he will never remember this, "I wish I could stop wanting you." I sit up, only mildly surprised when he blinks up at me, then highly disappointed when his eyes close and that drunk asshole's snores fill the room.

I HALF EXPECT the living room to be empty when I wake the next morning. It is, except for Quinn's boots next to the sofa and his coat laying across the coffee table. The noise from the half bath tells me that he's awake or at least trying to get himself to that point and so I take my time, showering, braiding my hair, washing my teeth before I make it to the kitchen. Quinn is sitting on the sofa, head down, elbows on his knees and doesn't look up when I reach for the coffee pot.

He only acknowledges me when I place a mug of coffee in front of him on the table. I get a nod of appreciation for my troubles and nothing more until half of the mug is empty. Then, Quinn abandons the coffee and sits back on the sofa, rubbing his face before he glances at me.

"I'm sorry."

That brings my eyebrows up, surprise keeping me speechless. "Wow."

Quinn turns, moves his head to stare up at me. "When I'm sorry, I say so."

"Then will you apologize to Carol?"

"For what?" He sits up straight, shoulders back.

"You missed the funeral."

"No," he says, fingers together as he stares down at the floor. "I did not. I just missed you and your lot."

"My lot. You mean Rhea's friends? Her family? Or do you just mean me, Quinn?"

This time when he looks at me, he doesn't frown. His mouth relaxes but he presses his lips together as though he needs a minute to collect his thoughts. Quinn runs his fingers through his hair, releasing a sigh. "I... don't do well with..." he waves a hand between us, "this sort of thing, do I?"

"How the hell would I know?"

Just then Quinn gives up the pretense of being grateful to me for bringing him out of the cold last night. "You needn't be a bitch."

"Get out." I don't bother to wait for a reaction. Instead I am at the door and it is open before Quinn even leaves the sofa. Even insulted, Quinn is cool, collected. His face looks pale and there are dark circles under his eyes and a large bruise forming under one where I popped him the night before. None of this makes me feel sorry for him. None of this makes me eager to watch him walk out of my apartment, either.

And when he reaches the door, I tell myself not to be upset that he's leaving. I tell myself that it is best that we keep our distance. I recall what an insufferable asshole Quinn can be, so I'm actually surprised when the door slams shut and Quinn is still in front of me.

"I'm too bleeding hung over for a fight so let's not have one, yeah?"

"And I'm too damn tired to deal with you. Go home, sleep off your hang over and forget you ever touched me." I reach for the door again and Quinn reacts, forcing me back, caging me between his long arms at the door.

"No, I don't think I can forget that easily, love. Nor do I want to."

"Quinn…"

"Sayo… shut up."

Rationally, I know I should reject him, force him out of my apartment, clear him out of my life. But Quinn is insistent to the point of being irresistible. Not many can turn him away. Especially not when he uses his mouth, his hands to convince and cajole.

"I've missed you," he admits, lips working along my neck, fingers in my hair guiding my head. "This skin, this body, I bloody crave it now." A squeeze against my ass and Quinn lifts me up, unzips my jeans.

I don't stop him. I should. I know I should, but I don't do anything more than follow his lead, forgetting that he abandoned me when Rhea died. Forgetting how I ached alone, wanting the forgetting he offered. It is too potent now, with Quinn touching me, pushing aside my jeans, my thong, with his fingers gripping, squeezing, insisting.

"What have you done to me?" He drops to his knees, working his tongue against my hipbone, down the top of my thigh. Quinn looks up, eyes, expression open, eager as he discards my clothes, as he touches, teases, keeping that heavy gaze of my face. I can't think, can't focus when he touches me like this, with his fingers and hands grazing, gripping.

"This is all I think about. This body." He spreads me apart with his thumb, rubbing the tip of one finger against my clit. "This beautiful, warm pussy." One lick against my lips and Quinn fingers me, slipping in two while he stands, grabbing my wrists to hold them together with his free hand.

"Quin... Quinn..." My hands shake against his hold.

"The way you taste, love, the way you smell, how tight you are, it's all I bloody well think about." When I start to pant, when my moans grow louder, more urgent, Quinn releases my wrists to pull my hips against his. "Do you think about me? Want me, Sayo? You want this?" And Quinn is bare, thick, that perfect cock pressing against me. "Tell me. Say it."

I'd rather scratch his eyes out, but Quinn insists—with his mouth on my neck, his fingers inside me, his dick teasing. I am helpless, pathetic. "Yes," I say, pulling him closer. "Yes, please. Now, Quinn."

And there is the forgetfulness I've needed. We are sensation again, mindless. Quinn touches me deep, holds my chin still to watch my expression as he takes me, pushing further, deeper and I take all he gives. Not thinking about saying no. Not admitting to myself that this is a balm that will not last. He is an easy fix that is not easy to deny. So I don't.

"This... this is good," I say, not looking at him, not thinking of Quinn at all. Not thinking of anything, just feeling. "This is... fine.

It's fine." And before I understand what I'm doing, before I register that my face is wet, that Quinn has released my chin, that the jarring thrusts he'd worked over me have eased, slowed, I am near to orgasm.

"It's… it's…"

"Sayo, love." And Quinn does something I never expect. He stops moving just to hold my face, just to kiss me slow, like I mean more than a balm. Like he means every touch and wants more.

"Quinn… what… please stop."

"You want me to stop?"

I glance at him, conflicted, confused, not quite sure why him being sweet, being tender unnerves me like it does. "I want… I don't want…"

"So, you want me to rub one out rather than finishing?" His voice is cold, sarcastic.

The crassness of his remark unnerves me. Can he really not understand? "Quinn…"

"No worries, pet. I can manage." He pulls out of me and I feel the temperature in the room drop. That mask is back in place and I am too shocked, too amazed at his response, to find the strength to even care. If that's the way he wants to be, then who am I to stop him?

He waits, lingers at the door and I wonder what he'll say, if I can manage to bring back the tenderness he almost let me see, but then Quinn smirks, shrugging like I am nothing and he is and through the door and out of my apartment before I can stop him. Before I realize how desperately I want to stop him.

TWENTY

LAYLA IS HAPPIER than I've ever seen her. Seeing her new baby, seeing the family Layla and Donovan have made together, takes away the some of the guilt I feel for all the time I missed with them as they went through their ups and downs, got married, bought a small house near Joe's and settled in to wait out the arrival of their daughter.

I'd spent that time grieving and numbing that grief with Quinn.

But now, here with my friends again, that pain is tempered some, the ache of missing so much is eased by the sight of that beautiful baby and the joy that lights Layla from deep inside. Autumn and I leave the hospital arm and arm, impossible-to-remove smiles lingering on our faces.

"Evelyn Meara Donley," I say, glancing at Autumn to see her chin tremble. "She's beautiful," I offer, my smile growing even bigger as Autumn nods.

Layla had named her daughter after Autumn's mother and her own. Two women who had given their daughters strength, who had taught them to fight, to thrive. It was a fitting honor to give to that beautiful baby. "Have you ever seen her like that?"

"Never, and especially not with Donovan."

We stand inside the hospital lobby, looking at the black clouds up ahead and the deluge that is covering the walk way and running down the steps. Still, neither one of us stop smiling and it's only when Declan opens the door and we both automatically step back to avoid the spatter that those ridiculous smiles dim.

"McShane. Wait here. I'll get the car." Declan offers us a smile, and Quinn, who stands behind us, one glare of warning. Quinn had not spoken to anyone while we visited Layla and the baby, but I caught our friends eyeing him and that bruise on his eye.

Declan runs out into the rain as Autumn and I step beneath the awning, laughing when Vaughn races out of the door and Mollie huddles behind us.

"It's absolutely pissing," she says, laughing when Vaughn steps in the center of the courtyard, arms stretched, head back, catching rain on his tongue.

"Is he crazy?" Autumn asks, laughing at the heat that colors Mollie's face.

"Yeah," she says, moving away from us. "He damn well is." And then she runs out into the shower, hopping on Vaughn's back, laughing as he spins them both around and around.

"Absolutely barking," Autumn says, but I notice that smile on her face hasn't lessened. It won't, not any time soon, not when our friends are happy, when the joy they feel is tangible, infectious.

To our left, Quinn stands on steps, gaze on me, watching, with an expression I cannot read. Autumn notices as well. "He's not nearly as smug as he was in the hospital room." Autumn glances over her shoulder at him, then turns back to me when he ignores her. "Are you responsible for the black eye?" She raises an eyebrow with the perfect rendition of a mother's glare. One day there will be ginger kids with Declan's attitude and Autumn's temper. I almost feel sorry for them being exposed to that glare for the whole of their lives.

Unable to bear the weight of even that facetious glare, I turn to watch the rain again, ignoring her for a moment, then I mumble weakly, "It looks worse than it actually is." Autumn's tisking tongue is ridiculous and I shake my head and chuckle despite myself, silencing her lecture before it comes. "It was an accident."

"Uh huh and that 'put me out of my misery' expression on his face?" Again she glances at him and I lean forward to watch him too before Autumn moves to stand in front of me. "That an accident too?"

"Friend…"

"Sayo," she says, pulling me closer conspiratorially, "You've got ten minutes before Declan gets back with the car. I'm going to run to the bathroom. Be wise with your time."

"Autumn…" but she is gone and I am left staring at Quinn, feeling stupid and silly. "What?" I throw it out as a challenge.

"I'm sorry." Quinn steps forward, close. My back it to the wall, I have nowhere else to go.

"Don't be."

He leans forward, resting one hand on the wall by my head. "You were crying. You were upset and I kept at you. I turned things around."

I shoot for indifference, shrugging, moving a step to the right when he reaches for the end of my braid. "You were being you."

His expression changes then, twists into something unfamiliar, something tender. Truly searching rather than bating. Something that makes my stomach twist. And then Quinn reaches out, stilling me with a soft touch of his hand against my cheek. "I'm sorry. I'm sorry I wasn't with you at the funeral. I'm sorry I acted like you weren't upset. I'm sorry I can't be more…"

"You might want to keep at those buggering apologies." Declan's loud, startling voice breaks us apart and what I was having with Quinn was gone, replaced by his typical brooding attitude. Declan, having no idea what he had interrupted, kept up the tirade at his half-brother. "What did I say to you the first fecking day you were here?'

"How the bloody hell should I know?" Quinn steps up to Declan, shoulders back, matching his threatening stance. "You kept yammering about. Like I could keep track."

"You wanker." Declan grips Quinn's collar but the younger man isn't put off by Declan's strength or size. "I told you to keep clear of her, of all of them. And what do you do? Especially Sayo… especially when…"

"Declan, stop, please," I say, but am completely ignored as Declan slams his brother against the glass behind us.

"You will fecking learn, little brother. You cannot treat folk the way you have your entire life."

"Enough!" Quinn shouts, managing to push Declan back. They both seem surprised by the movement. "You don't fecking know me. You don't know anything about me but what you were told. In all these months, have you once tried using a civil tongue with me? Have you once thought that maybe I am the way I fecking well am for a reason?"

Declan shakes his head, laughing. "There's no reason to be a prick."

"Says the man whose mum destroyed my family!"

Declan charges, grabbing Quinn again, knocking his head against the glass. "Don't you dare say anything against my mum."

Quinn volleys back, using his feet and thighs to keep Declan from slamming him. "It's the fecking truth! She lied. So did he. For ages and ages. I had a brother my whole life and he never once… it bloody broke my mum. It destroyed her."

"You think she was the only one?"

"Declan, stop." I yell, pushing between them with my hands on Declan's chest just as Autumn runs into the lobby. "The both of you. Maybe you both got screwed over. But time is short. God knows we've all learned that lesson." I look between them, feeling some relief when the hard set on their faces isn't quite as severe. Autumn pulls Declan back, rubbing his chest to calm him. "Quinn didn't do a thing to me that I didn't ask him for. He tried staying away."

"Sayo," Declan says, eyebrows shooting up as though he's convinced he heard me wrong.

"I went to him, to get away from the hurt I was feeling." I pause, glancing behind me at Quinn. "We used each other, that's all it was." I take a breath, knowing I was parroting the same thing he'd said that morning in my apartment. "That's all it will ever be. But that doesn't make him a bad person. In fact, how could he be? Rhea loved him." Autumn releases Declan and I step to the side so that the brothers are forced to face each other. "She loved him for a reason, Declan. Maybe you can find out why. Maybe… maybe you both can start over, put the past behind you? It's the least you can do because like it or not, you're brothers. You're blood."

I turn on my heel and walk out of the hospital, leaving the two brothers to their glowering and ebbing anger. I want nothing more than some liquid numbness, but the idea of going home where my thoughts will no doubt linger on the emptiness, doesn't sound appealing. Before I realize it, I'm already four blocks away from the hospital and heading for McKinney's. My umbrella is flooded and swaying in the wind, and I dart forward when I see the neon in the pub's window. Cars zip by me, flinging dirty water up from the puddles and I quicken my pace, jogging, making it to the pub just as the door slams open.

"You okay?" I hear, as I shake off my umbrella as I back into to pub, where I shed my sopping wet jacket.

"Yeah, I'm good," I say, gratefully taking the bundle of paper towels offered to me. It's only then that I look up to see who it is that has come to my rescue. "Sam."

"Hey." He smiles, reaching over the bar to retrieve a proper towel, smelling fresh from the dryer. It's still warm. "Here, this will work better than those paper towels." I let him dry me off, staring wide-eyed at his face, the strong cut of his angular jaw and those giant crystal eyes that I'd spent the better part of our short-lived relationship staring into. I'd never quite managed to figure out if they were gray or blue.

When Sam tilts his head, his smile lowering with concern, I blink, internally berating myself for gawking, and take the towel from him. "Thanks for the rescue." Patting my face dry keeps me from seeing his expression, from letting myself linger too long on his smile.

"It's not a problem. Here," Sam sits me down on a stool, moving my legs so I face the bar. "How about some hot tea or cocoa? I remember you liked both with Baileys."

So I let my ex-boyfriend ply me with Baileys-laced hot tea. I spent the next hour letting him flirt with me, joke with me, recalling all the silly things we'd done together, avoiding topics that led to our break up. By the time the door chimes with another customer, I am warm and a comfortable buzz warms my insides. Quinn O'Malley hasn't entered my thoughts once, something that increases that soft buzz.

"Here, have another, beautiful," Sam says, placing a cup of piping hot tea in front of me. As he walks away he touches my hand, moving his thumb across my knuckles—a gesture I realize he gives me to show affection, despite the mild buzz I have. He has a gentle smile and the touch is brief, likely not meant to be anything more than a kindness, but I didn't miss it what he meant by it. Neither, it seems did the two men at the end of the bar.

Declan and Quinn.

Sam sets two pints in front of them, earning a nod from Declan who tips back his glass, sending a quick toast and a smile my way. Quinn, however, doesn't touch his drink and when he stands, tossing a few bills onto the bar, he deflects Declan's hand on his shoulder.

"Where are you going?" I hear Declan ask but what Quinn whispers to him, is too low for me to make out. Quinn is out of the door, his pint forgotten.

When I look at Declan, he can only shake his head, downing half his drink in two gulps. "I don't know, love." He looks out the window, wiping his mouth. "I've no clue what to make of him."

Yeah, I think. *Neither do I.*

THE WAREHOUSE SEEMS darker, danker at night, especially after a storm. Quinn hasn't bothered with the lights or the heat. I climb the curved stairs like a woman on her way to the gallows, not sure why I am worried, having no clue why I feel guilty.

There is nothing between us.

Nothing.

We agreed. We made promises, unspoken, but sacred when this whole thing started. We wanted to forget. We wanted to not feel anything other than sensation. So why did Quinn glare at me as though I betrayed him? Why was Sam's attention the thing that had him leaving without so much as a backward glance?

The hallway lightens the closer I get to the room, from the single flame of his barrel candle in the center of his desk. There are forgotten sheets of paper strewn there, some with half sketches, some crumpled, littered around the floor. There are empty beer bottles and the lingering scent of food, but otherwise, no signs of Quinn, that he might be here at all.

Except for the candle and the shadow behind it.

He stands in front of the window in only his unbuttoned jeans. In Quinn's hand is an unlit cigarette and as I walk further inside, I catch sight of the lighter he flicks over and over, a nervous habit that is both soothing and irritating.

"Come to give me the toss?"

He doesn't move his gaze from the street below and in this light I notice how defined his body is, how the muscles beneath his skin are taut with barely any fat flawing his frame.

"How can I do that, Quinn, when there was no relationship between us?"

A jerk of his head and his gaze pierces beneath the shadows. "There was a relationship between us, Sayo." He moves away from the window and I pick up on the small stomp in his stride, the fists he makes as he stalks closer to me. "You had one with her. So did I. That's what was between us. Her."

The air becomes weighted, as though something dark, something thick filters through the vents. It is a sensation I know; the coil of lust and anger, the echo of desire. The hint of love. It all thickens around us, collects in the space between our bodies.

"Don't." I say, stopping him before he touches me. But Quinn is determined, stubborn, knows I don't want him keeping his touch from me.

"And now... she's gone. Now, love, so is that thing between us. Right?"

The rejection is forced. He's telling me to leave. He's telling me he doesn't want me. So why do I care? It's what I'd come to tell him. It's what being with Sam had reminded me of.

But Quinn not wanting me? Not craving me? The arrogant brat in me doesn't like that, isn't sure she wants to walk away.

"Nothing at all?" I ask him, watching his reaction, squinting to focus on the twist of his mouth, the tiny twitch that moves his eyebrow, any tell that gives him away. There. Right there—the small pulse moving the corner of his top lip and I know he's lying.

So I bluff. "Fine. If that's what you want." I turn, keeping my steps slow, trying desperately to keep my heartbeat steady.

"Sayo."

It isn't a question. It's not a demand. Somewhere in the middle, something in his tone, there is truth. It reaches across the room, keeps me rooted in place. He'd warned me before, admitted he'd take and give and would offer no apologies. But in this tone of his is something that sounds an awful lot like need, a lot like possession.

I should walk away. No looks back. No second thoughts. Just leave him, leave this warehouse and forget that he ever touched me.

"Sayo," he says again and this time that voice is closer. He'd moved like a whisper across the room and I hadn't noticed.

Two steps more and Quinn is behind me. Three more and he rushes forward, forcing me to the wall, bracing myself with my palms flat. "Quinn..."

"No," he says, leaning against me so I can't move. "No, love, you stay still and answer a question for me."

"Back off."

He does, only to slip his hand to my chest, to slide his fingers under my bra and cup my breasts. "You're so hot and cold with me, I never know who you'll be when you come to me."

Moving my head, I catch Quinn's gaze over my shoulder. "You never give yourself to me, O'Malley. Never."

He shifts, withdraws his hands to twist me around by the hips, not leaving much room between us, still holding me to the wall. "You might not like what you see in the real me. I don't much like him myself..."

If I thought he'd continue his awkward interrogation, I was wrong. His grip lessens, his body relaxing into mine and suddenly he moves his forehead against mine, breath hot over my face, smelling of warm beer.

"You want him? The blonde? You want to be rid of me, Sayo?"

"Quinn..." I try, wishing he didn't smell quite so good. Wishing that I didn't remember how much I love the way his arms wrap around me, how the stubble from his face tickles my chest when he rubs it there. I wish I knew how to walk away, to take what had happened between us for the lesson it was.

I wish I didn't want him so badly.

"Quinn..." I try again but he stands too close, feels too close and then our defenses weaken, they crumble and his mouth is on mine, his hands, mine, are everywhere, insisting, skilled, aching.

Bodies molding together.

Skin to skin, no room for regret.

There is only this sensation. This man. This moment.

Quinn touches me, takes me to floor, barely shoving my jeans off, hardly moving his pants down his hips before he hovers over me, sliding his hard dick against me.

"You don't want this anymore?" he asks, his breath shaking, his hands sure as he guides himself over my pussy. "Can you walk away from this, love?" He slips inside me in one fluid thrust and I gasp, gripping hold of his shoulders as he kisses up my neck. "Because I damn well can't."

Words flit into my mind, defenses that are likely logical, seem reasonable, but I don't speak them. Not with how well Quinn touches me, how he treats my body like a playground he's only just discovered.

He is deep inside me, and I'm not sure how to be rid of him. I'm not sure I want to be. But Quinn is a man of few promises. As much as I crave this, he is a wild card I'm not sure I want to play.

When his heartbeat slows and he continues to kiss me, mouth wet, slow against my lips, breath panting and pleased, I touch his face, keeping him still enough that he has to look at me.

"What do you want from me?" I manage to whisper.

Direct questions demand direct responses and I wait with Quinn on top of me, softening inside me as he watches, scanning my face, looking for something, but I don't know what that something is. And then, he closes his eyes, resting his forehead on mine and the faint hope I have dwindles into a dying spark.

Quinn's touch is light and tender, and for a fleeting second I think I might be wrong, that he will give me anything, everything. Then, he rolls away from me, lying at my side with his arm across his forehead.

"Nothing, love. Absolutely nothing."

TWENTY-ONE

AUTUMN AND I had taken the run up to Fanning Falls in less than an hour, sweating now despite the frigid winter weather. It was a trail I never tired of running, with a winding pathway that curled around the river and moved up the mountain. It was the best place to clear your mind, something I needed to do more often.

As we come to the end of Duncan Street, the longest lane that runs through campus before it straightens from its bend to head right into the large park near the athletic fields, Autumn laughs. Her steps quicken, like a kid who's just spotted an ice cream truck entering her neighborhood. She's likely drunk on the adrenaline pumping through her body, likely sexually frustrated since Declan has spent much of this week in Atlanta because Quinn had insisted on some night life that didn't include either Irish jigs or country music. Atlanta was the closest to that and Declan, Vaughn and even a reluctant Donovan had left for a boys' weekend four days ago. They were due back, and the smile on Autumn's face, I suspect, was a result of her spotting Declan's Mustang parked in front of the athletic building.

"They back already?"

She nods. "Declan said he wanted to stop to talk to Coach Mullens before he and Quinn went home."

"Awesome." But it wasn't, not to me. I had managed to keep out of Quinn's line of sight since that night after McKinney's. It was fine with me. Our little *Hey Now* was over. *Good riddance,* I thought.

We were ridiculous. Hot and cold, the pair of us, a fact I kept reminding myself of since I'd last seen him. But I hadn't expected to miss him. I hadn't expected that my mind would grow too full of thoughts of things that Quinn kept from me. Like when the chaos erupted around us, from our friends, my family, or the activity in Cavanagh when rugby matches ran over or ended with a win that combusted the entire town with laughter and happiness, none of which we felt at home in anymore. It was then that Quinn would come to me or I to him. We'd take each other to end the noise, to block out everything but sensation.

I missed how drunk he could make me feel. Like an addict.

"Gah, there he is," Autumn squeals, running faster as Declan leaves the athletic building and catches her the moment she jumps into his arms.

"Oh, baby… love," Declan mutters, then kisses her, holding her tight, giving back every hug, every touch she offers.

After a moment, Declan clears his throat, noticing me over Autumn's shoulder. "Sayo…" he starts but I wave him off.

"No worries. I'm used to the public groping by now."

"Sorry, sweetie," Autumn says, dropping her legs from their spot around Declan's waist.

"Miss me, did you, love?" Declan asks laughing when Autumn kisses his neck. "Ah, well, is it 'sometime' yet?" He asks even though he knows the response will be the same. But his smile falters when she only stands there, staring at him "What?"

"Yeah," she says, biting her lip. "It is."

There is a pause, a moment where Declan's mouth drops open, where he looks as though all the blood in his body flooded to his face. A pleased, shocked smile stretches across his mouth while he just stands there, staring at Autumn, utterly at a loss. And then, slowly, he recovers. "Are you… you're serious?" Declan says, pulling her by the waist so there isn't an inch of space between them.

"Yeah, I am."

It's the moment, the one he'd pestered her about for two years, and he picks her up and swings her in an exuberant circle, laughing as he puts her down again. But Autumn being Autumn doesn't let the shock settle. She simply accepts the way Declan kisses her, laughing at his excitement, and then she pats his chest, calming him as though she hadn't just made him the happiest man alive. "Hey, what did you do with Quinn?"

Declan shakes his head, gives Autumn a "we'll speak later," look and then frowns, looking around the parking lot. "No idea. I told him to wait in the car."

He looks around the building, moving his head, calling his brother's name with Autumn mimicking him and me itching to just walk away. And I almost do it, even take a few steps back thinking that Autumn and Declan are too caught up in each other, in the curiosity of where Quinn had disappeared to that they'd not think to ask after me. But then Declan and Autumn freeze, and both stare over my head just as I catch the high-pitched laughter of a girl coming from behind me. I know that laugh. Dammit all to hell, I know that vapid laugh.

I've hated Heather Matthews for years, even before she'd decided Declan was her target of choice and tried to take him from Autumn. She was a fake little poser, like most of the girls, the Cockies, that were always loitering on the pitch, hoping for a glance, even a half smile from any of the rugby players. She wanted to attach herself to someone with clout and in Cavanagh that meant rugby players. Or, it would seem, a player's half-brother.

I don't acknowledge Autumn at my side or Declan behind her as I turn and see Heather flirting with Quinn. I only know that the piercing ache in my stomach is too much, that the raw fury that pumps in my veins comes from absolutely nowhere and everywhere.

"Mother. Fucker," I hiss, jerking off Autumn's hand when she tries to restrain me.

"Sayo?" Quinn asks, taking a step away from Heather, from those fake nails rubbing against his scalp, from those oversized, store-bought tits that she rubs against his arm.

"Shit," I hear her say almost under her breath, and she retreats, backing away like she's just discovered Quinn is a risk she's not willing to take. She should run. She'd never gotten any retaliation from Autumn for trying to get between her and Declan. She'd never gotten so much as a tongue lashing from me for picking up Sam when I left him. She damn well deserved one now, but doesn't wait long enough for me to glare at her, let alone run her off. She quickly turned tail and walked off without a backwards glance.

"Mind yourself with that one," Declan tells Quinn as they both watch Heather cross the parking lot and head for a group of players hanging out near the pitch.

"Fast and loose?" Quinn asks, smirking. His tone is light and when he glances back at a shrugging Declan, adding, "Just how I like them," it takes more than Autumn's hand to hold me back. Hapless sod doesn't pick up on it until I am inches from his face. He takes a step back, his eyes wide as he looks at my face. "What the bleeding hell?"

"Do *not* mess with her." He retreats when I walk toward him, expression shocked.

"What…"

"You stay the hell away from her, O'Malley."

"Yeah?" he answers, seeming to acquire a little of his old attitude, probably more to save face than for any other reason. "And why should I not play with her a bit? You and me," he licks his lips, like the words have stuck in his mouth, "we made no bloody promises."

"She cannot have you, asshole." I've completely lost my mind. It's the only logical explanation for how high my voice has risen, how my hands shake and for the thick knot that clots my throat. "Not today. Not any fucking day."

"Sayo..." Autumn starts, but one quick wave of my hand and my best friend quiets. I can hear the low arguing between her and Declan, but don't catch more than him quietly telling her to let me be.

"Why are you making demands, then? Telling me my business."

"Calm down, the pair of you," Declan says, but Quinn shakes his head, giving him a warning glare.

"No, this makes no sense. She wouldn't..." he looks from his brother back to me. "The whole bleeding time it was 'don't talk to me, O'Malley,' and 'no emotion O'Malley, no attachments.' For feck's sake, you covered my gob when I'd compliment you and now what? Some bird gives me attention and you're not having it? Jaysus, woman, I'm dizzy from your back and forth moods."

"Wasn't just me, was it?" I step closer and this time Quinn doesn't retreat. "How many times did you just show up at my place? How many times did you act like you needed me?"

"And you welcomed me every sodding time. Don't play the martyr here. No one is innocent."

"Listen, both of you…" Autumn starts, seems shocked when Quinn and I both shout "Quiet!" at the same time.

"I don't know what you're playing at, Sayo, and you know, I don't much care." Quinn grabs my arm, voice low, lethal. "But you've no say in what I do or who I do it with."

And just like that the truth hits me, makes my chest constrict. He isn't wrong. I am behaving like a jealous idiot when I really, I have no rights. He gave me exactly what I asked for, when I wanted it and then I walked away. I was the one who made sure there was no connection. At least, I thought I did. So why the hell am I raving mad? Why am I making it clear to him that he couldn't have Heather?"

"God," I say, pulling away from Quinn. "I…"

"When did this happen?" Quinn asks, voice carrying less bite, but I can't answer, and I become the one to walk away, turning a deaf ear to their voices becoming faint and indistinguishable as I beat a hasty retreat.

WHY DO WE revert? Every single time? Why do we keep repeating past mistakes, conveniently forgetting that our choices led us down a road that we swore we'd never revisit?

I sit in the booth furthest away from the front door, far away from the bar to avoid the light crowd that McKinney's typically draws on a Sunday night. There is a group of sorority sisters near the front, downing dollar margaritas while some of the first year rugby players sing bad karaoke, trying to impress them. Declan had done that a couple years back when he wanted Autumn's forgiveness and he thought humiliation was the way to earn it. Maybe he was on to something. Maybe if I embarrassed myself in front of the town then Quinn would forget me acting like a jealous asshole.

"They'll be gone in half an hour," Sam says, sitting next to me in the booth. "But I can kick them out now if you want some quiet."

He smells like lemons and limes with a hint of sugar. I used to love it when Sam would come to my place after a shift, smelling of the fruit he'd cut to garnish whatever drinks were on special. That scent hasn't changed much. But I have.

"Why are you being so nice to me?" The question is out of my mouth before I even decided to ask it. It was something I'd wondered the last time I was here drinking his Baileys laced tea. It had been a long time since Sam and I had been an item. Why should it matter to him how I felt?

"I thought I was always nice," he says, brushing my hand before he leans on the table. "I gave you free tea the last time you were here."

"Yeah, I know." I turn, resting against the wall at my back so I can look at him. "You've never done that before and I've seen you plenty here since we broke up. It wasn't... wasn't until Rhea..."

"This isn't pity, if that's what you think, Sayo."

"Then tell me what it is."

Sam's eyes narrow as he thinks of what to say. He doesn't make me feel uncomfortable when he leans back, stretching his arm along the back of the booth, moving his lips like he was trying to gather his thoughts.

Finally, he exhales, tilting his head back to stare up at the ceiling, then back down at me. "I should have never let you slip away."

"What?"

He straightens, leaning on his side to face me. "Two weeks after we broke up, Tucker shows up at my place shitty as hell. He starts blabbing about Autumn, about what a whore she was, how she'd been sleeping with Fraser after meeting him once."

"That's *not* what happened."

"Yeah, I know." Sam shrugs, scrubbing his face. "Fraser and Donley, they hung out in here a lot. They'd come in for lunch, or after practice just to relax. You get to see all sides of people when you work behind that bar, and that semester when Fraser was running after Autumn, I saw plenty. But I didn't think about any of that when you told me what a shithead Tucker was." He shrugged again, shaking his head. "You know how it is, being friends with someone for so long, you sort of overlook their flaws. I did that with Tucker. But when he came to my place bashing Fraser and Autumn I realized you'd been right. Then, a few months later when Heather came around, well..."

"She distracted you."

He has the decency to look sheepish, shaking his head at his own stupidity. "I'm a guy and I'd gone a few months without..." Sam stops his explanation when I squint at him. "Fine. No excuses, but a few weeks with her and I knew you'd been right about both of them. But by then you'd moved on, and I had convinced myself that I didn't deserve you."

He reaches toward me, taking my hand. "I probably still don't, but I'd like to try." Sam has long fingers. There are several callouses on his knuckles, but the palms are smooth. "I know you're still hurting from losing Rhea. She was a sweet girl. I remember that from your sister's birthday dinner we spent with your family."

Around us the karaoke has grown drunker and louder, and the wait staff busies themselves with orders for pitchers, but Sam seems to see nothing but me.

"Sayo, I'm sorry I wasn't there." He inches closer, takes a hold of my hand. "I'm sorry you had to go through that at all. Maybe I can, I don't know, help a little." He takes my chin, lifting it as though he wants to pull me to him. "Maybe I can ease some of the ache for you."

"Sam," I say again, remembering that I had tried to take the ache away before. That hadn't worked out so well for me. That's what I think, where my thoughts are when Sam pulls me in, kissing me soft and slow.

That brush of his lips, the tenderness in his touch… he could ease my grief. He could, very easily make me forget…

And then another flash comes to my mind—the intensity of my clothes being pulled from me, the pulsing vibration of stronger hands, fiercer grabs. A mouth that possesses, controls, makes me crave that demand, eyes that are blue, not gentle, touches that are eager and sure. Quinn is everything Sam is not. He is more, so much more and as I let Sam kiss me, stealing some of my breath, a bit of my burdens, I feel… absolutely nothing.

"Oh God," I say, retreating, leaning back. Not letting him ask the question I know is threatening to leave his mouth. "Oh… shit. Shit!"

"What is it? What's wrong, Sayo?"

"I can't…" I make my lungs expand, keep enough air inside that I can think and reason. It's there—that knowledge, that sudden realization. "Son of bitch, Sam, I can't kiss you."

"Why the hell not?"

"Because," I tell him, pushing him out of the booth and grabbing my purse and jacket as I stand to leave. "I… I'm pretty damn sure I'm in love with someone else."

TWENTY-TWO

My life is not a Nora Ephraim-penned movie. Realizing I love Quinn is one thing. Seeing him, or God forbid, telling him? That's an entirely different matter. I wasn't about to go running through the sleepy streets of Cavanagh in a mad, dizzying rush to get to my man and profess my undying love. This isn't a John Hughes movie either.

One minute Sam was kissing me. The next I knew he shouldn't be, and then I did what any rational, red-blooded woman my age would do. I went home and hid under my blankets. Minutes went by. Hours. Before I knew it, two days had passed, and I was smelling mildly like the tub of roasted garlic hummus I'd eaten, (family size because I'm a pig) and still utterly unwilling to venture out.

Autumn's incessant calling, not leaving messages, texting and then calling again, finally got me out from under those blankets.

"Next Sunday at eleven. Don't make any plans."

"What have you signed me up for, friend?" I should have known there was some sneaky missive that Autumn kept to herself.

"Um, maid of honor duties."

My jaw literally dropped. I hadn't planned on that. I hadn't even expected it.

"No sense in waiting," Autumn explained. "Declan is due in New Zealand in a month. We may as well get married first." I was speechless, but she didn't waste any time leveling on the surprises. "Will you do it? Stand up for me?"

"Duh! Of course I will."

"Um, well, before you agree, I should tell you. Quinn is standing up for Declan."

"Quinn? Why not Donovan?"

"Donovan can't do it." She sounded annoyed, but I heard the half-truth in her tone. That woman had schemes afoot. "He and Layla are taking the baby to New Orleans to visit his family."

Autumn's breath went still, as though she was holding it. But dang, she had been my best friend since we were kids. There was no way I'd let Quinn O'Malley stop me from being there on the most important day of her life. "Sure," I finally said, ignoring the slow rumble that started in my stomach when I thought of looking at Quinn across the aisle. "Of course I'll do it."

I just didn't realize what a challenge that day would be.

AUTUMN WAS TYPICALLY calm. Always. Aside from panic attacks when her anxiety got out of hand, especially when things are out of her control, she never had an issue retaining her calm.

Her wedding day was the exception.

She looks beautiful. Her thick ginger hair is pinned up at the sides, and a simple gardenia accented with baby's breath nestles around the crown of her head. The dress she wears is simple, knee length with a classic pin up silhouette in white satin with a pleated skirt. She looks like a paler, taller, much more Irish Marilyn Monroe.

"Declan is going to lose his shit," Mollie says approvingly, zipping up Autumn's dress as I steam the hem. Autumn's reply is a non-committal grunt and I exchange glances with Mollie, shaking my head at our friend's distracted, edging-toward-flustered state.

There seems to be a lot weighing on her—the move to a new country, finishing her graduate work, closing up the house, finding a job in New Zealand... getting married. Added to that is the quickness of this wedding. It doesn't seem right that Layla isn't here, but family visits with the first grandchild outweigh impromptu weddings, apparently. Fortunately she and Donovan would be back before the New Zealand departure.

The church Autumn managed to rent for the ceremony is very old, at least one hundred and fifty years, with nothing but the framework to serve as a venue for small, intimate weddings. The structure is made up of a white washed brick frame and a half-roof that lets in the sunlight and casts beautiful light against the alter and the stained-glass behind it. The tiny building outside of the church houses the office and all around both buildings is a lush, well-maintained English garden.

Autumn fidgets, shaking her foot as she leans against the bathroom counter in the church office. We'd blocked the entrance, using the bathroom as a make-shift dressing room. I notice the way Autumn keeps glancing at her phone, how she mumbles under her breath.

"Sweetie, what's the problem?" I ask, touching her shoulder.

Finally, she exhales, rubbing her neck. "Declan wasn't worried before now, but we only have twenty minutes and Quinn's still not here."

"What do you mean?"

"If you'd been here on time, you'd have realized Quinn is MIA." I ignore the snap in Autumn's voice, chalking it up to pre-wedding nerves. Still, she manages to earn my forgiveness with an apologetic smile.

"I don't know why this surprises you," Mollie says.

"But they've been getting along so well," Autumn explains. The trip to Atlanta actually had gone well, and Quinn had started watching matches with Declan, Donovan, and the others on the squad. "He didn't even fuss when Declan asked him to be his best man," she said, plaintively.

"Really?" Mollie sounds skeptical and I had to agree. That did seem wildly out of character for Quinn.

"Well, I did get the impression that he was annoyed that he was Declan's second choice, but I can't see that being a reason to ditch us."

"No one's heard from him?" I say, stopping Autumn when she chews on her thumb nail. "Don't. You'll mess up your manicure."

"Do you have any idea where he could be?" she asks, holding my wrist when I swat her thumb out of her mouth.

I look at the clock sighing at the time. "Give me twenty minutes and I'll be right back."

"We can't start without you or Quinn."

"Yes you can, friend." When I smile at her, Autumn's shoulders lower as though I somehow will save the day. "But you better not."

TWENTY-THREE

Quinn has always disliked Cavanagh, that he's made abundantly clear. It is nothing, I assume, like Dublin. He is used to the excitement of a large city, the fast pace and diversity, the buzz of something always going down. Cavanagh is the opposite of all that, so Quinn took to his warehouse, hiding from his brother, from the slow pace of our lives and the natural environment of our surroundings. *Shitehole.* That's what he made of our small town. But it was Quinn who hid in near squalor. He was the one who chose to retreat to a run down, dank building and dusty room rather than join his family and the life he could have with us.

Nevertheless, that warehouse had been a haven for us, and it is where I hurriedly drive to retrieve him, to bring him back. I'm sure he'll be there.

I have no illusions about how he'll welcome me or if he will at all. I only know that returning to this place and dragging him to the wedding—kicking and screaming if I have to— will calm my best friend and make her wedding day the sweet, simple affair she's always wanted.

The sidewalk is empty of parked cars and there is little traffic that surrounds the building. I fuss with my dress—a simple, pale purple baby doll number with a understated beaded bust and a tapered skirt —adjusting it as I near the building. But when the mural on the side of the building comes into view, it stops me cold, save for the pounding of my heart in my chest.

He finally finished Rhea's mural.

It is everything she would have wanted—light and magic, a wonderful cosmic fantasy that seems to breathe like a living creature. The blues and blacks of the backgrounds are lush, the brilliant cluster of stars seems to blink and shine even in the midafternoon light. Rhea is positioned right in the center of the building—the mountains guard and protect the town as Rhea soars from the ground, away from the trees and mountains. She flies into the ether, arms outstretched, hair flowing down her back, cascading against her cape. She is fierce. She is power. She is amazingly free. And below her Quinn and I hold each other, watching her fly away.

Before I realize it, my face grows wet with tears, threatening to mess up my makeup. But as much as I want to just stand and stare at the precious mural, time is wasting, and I hurry into the building, traversing the cluttered lobby and up that massive stair case, listening for any activity, for any movement that might give Quinn away.

There is none. Not in the front room or hallway on the second floor, not in the makeshift bedroom he's crafted near the back of the room. But all around the small mattress stuffed in a corner, littering on the floor and pinned to the walls, are sketches—hundreds of sketches that paint a picture of the life Quinn has led in the month since Rhea died—or the life he wishes he had.

There is Rhea playing on the pitch with Declan—this version of the Irishman with a kinder, gentler face and a brilliant smile. There is Rhea and Carol sitting on the edge of a long pier, their feet floating in the still water with a brilliant sunset behind them. There is Quinn and Rhea leveling the villainous *Death Doctor C*, eradicating him and his poisonous needles with karate chops from their fists and fearsome kicks from their feet. Then Rhea, with wings that stretch and seem to flap, that beautiful green and blue fairy with iridescent skin and hair that fans out to touch her wings. She is remarkable, so beautiful, and I can only lay my palm flat below my collarbone to keep my heartbeat even and calm.

Quinn had drawn the world he envisioned. He'd left these characters here, illustrating the life he must have wished for, the one that existed in his mind. Rhea alive and happy. Declan generous, kind, how we saw him all the time, how Quinn had only just discovered his brother to be.

But there, next to the bed in the center in the wall, is a sketch that seems to have been carefully drawn. Time and attention had been paid to each stroke, the barest hint of erased and redrawn lines. The image is more finished than the others, an elegant depiction that staggers me, leaves me breathless.

Of all the things I have seen Quinn draw, nothing, not even that remarkable mural or the treatment he's given to my sweet cousin's image, felt as real, as alive, as cared for as this image.

My face. My mouth, my nose, the oval shape of my eyes, even the arch of my brows. Quinn had created me as he saw me. Beautiful. Luminous. Looking at the picture, I take in the smooth lines, the subtle curves. They feel kissed, touched by his hands, fashioned from whatever it was he felt for me and as I study the sketch my heart shudders again with the basic, absolute knowledge that Quinn loves me.

If I know anything, I know that.

Quinn loves me.

It's in the pout on my lips, the way they look well kissed and full. It's in the perfection in my imperfections, the scar on my temple that he somehow made to look flattering. It's in the arch of my cheekbones, how they are pronounced, not dulled by my full cheeks.

With every stroke he promises to love me.

With every line, he shows me what lives in his heart.

The sudden vibration of my phone pulls my attention away from the sketch and the sensation of want, of love and desire that courses through me.

Quinn is here. Get to here asap! Autumn's text reads and I nod, as though she can see me, not to acknowledge what she says, but to settle in my mind my intention.

I want to claim what's mine.

TWENTY-FOUR

THERE HAS NEVER been a more awkward moment in my life. Back straight, stomach twisted in knots, I stand across the aisle as my best friend marries her love. It is sweet, the way they look at each other—attention focuses, eyes never flicking away from each other's faces—there is real love, real trust and companionship in the looks they give each other. It was a long time coming—years, in fact. So many broken promises that became impossible hopes, that became guarantees that the past had been forgiven, and it all led here, in this moment as Autumn looks up at Declan, as they watch each other surrounded by the small congregation of family and friends.

I don't think either one of them listen much to what the priest says. Declan stretches his hand, touches her face as though he can't keep his hands to himself. As though he must touch her, just to see if she's real.

It's sweet. It's enviable.

And then, there's Quinn.

God help me, I can't look at him. It's ridiculous, really. I shouldn't be acting this way. The man has seen me naked. He's touched and tasted the most intimate parts of my body. He's rendered me breathless just with his mouth and fingers. And, damn it all, I love him. If I'm not completely wrong, he loves me too.

So why the hell can I not look at him?

"If there is anyone who objects to this union..." the priest's pointless words pull my attention back to the altar, to the smile illuminating Autumn's face—and the almost humorous glare Declan sends around the church. His threat isn't necessary. The only people in this building are friends and family, none of whom want anything more than for Declan and Autumn besottedly bound forever. There's a vain hope among us that marriage will calm them, possibly take some of the arrogance out of them. Those two think they invented romance and love. It's a little insulting. And endearing.

"McShane," Declan whispers, slipping on that ring that has burned a hole in his pocket for two years. Her name comes out like a wish and the big Irishman doesn't seem able to stop himself from kissing her forehead, from holding her cheek as she slips his ring on his free hand.

And then, the permission for the kiss comes and Declan doesn't wait, Autumn doesn't wait, and the couple kiss like their lungs will only fill with the touch of their mouths. All around us, Joe, Mollie, even Ava, claps, smiles and laughs as that kiss lingers. Declan kisses his bride and tears get in the way of my laughter as my best friend hugs me and the couple leave the altar. I hadn't needed to worry about Quinn walking me down the aisle when I returned from the warehouse. Joe had tugged him bodily to the altar, after making Quinn smooth down his hair and his slightly rumpled shirt. I suspect a long night and lots of whiskey had been the culprit that made Quinn late for his brother's wedding. But, no, I hadn't had him forced on me as I walked down the aisle.

But now I do.

His stance is too straight, his look mildly annoyed as we stand side by side and, as though it's an afterthought, Quinn stiffly extends his arm, offering me his elbow. But there isn't a hint of amusement in his eyes.

I take his damn elbow anyway just to breath in his cologne. Just to get a private flash of how warm he always is, how his muscles bunch and flex on their own.

Shit.

We stand like this—my arm wrapped in his, our legs touching, my fingers resting on his bicep—while the photographer annoys us with one picture after another. It seems like ages before I can break away, only to have that camera pointed back in my face and Quinn moved directly behind me as the photograph snaps "bridal party" pictures.

"Jaysus, aren't you done, mate?" Quinn asks the guy, grunting to himself when Autumn glares at him.

"Sayo, you look so pretty in that color," my best friend offers, beaming like a proud mother as the photographer checks the light and Declan gawks at his new bride, completely under her spell. But Autumn is devious and I know the game she's playing. Quinn, bless him, has no clue what sort of manipulator his brother just married. "She's beautiful, right, Quinn?" Autumn asks, stepping next to him and pulling his hand to my hip. "There. Lovely, right?"

"Autumn…"

"If I didn't know better, I'd say you two look like a couple."

"Autumn…"

"Is that what we look like?" Quinn asks, sliding his hand over my belly. "Perhaps you'd like an action shot?" And the Quinn twists me around, holding the back of my neck while he dips me. "Play as though you still like me," he whispers. And then, that smug bastard kisses me slow, taking his time, earning a few whistles from Joe and Vaughn. "See now?" he says, still bending over me with his mouth just inches from mine, before he lets me back up. "I'm not so horrible, am I?"

"You'll… you'll do," I manage.

Before I could give much thought into that kiss or the self-deprecating way Quinn handled me, we are directed away from the church and to McKinney's for the reception. You know, because what I need is to be surrounded by my friends and my whatever Quinn is under the scrutinizing eyes of my ex-boyfriend-who-recently-kissed-me.

Sure.

No potential issues could arise.

None whatsoever.

AUTUMN WAS A Fraser now. She'd take Declan's name because she was proud to be his. They had both been dealt some pretty rough blows in their lives, both taking their mother's maiden names, both had long-reaching daddy issues that made keeping those surnames an easy choice.

There was no doubt that Autumn loved her father, Joe. Anyone who met Joe Brady today, would be hard pressed denying how charming, how generous he is. Sadly, that hadn't always been the case, hence, Autumn being a McShane for most of her life. And now she was McShane-Fraser. Her children would be as well. But that didn't seem to matter a bit to Joe, at least not if that proud, wide grin on his face and those watery eyes were any indication.

Joe dances with his daughter, holding her hand between his massive fingers, looking down at her as though he'd had a hand in making perfection and no one could top him.

Sam and his staff at McKinney's have outdone themselves, working magic with purple streamers and thick swags of mesh netting. There are white fairy lights strewn in every free space, every nook in the ceiling. It reminds me a bit of Autumn's winter wonderland, and that thought had me smiling, remembering how magical Autumn had made that day, how pleased Carol had been by everyone's generosity.

"What's up, then?" Mollie asks, sliding next to me on the free stool, looping her arm in mine. "Aren't you supposed to be dancing with the best man?"

"Yes, well, he's disappeared. Again." Quinn had been scarce during the reception, something that didn't surprise me.

"That's a shame really. You look beautiful. Here," she says, laughing to herself, "you can borrow mine." Mollie waves over her live-in giant of a boyfriend and the former Marine bowed to us both, his eyes a little red and glassy. "Shit faced yet, Winchester?"

"Ma'am? Me? Indeed not." His wink came easy and he didn't bother trying to apologize for the way he wobbled standing there or why he smelled quite a lot like Jamesons.

"Good. Then you can dance with Sayo." Mollie pushed me toward her boyfriend with a pat to my back. "She's in need."

"We live to serve." Vaughn bowed, worked some sort of ridiculous hand wave and then tugged me off onto the dance floor.

He was at least a foot and a half taller than me so anyone looking at Vaughn's back would think he was dancing by himself. Ridiculous, but not exactly an unreasonable assumption to make since half the party was shitfaced. While the ceremony had been a simple, private affair, the reception was a debauched, proper Irish party. Between Autumn's godmother Ava, and Joe, no expense had been spared and damn near the whole of Cavanagh had been invited to celebrate the happy couple.

I was in a sea of loud, laughing, dancing depraved partiers, my folks and siblings among them, not to mention Aunt Carol and a hesitant, awkward Uncle Clay. He'd missed Rhea's funeral, most of the aftermath of her death, but was making strides, asking for forgiveness I wasn't sure Carol would give him.

"Never seen so many happy people in all my damn life," Vaughn says, twirling me around the dancefloor like I weigh less than a feather.

"Any excuse in Cavanagh to party will be used. Guaranteed."

He says something then, but the room is loud and his laughter is louder, then Vaughn spins me again and I lose hold of his hand, only to be twirled back around by Mollie, who kisses my cheek, then Joe, who hugs me tight, until all the spinning and twirling and bodies and moving this way and that among the loud music, the thick scent of liquor and the grasp of strange, friendly fingers and then, finally, I stop and find myself in Quinn's arms.

"Oh."

But he either doesn't hear me or doesn't care how awkward I feel. Quinn navigates us away from the crowd, dancing past Autumn and Declan, beyond the reach and ear shot of Mollie and Vaughn until we are next to the end of the bar.

"Thanks," I say, keeping my eyes on the bar, on the dance floor, anywhere but at Quinn.

"Are you ever going to bloody look at me again? And I don't mean to glaring at me, or otherwise giving me shite for one thing or another I've done."

"I don't give you shit."

"Jaysus, you do so." Hands in his hair, Quinn shakes his head, looking around the bar before he steps close to me. "God above, Sayo, you nearly ripped my throat out when that Heather girl was chatting me up."

"Long damn history, O'Malley," I say, with a bit of a growl in my voice, and he grins. "You should be thanking me for that one, trust me."

"Oh I bet you think I should be thanking you for loads of things, don't you?" Suddenly, he isn't really joking anymore.

"I never said that."

"Putting Rhea in my space," his voice is low, but gentle and doesn't match the angry frown on his face or the way he backs me away from the crowd. "Making me fall for her, worry over her, grieve her. And you," he says, reaching for my face, then dropping his hand at his side as if now is not the time nor place. "You invading my head space, making me think thoughts you damn well wouldn't want me thinking."

"You got something out of it."

"Did I now? Did I really?"

Quinn's hand on my arm is firm but not tight, and I can't decide if I still love or hate his touch on my bare skin. "You saying you didn't?" I work my way out of his touch, and watch the room, returning my attention back to Quinn only when no one pays attention to the rise of our voices. "You got what every man wants, didn't you? You got that a hell of a lot."

"That what you think?"

"I think you got more than you bargained for. I think you fell in love with that little girl and it hurt you when she... when she died." When I drop my gaze, blinking fast, Quin moves my chin, but I take a step away from him, needing to say my peace without him distracting me. "I think you did everything you could to make sure she got the treatment she needed and when it still didn't save her, you got angry. At me, at her folks, at the hospital. And then you shut yourself away from me, from everyone. Because being alone was better than the risk of caring for someone again."

"How do you know what I want? You're the one that made no promises. You're the one that made certain I gave you none either and then, when I do something as simple as flirt with some bird you act like a jealous girlfriend. The bloody hell am I supposed to think?"

Heather is the last thing on my mind. Yes, I lost it when I saw her pawing at him, but this all goes deeper than that tart wanting in his pants. This was about Quinn telling half-truths and failing to acknowledge what's his for the taking.

When my hand lifts, latches onto his wrist, Quinn's shoulders tense, as though he suspects an attack. "Did you donate that money?"

His eyes are peering, hard, but he says nothing.

"Did you paint the mural because Rhea asked or because you wanted to?"

There is a shift in his expression, those piercing eyes shifting, but still Quinn remains silent.

"You loved her, didn't you?"

Those thick lips move, press together until they are tight, as though he has to force himself not to speak.

"You…" I take the advantage, knowing he won't reject me, knowing he won't walk away from me; when I move my hand up his arm, Quinn watches my fingers, catching each touch as it crosses his arm. "You love me, don't you Quinn?"

His jaw works and the tension in his face eases but Quinn doesn't speak.

"I…"

"Sayo?" Someone calls, breaking us a part until Sam is at my side with a hand grazing my elbow. "Everything okay?"

"She's fine," Quinn says, stepping in front of me like a caveman.

"Sorry, man, but I wasn't speaking to you."

"Maybe you should be." He folds his arms, head tilted in a challenge I know Sam won't take. Living in Cavanagh and working at McKinney's has taught him better than to cross an Irishman who's been drinking. "Maybe you should stop bleeding talking to her altogether."

"Who the hell do you think…"

"She is not for you." He pokes Sam's chest, eyes sharp. "Get that through your skull right bleeding now and bugger off."

"The pair of you," I say, glaring at them both, waving a hand to silence them when they both look eager to argue with me. "Stop with the chest thumping. It's pointless."

The pictures have been taken. My friends are pie eyed. So while the boys play their pissing match, I simply turn and walk out of McKinney's, annoyed, irritated by Quinn and Sam's pissing match and feeling less hopeful than I had after I left the warehouse this morning.

Quinn. God how I wish Declan would have left him in Ireland. My life would be a lot less complicated if he had.

And I'd be miserable.

"But I'm already miserable," I say to myself.

"Why, love?" For a moment, I think I am imagining Quinn's voice, but he's real, and I haven't gotten more than a block from the bar before he's come for me.

"Because you're here." I expect him to frown, to drop his mask again, but he doesn't. This time, he reaches for me, turns me to face him, and his touch is gentle, almost sweet. When I look into his eyes, they are unguarded, sincere.

"You... you don't want me to be?"

"No." There is a crumble of concrete next to the drain on the street and I kick the small bits, toeing them between the grate. "Yes. Hell, I don't know. God you're just so..."

"Sayo," he says, holding my shoulders. "Just what is it that you want from me?"

I could say a lot things, each more ridiculous than the next. Finally I settle on what my heart tells me.

"I want real. I told you that. I want you to tell me the truth about the donation, about the mural about... about Rhea."

"And about you?"

I look down, unable to take the tease in his eyes. "You can't do that can you? You can't be real."

"Nobody is realer than me, love. Especially," he says, stepping closer, "not wankers with blonde hair and dimples whose greatest achievement in life is managing a bar in the smallest bleeding town in America."

I shake my head. "You're jealous of Sam?"

"Hardly, but that doesn't mean I like him sniffing around you, trying to chat you up."

That smug amusement twitching his mouth drops altogether when I tilt my head, frowning at him. "Oh he did more than that."

Quinn works his jaw, nostrils flaring as he moves a step toward me. "What did he do, Sayo and when did he fecking do it? Today? Last week?"

"The night I saw you with Declan. The night Layla had the baby."

I can almost see him thinking. It was the same night I went to him, the night he told me he wanted nothing from me. He'd touched me then and I'd never mentioned Sam or what he'd offered me. "And what did he do then? After I left?"

"After you ran away?" The wall behind me of the closed bakery hits my back as I move from him, but Quinn follows.

"Tell me."

"He kissed me."

Quinn is livid, but his rage is calm, collected. A purse of his thick lips, the dip of his eyebrows, his jaw moving as he grinds his teeth—I expect him to turn quickly, jog back to McKinney's and find Sam, maybe knock him around a bit. Instead, he retains his cool, stretching out one arm to rest his palm next to my head on the brick. When he speaks, that voice is lethal, low. "He kissed you."

"He did."

Quinn pops his neck, letting those nostrils flare once before he leans down, both hands now against the brick wall behind me. "And what did you do when that wanker kissed you?"

"Oh. Well, for a few seconds," I start, trying not to grin when Quinn's mouth thins out further, "I guess I kissed him back."

"A few seconds?" I nod and Quinn grunts, passing off the frustrated sound by clearing his throat. "And after a few seconds?"

"I told him to stop."

"Why?"

"Because I realized I didn't want to kiss Sam." I grab Quinn's collar, surprising him. He comes close with no resistance, leaning into me like he has no control. "Because as he was kissing me…" I narrow my eyes, scrutinizing, "as he let his tongue slip into my…"

"I get the bleeding picture, woman."

"Anyway… as he kissed me I realized he shouldn't be."

Finger against my forehead, Quinn brushing back my hair, licking his lips as he watches me. "And why is that, Sayo?"

"Because I didn't want him. I didn't want to be with him. Because, Quinn, I realized I didn't love him." He lifts his eyebrows, waiting. "I knew I shouldn't be kissing Sam because I was in love with you. God help me, that was when I realized how much I love you."

His expression shifts. He's fighting disbelief, mistrust, hope, but then his face transforms and he relaxes, releasing a sigh. "I... I don't know how to do this a'tall. I've never... Sayo, I think." Another exhale and Quinn rubs the back of his neck but doesn't step out of my reach. "I might, but I don't know how to..." He takes a breath. "It wasn't just you and you... Jaysus, I wanted to forget too. It wasn't just you. I needed you. I... I still do." When Quinn blinks, leaning toward me, I catch his face between my hands, breathing in deep when he rests his forehead against mine. "I've been alone a long time and family hasn't ever meant much to me but you... you and Rhea and shite, even Fraser, have given me pause. The only thing I know for sure, Sayo, is that you're the only family I want. I might not be good at saying the words..."

"It's okay." I didn't need to hear the words. I knew what was in his heart. That had been clear in his sketch of me. "I'll teach you, Quinn."

TWENTY-FIVE

Junior high. Mrs. Elton's third period History class. That was the day I met Autumn. Rory Callahan called me a filthy name, something to do with my oval eyes. I had never heard the slur before but knew from his tone it was meant to be an insult. Autumn decked him in the nose and got detention. When I asked her why she'd defended me, she answered very simply: "Because no one should be picked on for being different."

She was the boldest thing I'd ever seen and I'd spent the next twenty years watching my best friend grow bolder, get tougher, endure more sadness than most folks. And now, sitting on Joe's front porch, I watch my best friend say goodbye to Mollie and Layla and kiss that beautiful baby, Evie, like she'll never see her again.

"Oh, you have to send me videos and pictures, every day." Layla nods and Autumn ignores her to plant yet another kiss on Evie's round cheeks. "I mean it. Every single day, promise, Layla."

"I will. I swear, sweetie."

They've been saying goodbye for twenty minutes.

I can only watch, not willing to move from the swing, ignoring Declan and Quinn huddled near the hood of the car with Joe, muttering things that are probably complaints about how long it takes us to leave each other.

They'd never understand. What man would? There is a bond women have. There is a union that occurs when time, when circumstance binds you to another person. Who else but a woman could understand the heartache of a lost love? The wrenching pain caused by a failure or rejection because of who you are? Who else but another woman could understand the dull weight of frustration when others set limits our minds can't accept? When the world tries to enforce those limits? No man understands our sisterhood. How in the world could they understand what it is to let that bond go?

My thoughts weigh me down just watching Mollie and Layla crying with Autumn, making promises for texts and chats, visits on holidays. And finally, when they have exhausted themselves with tears, Autumn looks up at me, her smile twitching.

If I stay put, she won't be able to leave.

If I don't move, she won't be able to say goodbye.

It is a juvenile response—digging my feet into the metaphorical ground in some pathetic attempt to keep my best friend here with me. I can't find it in myself to care how ridiculous it is. I can't be bothered with how my reaction may seem to the others.

Quinn nods, encouraging me to leave the porch and though his mild smile is sweet, beautiful, it doesn't make me move. I think maybe Autumn will give up, settle for a wave and then text me from the car, but that doesn't happen either.

She makes her way up to the swing before I can tell her to stop. If she sits next to me, that will be it. She'll say goodbye and I will be left without my best friend.

I shut my eyes, squeezing them tight, trying to tell myself that the pain will ease. Most pain does. I try to convince myself that this farewell is not permanent. But I don't know that.

The swing moves and that familiar scent—the one that reminds me of sleep overs and braided hair, over long weekends in our PJs and drunken parties with faceless rugby players— swirls around me one more time.

"Sayo." There is no judgement in her voice, no admonishment that tells me she thinks I'm being a brat. Her tone is gentle and kind, and I realize that of the two of us, Autumn has finally become the adult. I may be older. I may have finished my education and set out on a profession before her, but right now, in this moment, Autumn is the one who truly grew up.

"Breakfast, every Saturday morning. What will you do?"

"Get up when Declan does and have a bite with him."

I flash her a glance, horrified by the prospect. "With a boy? Breakfast is for besties." My gaze shoots to Declan, laughing with Quinn, listening to Donovan's animated story that keeps them all smiling, and I shrug. "I guess he'll be good company. But God, Autumn won't you get lonely over there? He'll be practicing and doing matches all over the place."

"And I'll follow, when I can and when I can't, we'll adjust." She leans forward, crossing her ankles before she rests her elbow on her knees looking up at me. "I'll have Joe to keep me company when Deco's not there."

"I don't like it."

"I wouldn't either if it was you leaving me behind." She exhales, looping her pinky to mine with her voice lowering, sounding a little sad. "Aren't you... aren't you happy for me?"

My best friend had endured so much loss—Joe leaving her, her mother's death, Tucker abandoning her after two years. It wasn't until Declan stepped into her life that her smile returned and it hasn't left her in nearly three years. I glance back at Declan who now leans against the car, hands in his pockets next to Quinn. They both watch me and Autumn.

All I ever wanted for my friends is even the smallest hint of joy. Mollie got that with Vaughn, despite the obstacles thrown in their way. Layla and Donovan got that when they finally stop getting in their own way. And Autumn, my sweet friend, she was the first to take what she wanted. She took a risk, the chance that she might not be loved back due to her past and Declan's being so intertwined, the risk that in loving him might have caused too much pain.

And yet, my friends found their happiness.

"Of course I am," I tell Autumn, knocking my shoulder against hers. "It's just, God, Autumn you're leaving me with Quinn."

"Ha, friend, stop acting like that's a burden."

One quick smile at him and Quinn stops speaking to Declan, eyebrows up, curious. He was a conundrum, something that I wasn't sure I'd ever figure out. Gone was the self-centered asshole who thought the world owed him a favor. In his place was a self-centered asshole who was learning that he owed the world a favor for getting him through a sickened childhood and the heartache that loving and then losing someone always causes.

"He told me last night that he never wanted to feel what he does for me."

Autumn's gaze is sharp and worried, but I shake my head, and ease her fear with my quick laugh. "He's never had to worry about loving someone before. Well, someone who doesn't claim to love him for all the wrong reasons."

"It's a new world for him."

"Yeah," I say, moving the swing with my feet. "And it's ours for the taking." I look at her and our eyes meet. "All of ours." My best friend's chin shakes as she watches me and I think of a hundred different things I could say in this moment—promises that might make her wonder if leaving Cavanagh really was the right thing to do. Scenarios to test her loyalty, challenges that encourage her to stay. But in the end, if we love someone, we always do what's best for them, even if it breaks our heart.

"It's yours. Just make sure you do us proud."

"I love you," she says, hugging me in a rush that catches me off guard. Autumn kisses me, whispers a dozen promises I know she's good for and then we both leave the porch, arm in arm, at least until we reach the driveway.

Another round of goodbyes, more hugs and kisses and my best friend, her husband and father are off in Vaughn's car with Mollie, all heading for their new lives.

"Going to be a bit weird here," Quinn says, nodding toward Joe's house. "Me being the only one left behind, I mean."

"Hmm, maybe you can throw a wild party. Get a bunch of girls over and..." he silences me with a kiss, one that has little Evie staring and Layla trying to cover her eyes as she and Donovan walk inside.

"I don't want any other girls over here." Quinn hugs me, kissing my forehead, the tip of my nose before he lands a soft kiss on my mouth. "You're the only one I want."

"And why is that?" I ask, knowing the answer but still loving the hearing of it.

"Will you ever tire of me saying it?" I shake my head, nudging him to repeat the same thing he told me two weeks ago when he admitted he loved me. Quinn sighs, shaking his head as he indulges me again. "You're like a cigarette, Sayo. So bleeding bad for me and you get stuck, inside my chest. Everything inside me absorbs you and you fill me up." He's repeated it so often I could practically mouth the words before he speaks them, but I let Quinn continue, closing my eyes when he runs his fingers down my face. "You stay there, among the bits of me that are dying. The difference is, you heal it all. You clean away all that darkness."

"And that's why you want me? Because I keep you clean?"

"No, love. I want you because you made me catch peace. You made me realize how much I wanted it in the first place. I want you because I love you. Isn't that enough?"

"More than enough."

And it was, with him. I'd stay with Quinn because he drew pictures that brought life to Rhea's hope, because he'd given a dying girl the last bit of happiness left to her. I'd stay because Quinn had drawn me in curves and lines without shadows, with nothing more than who I really was. I'd stay because the hope we held between us was caught up in memory, in love and loyalty.

He says I made him want it, that it was me that had him catching that serenity. Really, it was there for us both, wanting to be held, waiting for us to hold it in our hands.

The End

ACKNOWLEDGEMENTS

THE SERENITY SERIES first landed on the page after my father died of pancreatic cancer three years ago. I find it ironic that his death brought life to a lot of emotion that has evolved into plots and metaphors that all these characters feel at some point. In many ways, it is my father's death, and later a dear friend and a brave young woman I did not know, their stories and inspiration, at least, that are woven throughout this series. That doesn't mean this is a series of books that focuses on loss and death. I think the opposite can be said of Autumn, Mollie, Layla and Sayo and the loves they found in Cavanagh. This place, these people, this series is about love—all aspects of it: chasing it, finding it, claiming it, catching it, learning from it, suffering for it and embracing it.

As with all things I consider accomplishments, I have to thank several people mostly for enduring my complaints and excuses, for rattling me when I needed it and for cheering me on when I thought I could not write another word.

Thank you to my editor, Sharon Browning for your insight and brutal honesty. It helps me grow and thrive. I could publish nothing without you. Thank you to Judy Lovely for stepping in at the last minute to copy edit. You are a life saver, my Lovely.

Thank you to Beth Bilbrey Simkanin and Teresa Matzek for the playlist suggestions and to all my girls (and Mike) at MBS, the Vixens Writers Group, Relentless Reviewers and, as always, my Sweet Team and betas: Trish Leger, Judy Lovely, Carla Castro, Naarah Scheffler, LK Westhaver, Lorain Domich, Melanie Brunsch, Michelle Horstman-Thompson, Allyson Lavigne Wilson, Chanpreet Singh, Emily Lamphear, Heather Weston-Confer, Betsy Gehring, Allison Coburn, Christopher Ledbetter, Heather McCorkle, Joy Chambers, Jazmine Ayala, Joanna Holland, Jessica D. Hollyfield, Tina Jaworski and Sammy Llewellyn.

To my beloved readers and Facebook, Twitter and GoodReads friends, thank you so much for chatting with me, sending me notes of encouragement and coming out to say hi at signings and cons. I'm so proud to have each of you along for the ride while I navigate this crazy business.

As always, my sweet work buddies Marie, Sherry, Barbara, Sarah and Kalpana, thank you for picking up the pieces when I need it and for making me feel like a rock star when things get really hectic and the Seventh Circle threatens to get to me.

Thank you to my nieces Jennifer Jagneaux, Kayla Jagneaux, Juli Wright and Joy Chambers for their support and blatant cheerleading and to my girls, Trinity, Faith and Grace who make me feel like a queen. Thank you to my Himself, for enduring the endless nights of tap, tap, tapping, necessary earplugs and promises of "just a half an hour more." You are my lifeline.

Thank you so much to Allyson Lavigne Wilson for the insight to childhood cancer and to the real struggles that families fighting this battle face every day. Thank you so, so much to RN Laing for your impeccable art, your friendship and your ability to slip right inside my mind and see these characters exactly as they are in my head. I am so honored to be part of your world and humbled by your love and friendship.

Thank you to all the bloggers and readers for supporting and encouraging me and for all of you who continue to have faith in indie authors. Your support is necessary!

Thank you to Chelle Bliss, Lila Felix, Penelope Douglas, Willow Aster, CC Wood, Kele Moon, Brenda Rothert and Ing Cruz for always being there, supporting, encouraging and helping me traverse this insane business. You are all fiercely brilliant and wonderful women. Thank you!

And to those of you who have fought battles and won, who are still fighting, I send you my fiercest prayers and unfailing faith. To those of you who have been on the road to Cavanagh from the beginning, thank you. Come back and visit anytime.

Be blessed.

ABOUT THE AUTHOR

Eden Butler is an editor and writer of Fantasy, Mystery and Contemporary Romance novels and the nine-times great-granddaughter of an honest-to-God English pirate. This could explain her affinity for rule breaking and rum.

When she's not writing or wondering about her possibly Jack Sparrowesque ancestor, Eden patiently waits for her Hogwarts letter, edits, reads and spends way too much time watching rugby, Doctor Who and New Orleans Saints football.

She is currently living under teenage rule alongside her husband in southeast Louisiana.

Please send help.

Find Eden online at the following:

Twitter: twitter.com/EdenButler_

Facebook: www.facebook.com/eden.butler.10

Blog: edenbutlerwrites.wordpress.com/

GoodReads: goodreads.com/author/show/7275168.Eden_Butler

Subscribe to Eden's newsletter http://eepurl.com/VXQXD for giveaways, sneak peeks and various goodies that might just give you a chuckle.

ABOUT THE ILLUSTRATOR

Based out of Northern Virginia, R.N. Laing is an artist who works in many mediums from traditional fine art to digital illustration and video editing. She was the recipient of the Bob Rauchenburg Fine Arts scholarship in 2004 at Edison College in Fort Myers, Florida, and continued her education at Florida Gulf Coast University and the University of South Florida. Since 2012, R. N. Laing has been working as a freelance artist with primary focus in digital art.

Connect with her on Twitter (@innabluebox (https://twitter.com/innabluebox?lang=en)) and Tumblr (n-a-bluebox.tumblr.com/). Artwork can be purchased at: https://society6.com/innabluebox

Made in the USA
Columbia, SC
30 August 2019